MOUNTAINS,
MALBEC, AND MEN

Noelle Cumberland

Art and cover design by Caitlin B. Alexander CBA Illustration
www.cbaillustration.com
Editorial services by Sage Taylor Kingsley
www.SageforYourPage.com

Library of Congress Control Number: 2024907039
Paperback ISBN 979-8-9899912-0-4
Ebook ISBN 979-8-9899912-1-1
First Edition

Published by Red Cypress Bluff LLC
Contact www.noellecumberland.com

Because on days when Hope hides,
You find her for me
And for that, I am eternally grateful.

Table of Contents

PART 1:

TESTS, TESTAMENTS, AND TESTIMONY

1.1 ROCKY TOP

The solitary pink line on the test strip mocked me. A dash. A hyphen. A minus. A fill-in-the-blank, begging to be punctuated by ... something. Its dark pink was almost purple, reminding me of intoxicating ditto ink that I loved inhaling back in grade school. Grade school—a simpler time, when if I followed the rules, I was rewarded. But adulthood had no syllabus.

The metallic taste of blood tickled my tongue. I unclenched my teeth, freeing the inside of my cheek. I tore my eyes away from the test strip perched on the granite bathroom counter and grabbed my phone:

Atlanta	Tokyo
3:03 a.m.	5:03 p.m.

No new notifications. I thought my best friend, Lenny, was back from sea and would've responded by now. I needed some other way to process the panic swirling in my head. I checked the weather forecast at Thunderhead Mountain: Clear skies. A sixty-four-degree high at the summit. An early taste of spring in the Smoky Mountains. I turned to scan my closet.

I reserved the top row for work attire:

1. Shirts – Ten white, button-down, cotton-blend, long-sleeve shirts.
2. Pants – Five pairs of black slacks; two pairs of jeans.
3. Skirts – Two black pencil skirts; one gray pencil skirt; one A-line black skirt.
4. Blazers – Two black blazers; one blue blazer.

Long ago, I had adopted a work uniform to thwart decision fatigue, something that increased with each promotion. When I was forced to take a product owner position three years ago, no one prepared me for the twelve-hour workdays and monthly software release weekends. Work-life balance was a myth, but in spite of the long hours and the stress, my current job was more rewarding than any process engineer job I'd ever had.

I housed my outdoor attire on the bottom row of my closet:

1. Shirts – Five white, button-down, polyester, long-sleeve shirts with UPF.
2. Bottoms – Seven pairs of hiking pants in an assortment of grays, blacks, and tans; five pairs of black cycling shorts; one gray hiking skort.
3. Mid-layers – Three blue tops in varying degrees of thickness.
4. Jackets – A pink hard-shell; one orange, puffy jacket.

I pulled a shirt, a mid-layer, and a gray pair of pants off their hangers and then dressed. I grabbed a neck gaiter from a dresser drawer and slipped it over my head. I left my bedroom, averting my eyes from the closed door of my second bedroom down the hall. At my house's back door, I flung my backpack onto one shoulder and grabbed my boots by their laces. My gear stayed in go mode.

I checked my phone again.

No new notifications. I navigated to a message thread. My thumbs made quick work on the screen, logging my hiking plans with Mel. I'd met her at Virgin Falls a few years back. She had recently relocated to Tennessee after an early retirement, and we had become fast friends.

Me: *Hey, you're probably asleep by now but letting you know I'm headed up your way. Going to Rocky Top. ~2-hour drive then hike. Figure I should check in no later than 3 pm. Please ping me if you can join me.*

Mel: *I'm up! Damn dog wet the bed AGAIN! I thought this was your hiking bye week.*

My fingers paused as I debated my response. While Mel and my bond extended beyond hiking, she wasn't Lenny.

Me: *Woke up craving mountain air! I'll do a bye next weekend.*

Mel: *Wish I could join you girlfriend but I'm volunteering with the chamber and then dinner with some friends. Want to join for dinner?*

Me: *Thx for invite, but I'll pass. Feeling super introverted rn.*

The opening beat to Bill Withers's "Lovely Day" cried from my phone. I dismissed my alarm, plunging me back into silence. I tucked my phone in my pocket and opened my back door. One-Eyed Willy bolted from my patio chair. Her tortoiseshell fur blurred to black as she scurried from my yard. She sprinted across the street, toward her two-story Victorian home, which was occupied by the hipster neighbors who owned a menagerie of domesticated animals. I wasn't sure of her real name, as she never allowed me close enough to read her tags, but every day, my door cameras caught her napping on my chair. If I had one eye, I reckon I'd be skittish as hell too.

I set my backpack into my sixteen-year-old Camry's passenger seat. My car was my first big, post-college purchase. Over the years, I had been tempted to get something new, especially as my ex-husband traded in for new cars every two to three years, but now I couldn't fathom driving anything else. While I was placing my boots next to my trekking poles behind the driver's seat, my next-door neighbor approached, wheeling a shopping cart. I racked my brain, struggling to remember her name. It never stuck.

"Going for another hike, Allyn?" my neighbor asked. Her tongue slithered between her missing upper teeth. She was one of the four women who rented the house next door. From the stories she told, they had a slumlord. They were dirt-poor with hearts of gold and would inform me of strange people hanging around my property. I'd buy them fresh fruit and toiletries from time to time. Each Friday morning, I'd set out my trash, and when I would drive onto my parking pad, she would wheel my empty trashcan back to my house. Truthfully, I think she dumpster-dove.

"It's easy to take off when you don't have kids," she said.

My breath caught in my throat as if she had punched me in the gut. My stomach free-fell. I locked my knees to keep them from buckling. Beads of sweat puddled at my temples. I wiped them into my hair with the backs of my thumbs. I shut my eyes. *Get it together.* I reopened them and flashed my twice-orthodontia-corrected smile. "Yeah, I guess you're right." I missed the comforts of a car garage the most on days with rain—or random neighbor conversations.

"That's what we've been telling my niece. You've met her, right?"

Her niece was the young girl with tawny skin, caramel curls, and the swollen belly that grew every week. Some neighbors likely thought she was my sister despite my tighter curls and more melanated skin. People back home would see all our differences, categorizing her as mixed and me as redbone. We'd never met, but I was familiar with her presence, so I nodded.

"We told Stevanie to leave that Guatemalan boy alone," she said.

I scrunched my face into a frown.

My neighbor's eyes widened. "Not that anything's wrong with him being Guatemalan," she said. "We love everybody, but my sister had her young, and then there was one setback after another…. Anyway, Stevanie knew about safe sex. She's a smart girl, too. But what can you do? Kids think they're in love, and that'll save 'em." Her tongue prodded at her exposed gums where her front teeth used to be.

If you don't have anything nice to say, don't say anything at all. Maybe I don't need a garage, but a privacy fence could suffice. My eyes darted to my backpack, where it waited for me inside the car. "Well, I'd better get going before traffic picks up. Thanks again for always bringing in my trash."

"All right then." She half-saluted then walked due south on the street.

I settled into the driver's seat, not bothering with GPS. I knew my way to the Smokies by heart. I drove past my dumpster-diving neighbor and waved. She didn't see with her face bowed to the road. I left my historic neighborhood of Victorian and Craftsman homes rooted in yards with mature maples and oaks. The rocking-chair dotted, fairy-lit porches gazed upon manicured turf lawns contained by picket fences and also gave side-eye to the adjacent ivy- and clover-choked lots with their homes of peeling paint, boarded windows, and sagging roofs. I merged onto I-24

East and followed that until I exited onto I-75 North, leaving Chattanooga behind.

Hours later, I pulled into the Cades Cove picnic area and geared up, pulling my dark brown spirals in a topknot, applying the dark sparkly pink of my favorite Urban Decay Psycho lipstick, pulling on wool socks, lacing my boots, buckling the hip belt of my orange Gregory backpack and cinching it taut, checking that the shoulder straps supported my pack weight, and finally clicking my sternum strap and pulling it tight across my chest. The security of my straps was like a welcomed hug. I set off on the Anthony Creek Trail.

With each step, my tight muscles loosened and settled into a familiar rhythm. The trail was an old frenemy, listening to me curse and cry out in pain as my quads begged to quit. It didn't coddle. It didn't boost my self-esteem. It couldn't pass judgment, and because of that, I came to it raw and unfiltered. And so it allowed me to deal with the demons that plagued my mind. It tolerated countless monologues as I worked through pros and cons lists of: "Do I stay the course or move on?" Given that this trail had helped me obtain the clarity to stay in Chattanooga after ending my marriage, it should also help me sort out that single pink line.

As the trail paralleled Anthony Creek, my pace quickened, matching my racing mind, which busied itself identifying all the variables that had gotten me into my current predicament. I separated them by type: quantitative versus qualitative. Quantitative data was my jam because numbers don't lie.

I reached the Russell Field trail intersection. The wood trail signs stacked perpendicular to each other akin to a street intersection:

Anthony Creek Trail
← Crib Gap Trail 1.4
← Picnic Area (Trailhead) 1.6
→ Bote Mountain Trail 1.9
Russell Field Trail
→ Appalachian Trail 3.5
→ Russell Field Shelter 3.5

I didn't need any trail signs to guide me. I knew this path better than I knew my own home. Russell Field provided an easier route to Rocky Top, but I turned to remain on Anthony Creek Trail. One-point-nine miles to the Bote Mountain intersection. As the trail climbed away from the rushing waters and up the ridge, my pace slowed, and I sifted through the inventory of messy, qualitative data. The threat of coming tears burned my nasal cavity. Despite three years of healing, some memories remained fresh. Numbers don't lie, but ex-husbands do.

With her love letter clutched in my hand, I cornered my husband in the kitchen that we had designed in our forever home. For us, forever translated into five years. Even though neither of us were fond of cooking, we had hand-selected the custom white cabinets and the black quartz countertops. I had convinced him that the counters had to be black because Black withstands almost any stain while every imperfection showed. Then there was the Moroccan tile backsplash, the Sub-Zero fridge, the blue Wolf range, the farmer's sink, and an island to top it all off.

"How could you do this? We were trying to get pregnant." I wanted an answer, but no answer could justify his actions.

"I never wanted to be a father." He narrowed his blue eyes while his thin lips curled into a sneer.

"What?! I've never met anyone who didn't want something but still tried for months to get it. This isn't Stockholm syndrome. No one put a gun to your head. We talked about becoming parents, and you very much wanted this."

His smug smile dissipated.

I continued, "But I don't know you anymore. You lie as effortlessly as you breathe, so who knows if anything coming out your mouth is true. Or ever was. I knew it had to be her. I fucking saw her long, straight hair clinging to ketchup bottles in the fridge, and you brushed it off as me being crazy. Guess I'm not fucking crazy after all."

Even if I burned the letter, its words had already seared into my mind. Her large and curly cursive on scented stationery—revealing their pet names, the long glances at work, the parking lot talks and hugs—had confirmed I had lost him and the possibility of a baby long ago.

I didn't blink. My eyes stung. I paused, waiting for a response, always waiting for him to do the things he never did. "I suspected this nine months ago. Nine months!" I couldn't shake that number's significance. Instead of creating life, he used that time to destroy mine. "You've been lying to me for fucking nine months! The long workouts after work. Hiding your phone messages. Locking yourself in the bonus room to play video games. Accusing *me* of being paranoid whenever I questioned anything. All the fucking hair products you use now. Did you really think I'd never figure it out?" I tossed the love letter on the counter.

He could no longer refute my claims in the face of evidence. Quantitative data. I crossed my arms and cocked my head. "How insulting for you to think you could outsmart me."

I paused, again expecting a response that wouldn't come. He stood there with the same glare. Probing for some sign of life, I said, "You've lived this double life. My gut told me you were fucking around with her, but I trusted you instead of my own gut. You're a piece of shit."

"We didn't have sex," he said.

"We've already established you lie about everything. How can I believe anything you say?" Emotions constricted my throat. My face contorted, trying to spew the words out. "You allowed yourself to get caught up with your coworker! A, a"—I struggled to find the words to string together a complete sentence—"a *married* woman with a five-year-old son. All while you were trying to conceive with *your wife*. And you say you didn't want to be a father? Well, riddle me this: If you didn't want to be a father, why have an affair with a mom?"

A vein bulged on his forehead. He leaned back against the counter and crossed his muscular arms. I couldn't recall the last time they held me.

"I would've been fine being a dad to her son because she's a good mom. You'd be a horrible mom."

I was stunned into silence. I stumbled back as if his words had balled into a fist and uppercut my chin. I gripped the Blackness of the kitchen island, struggling to regain my composure and confidence. Whoever said, "Sticks and stones can break my bones, but words will never hurt me," lied.

I could have handled him making a mockery of our marriage but calling me a bad mom was something I couldn't forgive, something we could never recover from. Even if he had said that out of anger and spite, even if I knew he was a habitual liar, he had just articulated my worst fear. Torn me open.

"Well, I've been on mom duty for the last ten years," I said. "Cooking, cleaning, picking up your dirty drawers and socks off the floor, filing taxes, scheduling all the doctor appointments, making sure you save for retirement—"

"But you couldn't even care for a cat."

I scoffed. "Seriously? That was, like, seven years ago! We were both stressed coming home to cat piss on the bed, and crating him for ten-plus hours a day seemed cruel. I don't think rehoming a cat constitutes bad mothering."

"You just push, push, push. Everything has to be done a certain way, and if it isn't, you freak out."

"Well, I don't hear you complaining about all the vacations and that Tesla in the garage!" I blurted out. "It's a far cry from me having to cosign for your Camaro when we first got married, isn't it? If someone pushed me from being a college dropout, answering help desk calls, to becoming a highly paid network architect with all the bonuses and stock options, I'd be damn well appreciative."

His hands gripped his hips. "Yes! I like the things we have, okay?" His right hand moved to touch his hair. Before his fingers could disrupt his gelled hair, he threw them in the air. "But have you even noticed how miserable I've been? You just, you just get laser-focused on achieving some goal that ... that—"

My eyes widened in anticipation of something pro-phetic. Something logical to explain why the easygoing, quiet man I married, who had supported all my dreams, had been wilding out.

He folded his arms. "You just pushed so much that you pushed me away, okay?"

When a trail sign came into view, I filed that kitchen-scene memory back in my mental divorce folder. Like scenes from my failed marriage, I could recite the sign from memory:

| Anthony Creek Trail |
| Russell Field Trail 1.9 → |
Cades Cove 3.5 →
Bote Mountain Trail
Lead Cove Trail 1.2 →
← Appalachian Trail 1.7

At the Bote Mountain Trail intersection, I broke for wa-ter and prepared to power through the 1.7 mile climb to the Appalachian Trail, or "AT," as us hikers called it. Powering through was kind of my MO for life. I had clung to my mar-riage for another six months after that fight before I re-signed myself to the fact that the Happily Ever After I sought could never be with him. It was hard to accept after all the investments I had made in us. A year after our di-vorce, he had a whirlwind romance with some woman he had only been dating for three months, an elementary school teacher. He remarried, and six months ago, he sent me a photo birth announcement. Seeing my ex's arms wrapped around a stranger holding their baby sent me into a tailspin. My friends called him an asshole for sending the announcement. My gut reaction agreed with them, but I had spent the last few years working hard to not breathe life into negative energy, so I sent the happy parents a gift, wishing them well. All new life was a blessing that should be celebrated, but despite me trying to see the silver lining of being replaced, Bordeaux drowned my bitterness in the months that followed. Another woman had reaped the rewards of my efforts. I suppose my ex had found his Happily Ever After, and here I was, back on the trail, staving off an emotional breakdown over a damn pink line.

What the fuck was I doing with my life?

I spotted the AT trail sign as it started to drizzle:

Appalachian Trail
Eagle Creek Trail 0.1 →
Spence Field Shelter 0.2 →
← Jenkins Ridge Trail 0.3
Bote Mountain Trail
Anthony Creek Trail 1.7 →
Lead Cove Trail 2.9 →
Laurel Creek Road 7.2 →

Northbound was another 1.5 miles and a final, quad-killing push to reach Rocky Top. At the trail sign, I slid my pack to the ground and guzzled water. Scents of raspberries, cedar, and vanilla wafted toward me on a light spring breeze. I turned my head south, in the direction of the perfumed air. A couple wearing matching pink, cotton-blend Breast Cancer Awareness shirts and daypacks approached the trail intersection. Not thru-hikers.

"Hey," I greeted them in between sips.

"Hi," they acknowledged me in unison. The woman asked, "Are you hiking to Rocky Top?"

"Yeah, how about you guys?"

"Oh, no. Spence Field was our final destination. We came up Russell Field and are heading down Bote," the man said, nodding in the direction I had come.

"Was the weather this dreary your entire time on the AT?" I asked, looking up at the tree-filtered sky. If they had taken the Russell Field Trail, I calculated they had hiked for an hour and a half along the AT if they kept a two-miles-per-hour pace.

"Yeah, for the most part. We had a break in the clouds for a little bit but not long," she said.

"Somehow this trail curses me. I've never had a clear-day summit at Rocky Top," I said.

"What time did you start this morning?" she asked.

"Around seven."

"You're making great time," she said with a smile.

"Thanks."

They took a few photos at the trailhead before the man tilted his head and asked, "Are you from around here?"

"Oh, no. I live in Chattanooga, but I come up to the Smokies fairly often. I have a friend who lives in Sevierville. She and I hike together a good bit."

"Oh, you're Allyn 'No Facebook'!" the woman said. Her face lit up like a Christmas tree.

Allyn "No Facebook" was how Mel and others in the 865 hiking community tagged me in photos. I chuckled. "Yeah, I am. How'd you know?"

"Well, you looked familiar to us when we were coming up. Your lipstick and clothes are kind of like hiker preppy. And then when you said you were from Chattanooga with a friend who lives up here"—she glanced at her hiking companion and giggled—"we knew."

I was unconvinced my lipstick and hiking uniform were the only inputs to that conclusion. I suspected my rare status as a minority on the mountain was a bigger contributor to her guess.

"Would you take a photo with us?" he asked while removing his phone from its holster belt.

"Sure." I picked up my pack and fastened my hip belt. As if we were members of a cheerleading squad, we positioned ourselves around the trail sign, squeezing and crouching in sync, ensuring our faces, packs, and sign were in the shot. I smiled wide, exposing my molars. Satisfied with the photos, he fastened his phone back in its holster.

"Well, I'll have to let Mel know I ran into you," I said.

"Oh, Miss Melinda doesn't know us. We've only been on a couple of group hikes with her, and we're always in the back."

"I'll still let her know I ran into you." Thanks to Facebook, Mel would know before I made it back to my car. "Well, I better head off. I hope you two have a great rest of your hike."

"You too," they replied in unison.

I turned north to follow the AT as it loosely matched the Tennessee and North Carolina state border. I passed a patch of blackberry bushes that signaled the point where my ex-husband and I had turned around on my first summit attempt.

He and I never summited Rocky Top together; in fact, we'd never returned to this section of the AT after that July Fourth hike, when he said his leg pain was too unbearable to continue.

Years later, I came back alone, and I summitted. In doing so, I learned that alone I could achieve what I could never have done with him.

But could I, or was that just the pep talk I rallied behind?

I blinked. The drizzle camouflaged the salty tears that trickled down my face.

My divorce had maimed me in ways I never let on. I was convinced everyone saw my failure as if I had a scarlet "D" branded across my left breast. *Divorcée.* Over and over, I asked myself, "What did I do to deserve this?"

I had done what I was supposed to do. I followed the syllabus, but I still flunked.

- √   Earn college degree
- √   Obtain lucrative job
- √   Buy home
- √   Get married
- –   Start family

A dash. A hyphen. A minus. A fill-in-the-blank of anything but that check mark.

I channeled my frustration into powering through the final push to Rocky Top. As I was huffing and puffing and grunting, laughter echoed ahead. I used my poles to push my body up to the summit. Four backpacks taller than most human torsos sat on the ground. Sandals and folded, silver sleeping pads were strapped to some of them.

Two women—one tall and blonde, the other short and brunette—and two lanky men stood near the packs. The brunette woman busied herself with a sketchpad. Oil and sweat muddled with the scent of an approaching spring. Thru-hikers.

Rocky Top was quintessential East Tennessee, and its location had inspired the namesake song, which happened to be one of Tennessee's ten official state songs. I smiled, knowing Rocky Top's peak was actually within North Carolina's borders. Once I'd caught my breath and chugged a bit of water, I engaged in conversation, maintaining my distance per the six-foot CDC recommended guideline to combat the spread of coronavirus.

"So, are you guys thru-hiking all the way to Maine, or are you flip-flopping?" I said. This time of year, they must have been trekking northbound, or "NoBo," as us hikers called it.

The short woman with dark-haired, stocky legs answered while continuing to sketch. "Well, my goal is Harpers Ferry since I did the north section last year, but at this point, I'm going as far as I can because we may not be allowed on the trail much longer. In fact, we're being advised to leave the trail. Technically, we're not allowed to sleep in shelters anymore, but it was so cold last night, we slept at the Spence Field Shelter."

The thin, blonde woman beside her said, "Hiking as far as I can go. The goal is Katahdin." She grinned. "You thru-hiked this before?"

"Oh no," I said while shaking my head and letting a chuckle escape. "I have no aspirations to thru-hike anything. I like flushing toilets and hot showers too much for that, so I'd only last a couple of weeks. But I have a few friends who have thru-hiked a few trails, and I admire the mental grit it takes. Where are you from?" I asked the blonde. "I can't place your accent."

"I'm German, but I live in England. I married an English man." She blushed. "I've planned to thru-hike for over a year. I'm unsure how I can get home now that countries are closing borders, but I'll worry about that when I'm done."

The woman who was sketching added, "All of our normal supply sources have been wiped out with the panic buying. Even if we stay on the trail, we may not have a food source."

My heart ached for them. Many thru-hikers dream for years of trekking the AT. They spend at least a year planning logistics and often quit their jobs or take a sabbatical if they're not already in retirement. The mental effort of overcoming the Appalachian Trail surpasses its physical toil. Their pain resonated so deeply with me: dreaming for years, planning and investing, and then meeting an unexpected outcome. But their fight wasn't done; they were clinging to hope. And why shouldn't they?

"I have four protein bars I'm willing to give you," I said. "I swear I don't have coronavirus. I live alone and hermit in my house when I'm not on the trails. I can lay the bars on this rock in between us." I had packed four protein bars that I wouldn't eat on my trek back to my car.

They hesitated, but ultimately they wanted the bars. After sanitizing my hands, I placed the bars on a rock six feet equidistant from us. Once I backed up, they snatched the bars like starved squirrels. They ripped open the packaging and moaned in satisfaction, resisting the urge to inhale the bars whole.

Despite the gloomy day that matched their outlook, I wanted them to treasure that moment and bond with that peak the way I had. When there was a break in the clouds, I pointed south. "Do you see Fontana Lake?"

"Wait, no. Is that it?" the blonde asked, standing on her tippy-toes and then a boulder.

"Yeah," I said.

"We were just there yesterday," the sketcher said.

All four in the group marveled as clouds played peek-aboo with the lake.

"I hope you guys stay on the trail long enough to see Max Patch and Carver's Gap. Carver's Gap is really a slice of heaven. Three-sixty views for miles. It's less than a hundred miles south of the Virginia border."

They continued in conversation about needing a double-zero day as I maneuvered around them, taking photos. I stowed away my camera, lifted my pack onto my back, and called out, "Good luck on your journey." I turned my back to them and headed south, passing at least five thru-hikers on my way to the parking lot. I empathized how disappointing this all must have been for them. I wished I had packed more food.

The test strip remained on the counter, untouched since the predawn hours. I twisted my mouth. While my hike had been productive, there weren't enough miles to sort through the entirety of my qualitative list. What was I going to do?

My phone buzzed. I glanced at the screen. Lenny's WhatsApp photo stared at me—an Ankara headwrap covered her updo while her gold hoop earrings kissed her shoulders.

Lenny and I had been dorm mates our freshman year at Georgia Tech. Our first semester on campus, we were cordial, exchanging greetings as we passed each other, entering and exiting the communal bathroom, the dining hall, the Student Center, and Skiles. For spring semester, we signed up for the same Calculus II class and section, where we had a well-meaning but ineffective teaching assistant who struggled to solve integrals as much as we did. We teamed up as study mates. We went on to earn As in that course and became best friends. In the almost two decades that followed, our friendship had collected four degrees; spanned five continents; and survived "don't ask, don't tell," a death, a divorce, and a hysterectomy.

I answered the voice call.

"Hey, I'm so sorry it took me this long to get back," Lenny said. "We were held up at port. Things have been insane with this coronavirus. They're looking at cutting my assignment short to get me back stateside. It's a good thing you visited over Thanksgiving."

"Is it really that serious?" I asked.

"Yeah. You know the Japanese don't play. Are things not in lockdown there?"

"I mean, it depends on where you're at, really. Like, I'm so thankful I didn't go home for Mardi Gras this year. Things are pretty locked down there, but my family's okay. But here?" I blew a raspberry. "It's not the massive lockdowns like you hear about in the bigger cities. Our corporate campuses are still open, but they've limited in-person meetings. It seems like it'll blow over in a month."

Lenny sucked her teeth. "I don't think it will. But whatever, we can talk about that later. How didn't I know you already bought sperm, much less had three insemination rounds?!"

"Sorry, you were out at sea, and it's been way too much to email, text, or send an audio message. And I know you've had your own challenges with your tour. I didn't want to burden you."

"Girl, stop. Tell me what's going on. How are you feeling?"

I pushed out all the air from my lungs, forcing my belly button to my spine. "Disappointed. I don't know if that's the right word. Fuck, I'm angry."

"Angry? What happened?"

I glowered in the direction of the test strip and recounted my last visit to the fertility clinic.

1.2 HAIL MARY, FULL OF GRACE

Following medical guidelines, I guzzled two thousand milliliters of water en route to the clinic because a full bladder was desired to allow the physician to better see the uterus. Once there, I signed in, noticing the date would've been my thirteenth wedding anniversary.

I found a seat across from a young couple and crossed my legs, waiting to be called to the exam room. On prior visits, I had been called to the exam room within ten minutes of arrival, but as ten minutes turned to twenty, I continued to wait with my legs crossed and squeezed.

The fourth of March—my former anniversary. What were the odds of that? I was never great at probability but tried to recall the equation to calculate the odds of my ovulating on this date. After failing to recollect it, I chuckled at how I was spending the day. Instead of a good old-fashioned dinner followed by married-people sex, I would have the pleasure of a threesome: physician, nurse, and patient.

"Allyn, we're ready for you," an employee said, disrupting my thoughts.

I glanced at my phone. My bladder and I had been waiting thirty minutes.

In the darkened exam room, I undressed from the waist down. I tucked my panties into the pocket of my slacks because even though the medical staff had seen plenty of my vagina, something about them seeing my panties was too personal. I then folded my pants and set them on a chair. I climbed on the exam table and covered myself with surgical drapes to maintain my modesty. Ten minutes later, a nurse entered the room. She presented my donor card and the accompanying sperm vial. I read my donor's alias and verified his numerical identification. I knew that number like my own social security number.

My donor was an Arizona State University engineering student. On paper, he checked all my boxes—CMV negative; confirmed live births; open donor; not a carrier for any genetic disorders; over six feet tall; athletic, as he was on the swim team; and analytical because he was a Rational per the Keirsey test—but listening to his interview had sealed the deal. I listened to it daily. He discussed being a first-generation college student and the black sheep of his family because he preferred being active outside rather than indulging in city pleasures. I empathized. All of my family and most of my friends were city people. Hell, I was, too, until I experienced the freeness that came from the trails.

I verbally acknowledged to the nurse that my donor details were accurate, and she left the room. I crossed my legs, damming up the floodwaters that were pushing for release. How much longer would I have to wait?

Ten minutes later, my physician and the same nurse entered. This wasn't my first rodeo. I scooted my bottom to the edge of the exam table and rested my feet in the stirrups. He turned on the procedural light and prepped the catheter. He then inserted the catheter, bypassing my cervix, and flooded my uterus with donor sperm. It was a sixty-second affair.

"You can leave after lying for fifteen minutes," he said.

I nodded. Fifteen minutes allowed sufficient time for virile sperm to travel to my egg. If I had waited fifty minutes to use the bathroom, what was another fifteen?

They left the room. The ticking of the red second hand commanded my attention. I potty-danced lying down. I counted ceiling tiles. I contemplated why physician offices didn't commission artists to paint the ceilings like Egyptian temples or Italian Renaissance churches; I'd much rather look at something other than randomized patterned dots. I hummed the only tunes that came to mind, nursery rhymes, then checked the clock. Four minutes had elapsed.

Why had it taken so long to get me to the exam room? My mind-trick powers waned; the pressure in my bladder was unbearable. Like a child, I clamped my bent legs together in an effort to hold not only my urine but the sperm in.

After ten minutes of trying to distract myself, I was certain that I was going to pee all over the exam table. I prayed that my donor's sperm swam as fast as he did because I couldn't endure another second of waiting. I slid off the exam table to a standing position as I was afraid the very act of sitting would fool my brain that I was seated on a toilet, and it'd be game over. I considered throwing a bunch of paper towels on the floor like a potty pad and relieving myself then and there. The staff would understand, right? Hopping and wiggling from one foot to the next, I pulled my panties from my pants pocket and put one leg through and then the next. I rocked my hips as if I were balancing a hula hoop—if I were too still, I'd relieve myself all over the floor. I raised my slacks up both of my legs at the same time. I didn't have the mental focus and dexterity to zip and button them. I flung open the door, flooding the exam room with the harsh fluorescents of the hallway, and fast-walked, like a mall walker, to the bathroom. If anyone stood in my way, I was going to tackle and then golden-shower them.

I tackled the bathroom door instead. As I locked it, a trickle escaped. I chided myself. *Oh no, Allyn. You are too damn old to pee yourself.* I had neither the strength to hover over nor to line the toilet seat, so I sat on my hands. As soon as my thighs touched the backs of them, serenity swept over me, and I released Niagara Falls. Anyone walking by would have sworn an elephant was using the facilities.

As I washed my hands, anger conquered my peaceful-ness, along with the thought that prodded at the back of my mind. Why had I been in the waiting room for thirty damn minutes? There was a reason for appointment times. I had done my part in showing up on time. I shouldn't have to suffer for someone else's inefficiency. My breath short-ened, and my chest heaved. *Did I wait long enough to allow the sperm to travel to my egg?* The thought that my egg wasn't fertilized consumed me. It grabbed hold of my uterus and twisted it into a knot.

I sprinted out of the clinic and into the safety of my Camry. *What if it didn't take?* In a panic, I called my ex-boy-friend on my way to work.

"Hey," Ryan answered. His "hey" occupied two sylla-bles. I always had been attracted to his drawl. He punched above his weight with his voice combined with his wit, as he would say.

I hard-swallowed, attempting to alleviate my cotton mouth. "You need to come and have sex with me, like, now." While we talked daily and considered ourselves good friends, it had been nearly nine months since we had broken up. From the start of our courtship, I hadn't been shy about expressing that my main desire was becoming pregnant. While I sometimes questioned how much he supported my goals, our friendship wouldn't be rocked by my request. It was a low-risk plea for an immeasurable reward.

"What?" he asked.

In one breath, as if I were an auctioneer, "So, I went for my last IUI today, and I just want to ensure that I have *the* best chance for pregnancy. You know, I read that sperm competition can increase my chances of pregnancy, and I'm ovulating *today*. It'd mean *the world* to me if you would come and give me your sperm." Then I smiled. He prided himself in his ability to hear my smiles.

He sighed as if I had asked him to stop watching football and fix a leaky toilet. "I'll see what I can do."

Was that a yes? Was that a no? *Why can't he just be straight with me? I didn't ask if he was free to grab a drink after work.* My life's happiness was intertwined with getting pregnant. For almost a year, fertility had been my second job. And Ryan knew that.

First, I found the best fertility specialist for me. Next, I had to get on the schedule for the consult where we talked about LH, FSH, CMV, IVF, IUI, and a host of other topics. I went through many rounds of testing, proving that I did in fact ovulate and that I had a sufficient number of ovarian follicles. I discovered that I was CMV-negative—a rarity in the adult population. Exposing myself to a CMV-positive donor had the potential to increase my child's risk, albeit small, of birth defects and congenital abnormalities. I couldn't accept that risk—no matter how small. Then, I got an HSG, where my physician flooded my uterus with a dye, revealing no blockage in my uterus, though I did have one partially blocked fallopian tube. All these tests proved that I was capable of a natural pregnancy.

My physician cleared me for IUI even though IVF could better manage my ectopic pregnancy risk. I narrowed down to a donor, but by the time I was ready to purchase his sperm, someone else had depleted his inventory. So I found another suitable donor. I bought and shipped the sperm to my clinic. I cleared treatment with my insurance. I performed countless LH surge tests and religiously tracked my basal body temp to determine when I was ovulating. I decided what would happen to the unused sperm in the event of my death. I experienced two failed rounds of IUI. And after all that commitment, I was being transported back to the beginning—subjected to the whims of a man bestowing his semen.

I survived my workday without hearing back from Ryan. I resolved my fate had been settled eight hours ago—the moment I got up from the exam table. Defeated, I entered my home and freed my tired feet from my heels when my phone buzzed.

Ryan: *OMW*

I hopped in the shower, and after I freshened up, I had at least ten minutes before he would arrive. I wiped up incense ash, restacked the disheveled books on my coffee table, lined up my remotes in height order, folded spare blankets and draped them over the sofa back, and fluffed pillows. I sat on the edge of my sofa, drumming my fingers on my knees. *Did too much time elapse? My egg could be dead for all I know.*

My doorknob jiggled. When our relationship was new, I used to unlock the door for Ryan before he arrived. Then he had earned a key, then unearned it, and now he had to knock like everyone else. Despite the favor I was asking of him, his door privilege remained unchanged. Did he think otherwise? A chime alerted when I opened the door.

"Hey." I welcomed him in, sweeping my arm Vanna White–style toward my living room. The scent of cedar-wood and bergamot entered the room.

"I heard you were in need of my services," he said while slipping off his Chacos. No shoes in the house; he re-membered. The overhead light reflected off his head, and not a hair was out of place on his beard.

I laughed. He had a way of turning uncomfortable mo-ments into laughable ones. His ability to make me laugh was both why I had fallen in love with him and why we remained friends.

"I really do appreciate you doing this for me." I smiled, bit my lip, and looked up at him.

He placed his hands on my hips and bent down to kiss my neck. I twisted away and walked to my bedroom. He couldn't kiss me. That was a level of intimacy I wasn't seek-ing. He had lost access to that part of me. I slid under the covers and undressed. He flung off his hoodie and work clothes, no longer embarrassed about his belly or the dim-ples and folds of his pale skin. He attempted to kiss my lips. I turned my face, presenting him with my cheek and neck. I had long since divorced myself from all romantic and sex-ual desires; sex was no longer for pleasure but only a means to procreate.

While he was doing his business, my mind drifted to thoughts of patrimony. When our relationship was new, I thought he'd make an amazing dad, so I waited for him to be ready. I even told him I'd be open to him being a stay-at-home parent. *That was then, but now? Would I want to know if he fathered my child instead of my donor?* I grimaced. I hoped my egg was already fertilized. I had developed this weird attachment to my donor, a man I knew only by his alias and donor number but whose voice I could pick out in a crowded room. I closed my eyes as my lips mouthed the words from his interview. A silent prayer of sorts to Drukpa Kunley—the fertility saint.

My mind snapped back to my bedroom when Ryan's groans grew guttural. I was ready to receive the gift. Ready to lie there for a full fifteen minutes. I was so focused on sperm that I thought of little else. *Yes, anoint my cervix with your sperm.* And then he pulled out. He ejaculated on my stomach. *WTF?!* My eyes widened, watching his penis spasm until it went limp like its owner.

I considered scooping and sliding his semen inside of me. I had become so superstitious about fertility that the normal laws of science did not apply. I had lost all reasoning and logic. I had transformed into a woman who was not above trying sorcery if it meant a healthy pregnancy.

I couldn't believe he had come over and reneged. *How could he do this to me? He knew what I wanted. He knew the deal!* I wanted to sink into my mattress where I'd suffocate in my sadness. *I will not let him see me cry.* I leaped out of bed, grabbed my clothes, and went to my bathroom to clean up, dress, and compose myself. Growing up, that was what my mother had enforced: go to the cry room; let out all your emotions; and when you are ready to be civil, rejoin the family. It was kind of like the cry room at a church, but my sister and I were left alone to sort out how to soothe those big feelings when they burst through. My sister didn't visit the cry room as much as me. Each week, I spent countless hours in the bathroom, wrangling my savagery. Some habits were hard to break.

I splashed my face with water. Anger slayed my sadness. I wanted to punch the fuck out of Ryan. I wanted to gouge his eyes out. I wanted to rip off his balls. He showed up to make a deposit, and all he did was withdrawal.

I opened the bathroom door. He had put his clothes on and was lying on top of my bed. I clenched my teeth. How had he remembered no shoes in the house but forgotten no outside clothes on the bed?

Anger. Disappointment. Hopelessness. Sadness. Emotions cycled through my body, up and down, round and round. I was on an emotional carousel that I couldn't escape. I braced my arm on the bathroom doorframe and timed my breathing to steady my tone. "Why'd you come over if you were just going to pull out?"

He sighed as if he had been anticipating this conversation. "Because if I didn't come over, I knew you wouldn't let it go. You never let anything go. Once you make up your mind, once you set your goal, you will do it at any cost."

Wrinkles stamped my forehead as I glared at him. "That's not fair. You're criticizing me for accomplishing my goals? You know, at least I have goals. It's cowardly that you just couldn't say no."

"I didn't know until the last minute."

"Bull-fucking-shit. You knew the moment I first asked the question that you weren't going to do it."

"Allyn, you never ever leave me with any choice—"

"That's not fucking fair. You're crossing a line you may never be able to come back from." My hands shifted to my hips where they dug into my flesh, turning my fingertips white.

He sprang from the bed. Tears escaped from his eyes. "What am I supposed to do? I still love you." His hands flailed around him as if he were performing an interpretive dance of the story of his heart. "It's not that I didn't want to have a child with you. I just needed you to be more stable."

I hated when he cried, but I hated the conversation about stability even more. I needed to diffuse this. I closed my eyes and swallowed. When I reopened them, I clenched my fist and spoke as if I were reading from an organic chemistry book: "I will always have love for you, and I do acknowledge that you have shared a couple of times that you could see yourself fathering my child, but you're not going to insinuate that I am an unstable person. That's not even remotely accurate."

Truthfully, there had been many times in my three IUI cycles where I wasn't stable. I lived and died by the presence and darkness of lines on pee sticks. They controlled me, dictating how happy or sad I was on any given day.

"Fine. Consistent. I needed you to be more consistent."

I unclenched my fist and surveyed the four dark crescents etched into my palm. Emotion crept into my voice. "I am not having this conversation again with you. You cannot put the weight of this solely on my shoulders." I crossed my arms. My knees locked, and my shoulders nearly touched my ears.

"You were so hot and cold," he continued speaking, ignoring what I had just said.

"When a late-thirties, goal-oriented woman tells you, 'I will have a child with or without you,' maybe you should believe her. Did you think I'd wait on you forever? Why are we even talking about this? It's completely irrelevant."

His hands continued to dance out his pain. "And then you gave me no choice, Allyn! You just woke up and said you were going to get a donor."

"It was not that sudden. You always knew it was a possibility. You had a choice. You chose not to, and I wanted this. I needed this. You've always made my wanting to get pregnant about you, about us. It never was—"

"You were going to leave me!"

Bingo. That's what it had been about all along. I glowered at him in silence.

He crossed his arms, tucking his hands into his armpits to control them. "You said it in jest, but I knew you were fully capable of getting pregnant and disappearing. You would *Black Mirror* "White Christmas" me. It was never about a child for me. It was always you. I wanted you, and if you wanted the child, then fine, but I needed *you*." His voice softened. "I needed you to be consistent with loving me."

Truth sometimes has a biting bitterness. Even though he said he loved me, he didn't love me enough to give me the one thing I wanted—the one thing I needed from a man. He had dangled the carrot of him coming around to fatherhood to keep me on the hook: *One day; Soon; I'm closer than ever.* His love was selfish. He struggled seeing beyond himself and his own perspective. In fact, his myopia led to our breakup.

I was done with the conversation. I was done being reminded how much he loved me. His arms still squeezed tightly when we hugged. His hand continued to brush against mine when it handed me a drink. His eyes still lingered on my face the way a lover's would. But I had moved on. After him, I had turned over my entire being to ready my life for motherhood. I was done feeling guilty for choosing myself and my future baby above all.

"I know you think me 'getting myself pregnant' is selfish, but what you just did to me, pulling out, was immensely selfish. And it hurts. And if I don't get pregnant, it's going to take me a while to forgive you."

His face had dried. "I understand."

In silence, we walked to my glass front door. I opened it for him to pass through and then closed it behind him. I watched him get in his Honda Element and drive away as I had done countless times before. I turned around. My knees buckled. I rested my back against the door and slid down to the floor. I fought the tears, clamoring to break free.

And weeks later, while I was recounting the story to Lenny, I still fought the tears begging to break free. "Lenny, for the next week and a half, I waited. Tuesday. Wednesday. Thursday. Friday. Saturday. And then there was spotting. I always spot, but was this spotting implantation bleeding? And then, the bright, red blood. *The Shining* elevator blood."

"That sucks," Lenny said, "but I don't get what you're so angry about. Surely it can't be your ex. I could've told you he wouldn't follow through."

"Well, that's partly it, yes," I said, tilting my head and scrunching my face.

Lenny groaned. "Him, your ex-husband ... I don't know why you wasted so much time on those weak-ass men."

"For starters, you know I married young after a very short courtship. I didn't have a grasp on what I wanted in a man, and you know I bonded with Ryan over flattery, good sex, and us commiserating over our dead fathers and dysfunctional mothers. But it's not just that. I just thought I'd be pregnant. I thought if I did this in a controlled environment, with all variables known, that it'd work."

"So, why not do more treatments? I don't understand what the problem is."

"Well, I'm out of sperm, so I'd have to buy more. And given my age, my physician wouldn't support another round of IUI without the use of hormones. The data show if you don't get pregnant after three rounds of IUI, you need to take more aggressive measures, and I want to conceive as naturally as possible. Hell, he'll probably push me to go straight to IVF. And those hormones would increase the chance of multiple births. I don't want to be Octomom."

"I don't get what there is to be upset about. You have a damn uterus and still have options. If you want to get pregnant, take the hormones."

I sighed. *If my own best friend doesn't empathize with my dilemma, who will? Am I making mountains out of molehills? Am I too close to the issue to be pragmatic?* "I just don't want this to leave me financially and emotionally bankrupt. Besides, I told myself, 'Three months and stop.'"

"Allyn, if there's anything I know about you, it's that you are determined, and you will find a solution even if that solution is to stop. Whatever you decide to do, you know I got your back."

And with those words, I knew not to press further on the topic because if I did, she would say the words she didn't want to say. We were fluent in Southern subtleties.

"You're right. So, when do you think you'll be back stateside?"

"Hold on a sec." Lenny's muffled voice spoke to someone else. "Hey, sorry, I got to go. I'll message you when I can. Hang in there. Love you, girl."

"Love you, too," I said to the phone. She had already hung up. I scrolled through my contacts. Ryan, Lenny, and my sister were the only people in my circle with whom I shared my fertility journey.

I messaged Ryan.

Me: *Not pregnant.*

I stared at the screen, waiting for a reply. After a minute, I typed a message to my sister.

Me: *What's going on?*

Sister: *Lesson plans. The district is driving me crazy. It's like they don't understand the student demographics. Nearly all my students work to help pay the family bills. Everything is shut down, so they're likely stressing a/b how they will pay bills. And then over half of them don't even have computers or internet. What are they expecting me to do? How successful do they think I'm going to be teaching these kids online? It's a clusterfuck.*

Ryan still hadn't responded.

I messaged my sister back.

Me: *WOW!*

I tossed the test strip into the bathroom trash and then took my bathroom trash to the outside bin. I imagined my neighbor finding all my test strips. It's not like she would ever say anything to me, just like I wouldn't confront her for her raccooning in trashcans. Shame kept the best secrets.

I checked my phone. No new messages. I placed it on my nightstand and then plopped down on the white duvet covering my California king, in the hundred-year-old bungalow I owned outright. I buried my face into the white, percale pillowcase and wept myself to sleep.

1.3 A STOIC SUFFERING

Bill Withers's "Lovely Day" woke me at 4:30 a.m. the next day. My hand slipped past my nightstand's crystal collection and grabbed my thermometer. Out of habit, I placed the thermometer under my tongue before I grabbed my phone. No new messages. The thermometer beeped: 96.4 degrees. I didn't bother recording it. I rolled out of bed to start my workday routine: spin class, shower, work, adulting, yoga, sleep.

I mimed my way through work. I half paid attention on video calls as my heart questioned what the fuck I was doing with my life. I'd find myself staring out into the distance—at a window, a wall, another coworker's desk—with tears welling up at the emptiness of it all. An occasional coworker would walk into the path of my faraway gaze and ask with concern, "Allyn, are you okay?"

I'd blink away my misty eyes and flash my clinically whitened teeth and respond, "Just some exercises to manage a bit of eye fatigue."

I had mastered the appearance of a calm exterior while inside I battled a hurricane of emotions. Throughout my career, I had observed Black peers categorized as emotional, difficult, or "not a team player" for the same behaviors for which a White peer would be categorized as passionate, accountable, or a trailblazer. And while passionate, accountable, and trailblazer translated to promotions, emotional, difficult, and "not a team player" were acceptable corporate speak for labeling a Black person as angry to justify stalling their career. Thanks to my mother's cry room and Corporate America's suppression tactics, I excelled at containing my savagery and smoothing difficult subjects over with the right words and a friendly smile. No one ever probed further.

My phone buzzed. Unable to fight my conditioning, I checked it.

Ryan: *Sorry. Grab lunch? Drinks after work?*

A scoff accompanied my eye roll. While a part of me wanted to burrow into his arms and erase the last year, I was neither the rescuing nor the forgetting kind. I managed to complete the day, avoiding further attention and triggering messages, but I still had to face home.

My sweaty thighs suctioned to my bathroom's tile floor. I navigated the fertility clinic's phone tree in order to report my cycle as I had done twice before.

"If you are not in a treatment cycle and have a general question, which can wait until the next business day, you can leave a message for the nurses by pressing four."

I moved the phone away from my face and pressed four. I waited for the familiar recording, instructing me to leave a message but was startled when a "Hello" answered.

My heart fluttered. I inhaled through my nose, willing my galloping heart to a trot. "Hi. My name is Allyn Thompson. My date of birth is April 16, 1982. I'm calling to report that yesterday was the first day of my cycle."

"One moment," the voice said. Faint clicking sounded. "Ms. Thompson, we don't have any more vials to use. How would you like to proceed?"

Was it as simple as Lenny had said? Buy more sperm and start IVF?

If I want this, I wouldn't have set a time limit, though, right?

If I want this, I will be willing to deplete my savings and finance against my house like so many other hopefuls, right?

Do I want to be injected with fertility drugs?

Do I want my eggs harvested?

In the event I get pregnant, would I carry a healthy baby to term?

If I am wrecked simply from not getting pregnant, how would I handle a miscarriage?

If something this small could set off depression dominoes of this magnitude, how do I ever think I could handle being a parent?

Tears banged against my eyelids. I clenched my eyes, shooing them away. I vowed to not crack, to not unravel into a blubbering mess. "I'm not proceeding with any fertility plans," I told the voice on the other end of the line.

"Okay. Well, we're here if you ever change your mind."

For pregnancy hopefuls, a fertility clinic was no different than a casino to a gambler. They hooked you on an improbable possibility. I cracked open an eye and tapped the red phone receiver icon to hang up. I wanted to chuck my phone across the room, but instead, I stared at it until the screen went dark. Its darkness reflected the veneer of my stoicism splinter and collected the tears I could no longer hold back.

Why is it so easy for other women to get pregnant? I mean, some women sneeze and are pregnant. I can't achieve a fundamental, natural act of being a woman. In another time, I would've been cast aside as worthless because that was all women were good for, vessels to bring forth life. And despite directing the work of at least ten men, I can't birth a single one. I am biologically broken. Barren. A new scarlet letter, B, branded my skin.

I unglued my thighs from the floor and beelined to my bar cabinet, untouched since I'd started testing for ovulation. While I could have indulged each treatment cycle prior to ovulating, I had refrained to reduce any risk of residual alcohol impacting my pregnancy chances. I surveyed the alcoholic stamps of my passport book: Chilean carménère, Argentine malbec, South African chenin blanc, New Zealand sauvignon blanc, Chianti, French rosé, ouzo, ruou, ara, and K5 and Japanese whiskies. I grabbed a bottle of malbec and uncorked it. I ignored the decanter and guzzled from the bottle, returning to the comforts of my bathroom.

I ran a scalding bath, undressed, and sank into the water. With the bottle in my hand, I hugged my knees to my chest and stared blankly at the faucet, depleted and unsure how to cope with the loss of something that never actually was.

Statistically, I shouldn't have been depressed; not being pregnant was the most probabilistic outcome. My physician had reviewed the data with me. For my age, the IUI success rate was about 10 percent per cycle without hormones; for IVF, roughly 25 percent. If I wanted a baby, IVF would provide the better outcome.

And yet I was terrified of IVF. I had struggled deciding the fate of unused donor sperm, so how would I fare with preserving or destroying embryos? Also, the hormones could throw my emotions into a tailspin and foster fatigue, to the point that I couldn't hike. And without hiking, I was unsure how I'd maintain the little balance I did have in my life.

And to think I'd lived a whole life before hiking, chasing checkmarks on my list. Education, career, marriage.

Then, after my ex-husband and I built our forever home, nesting consumed me. I was ready to check the next box. He asked for more time—he wanted to focus on his career—but how much more time did he need? They said there was never a right time to have a child, so I couldn't understand why, after five years of marriage, we needed to wait.

His long nights at the office translated to dinners alone and a cold bed where I would roll over and hug a pillow instead of him. And when his weight slipped under the flat sheet at the witching hour and his warm hand found my breast or ass, I swatted away his advances and scooted to the far side of the bed. When I stopped kissing him goodbye in the mornings, when he stopped reaching for me in bed, when we stopped texting during the day, I confessed my melancholy to Lenny. A roommate had replaced my husband.

Lenny suggested counseling. She said it had helped her when her mom passed. I tried to picture therapy. A quiet, seated figure. Notepads. Ambient lighting. Couches. He said. She said. Tissues. Would talking to a stranger return my husband and give me a child? I proposed it to my ex. He declined, so I went alone. I learned no one was responsible for my happiness but me. I couldn't blame him for enforcing his boundary, but it was my decision if I wanted to remain miserable.

I didn't want a roommate, but I also didn't want a divorce; divorces didn't beget children. This left only one course of action: I had to figure out how to shift him back to being a husband. My therapist asked what we used to do, what qualities had first attracted me to him. In our six-month courtship, we had done nothing but dinner and movies, so we tried weekly date nights where we ate and watched movies in silence. Then I suggested we hike to Edwards Point. He scrunched his face at the suggestion. His wife, who wouldn't check the mail without heels, a hint of color on her lips, and hair worthy of a shampoo ad, wanted to hike. But, like all my other suggestions, he agreed.

He offered me his hand where erosion had washed out trail steps. He dressed my wound when my knee banged a boulder. He encouraged me as I clawed my way back to the trail after a Rainbow Falls detour. And when we sat with our legs dangling off Edwards Point, marveling at the Tennessee River Gorge, he reached to pull me in, and instead of recoiling, I rested my head on his shoulder and let him kiss my sweaty head.

Hiking superglued my marriage.

Instead of chasing my final checkmark, we chased trails instead.

Chasing trails staved off my want for a baby for only so long. After a couple of years, I was back to chasing a pregnancy while my ex-husband chased a connection with another woman. After our divorce, I questioned if trails were an us thing, only to be enjoyed in the company of another. But alone, without conversation, without the beat of someone else's breath or footsteps creating a rhythm with mine, my love for trails deepened. Hiking didn't just gift my marriage a few more years; it saved me.

When the world seemed to be imploding, when I was spiraling, when depression lunged for my hand, all I needed was a few miles on the trail to put everything in perspective. As my legs carried me to waterfalls, canyons, summits, and valleys, I found solace in how beautiful nature's destruction could be. There was nothing like a trail to show the ephemerality of human life. To help me respect nature. Be grateful. Be kind. Focus on the now.

Trails were freedom. Freedom from work, freedom from the empty bedroom that could be a nursery, freedom from judgment. Because trails never judged.

Yet while trails didn't judge me, my mother did.

I gulped more wine. "Humph, my mother." She would never support my fertility journey. I imagined her denouncing it as "unnatural." But in reality, even if it was done naturally, I questioned if she would support me being a mother at all.

When I was barely old enough to menstruate, my mother took me to her job at the hospital's maternity ward, where the majority of patients were teenagers. She grabbed my arm, dragging me from room to room, peeping in on pain through half-cracked doors. With gritted teeth, she said, "You better not get pregnant and bring a baby home." Her hushed voice was barely audible over the screams of labor. "I'll cook it in the microwave."

Around the same time, she taught me how to put on a condom. "Never trust a man to do it." She would drill me at random moments. Unpeeled bananas still provoked my anxiety. I figured my mother's greatest fear was that I'd ruin my life by becoming a teen mom. My mother had been only a few years removed from being a teen mom, and my grandmother had mothered three kids before twenty, but times were different then. I couldn't recall any teen moms at my schools. It seemed a thing of the past, but Stevanie, my neighbor's niece, reminded me that it was not.

When my teenage years yielded to my twenties and I told my mother I was getting married, when she learned my husband was White, she instructed me to never have

children. When I questioned why, she explained that biracial children grow up confused, not knowing where they
belong. They were sentenced to a life of emotional struggle
and social ostracization.

Many times, I wondered if I had married Black, would
my mother have conjured up some different reason why I
shouldn't have children? Would my child be too Black?
Would the world be too cruel? I couldn't drink down the
discomfort that my mother just didn't think I should be a
mom without the right kind of man. Southern subtleties.

The water grew tepid, the bottle empty. I hiccupped and
then released my knees, reclined, and floated. My skin
goose-bumped. I stared at the white ceiling. Thoughts
overloaded my brain to the equivalent of a blue screen.
Numb.

I drained the tub and dressed. After cleaning the tub, I
found my way to bed and checked my phone. No new messages. I checked the local news app. Ads of gummy smiles
and chubby cheeks that evoked that intoxicating newborn
smell popped on the screen. I flipped my phone over and
buried my face in the pillow.

I'd survived my divorce, but I was unsure how I would
survive not being a mom. This was something bigger. But
maybe my mother and ex-husband were right. Maybe I
wouldn't have been a good mother.

I rolled over and grabbed the hematite palm stone that
rested on my nightstand. "God, grant me the serenity to
accept the things I cannot change, courage to change the
things I can, and the wisdom to know the difference."

And then I sobbed until my throat croaked, and my reservoir of tears dried.

The following week, I puppeted my way through life, following more or less the same routine: spin, work, adulting, yoga, sleep.

I wasn't sure what to do. I was hollow. I was crushed. I was unraveled. I needed some sort of catalyst to disrupt my routine, to guide me to a path.

And then my work's corporate campus closed due to the coronavirus, mandating all employees to work from home.

Two days later, my gym closed.

Two days after that, the Great Smoky Mountains National Park, as well as many other nationally protected lands, closed.

A week after the Smokies closed, Tennessee state parks closed.

They said that they would reopen in two weeks.

This wasn't the catalyst I was expecting.

1.4 MANDATES

When the two-week shutdown extended, to be reassessed at the end of April, my neighborhood protested sheltering in place. The Virginia Avenue Greenway behind my home crowded with cyclists, runners, walkers, Rollerbladers, and anything else nonmotorized that moved. I'd peer out my windows and chastise their lack of responsibilities.

I remained locked in my dungeon, where my sixty-hour workweek mushroomed to seventy. Coworkers battled their partners, pets, and progeny while my home echoed silence.

Wake up, dress, walk ten paces to my desk in the dining room, avoid eye contact with the other bedroom, work, eat, adult, shower, sleep. I drank myself to sleep most nights, hoping I wouldn't wake up because, as despondent as I was, I wasn't brave enough to actively take my life. *How did I go from wanting to bring forth new life to wanting to end mine?*

The lack of my 9 a.m. daily huddle reminder became my only indication of the weekend, and then I drowned myself in more wine. Only a couple of bottles remained in the bar cabinet. I needed adult grapes to quiet the voices that plagued my mind.

Night bled to day bled to night until one afternoon, a hiss and a growl sounded too close for comfort. I yanked aside the gray, Roman shade covering my front door. One-Eyed Willy and my neighbor's red husky eyed each other in preparation for Mortal Kombat. I opened my door. One-Eyed Willy bolted, and the husky stared at me with his pleading, icy-blue eyes. I slid on my Chacos and stepped onto my front porch. The brightness stung my eyes. How had I transformed into a Morlock so quickly?

I walked the husky back to his home across the street and latched the gate closed. Shielding my eyes, I turned to return to my sanctuary of suffered, solitary confinement. A bike whizzed by, nearly crashing into me and whipping up my frizzy flyaways. I stumbled out of my autopilot stupor, ready to shout some expletive at the back of the bicyclist's helmet, but the newly leafed trees on Lookout Mountain shushed me. They called me home.

I walked west, venturing beyond my home. Virginia, Saint Elmo, and Alabama avenues separated me from the mountain. I approached the Virginia Avenue intersection. Training wheels, strollers, and squeals of delight assaulted me. I aborted my mission to Lookout Mountain and ran to my house to beat the forecast of my tears. I freed my feet from my Chacos and bolted to my cry room to let the monsoon flow.

Why am I running away from what I want? Why can't I just do like Lenny said and surrender to the hormones? I want it bad enough, right? So, why can't I just buy more sperm? It's as easy as buying a pair of shoes. Search, click, add to cart, check out.

My phone vibrated, an unprogrammed yet familiar number displayed. I had completely forgotten about my appointment. I sniffed up snot, cleared my throat, and windshield-wiped my face.

"This is Allyn."

"Hello, is now still a good time?"

It was strange not sitting in the room with her, with the couch, with the soft glow of a lamp, with the box of tissues on the coffee table, with the church bells ringing at quarter to, signaling us to wrap up our fifty-minute session.

"Yeah, definitely."

"I hate doing this part, but can we talk business first?"

"Yeah, sure." We discussed payment. Even though my health insurance covered a limited number of mental health visits a year, I had opted to keep my sessions off the record, paying in cash. Without being able to exchange cash, I used a payment app instead.

Once she received payment, my therapist opened with, "So, what's on your mind today, Allyn?"

From my initial desire to have a baby to my divorce to Ryan to work-life balance to fertility treatments, and everything else in between, I had been seeing my therapist on and off over the last few years. Whenever my train went off the track, she was there to guide me back.

How should I answer? I had experienced setbacks when life didn't go as planned, but I had recovered from them. I had never been on this Groundhog Day loop with nothing to jerk me to another path. "Yeah, wow, there's just so much going on, and I'm feeling a bit stuck."

"Is it the pandemic? Is there something else? Talk to me about it," she said, accustomed to pulling things out of me.

"I wouldn't say it's the pandemic. So long as trails reopen, I'll be fine. I've never been a social butterfly. But, yeah, my final fertility round didn't take, and … and I can't get past it." I paced through the rooms in my two-bedroom bungalow, adorned with its original two-and-a-quarter-inch wood plank floors, gray painted walls, and carefully arranged Stickley furniture. I cast my eyes downward whenever I stepped in the hallway with the closed bedroom door and its crystal doorknob—the only of its kind out of the fourteen doors in my home. When I started fertility treatments, I changed the knob to that room and vowed to not do anything else to the space until I became pregnant.

"I'm so sorry to hear that," my therapist said. "What can't you get past?"

"Thanks. I appreciate that. I haven't accepted the outcome."

My therapist cleared her throat. I sensed her shifting her weight onto her other hip while writing in her notebook. I continued, "And I know I've done a lot of work on detaching from outcomes, but I'm in disbelief that I'm not pregnant. I just didn't think it *couldn't happen* if I controlled all the variables. I mean, it's what I do. I set goals. I create a plan. I meet goals. I had three tries to make it happen."

"I know you were very selective in who you shared this fertility journey with. What have they said about you feeling stuck?"

"Well, I haven't shared with them that I feel stuck. They all know about the 'three tries and done.'"

"Why haven't you shared?" she asked.

"For starters, I think they're used to me unsticking myself given enough time, but honestly, they're all so busy, and I don't want to burden them with this. I mean, people are dying and losing their jobs, and I'm so self-absorbed in my desire to have a baby that it all seems rather silly."

"I don't think it's silly or self-absorbed at all. This is something you've wanted for years, something that spanned two significant relationships. And many women and men have the desire for a family. So let's get back to why you feel that you cannot walk away from this. You seemed very realistic about the data. What changed?"

There was no way anyone could fathom how this loss had knocked me down so much that I had fallen into an existential crisis. I paused, formulating how to respond, mindful of my word choices so that she wouldn't scribble any suicidal notes. "Because despite the statistics, I didn't really believe it *couldn't* happen. I know years ago we talked about me overcoming my fear of failure about divorce and how I felt I walked around with this scarlet letter. Well, I'm barren, and that feels like the most primal of failures. Like, how dare I even think I could be a mom? My own husband and mother didn't think I'd be a good mom. My mother even said she was happy her maternal daughter had children, and—"

"I'm going to stop you right there, Allyn. You *know* you would be an excellent mom. You told me that you work release weekends with your team even though it's not required of your job."

"Yes, I do. If they're having to spend a Saturday deploying code that I instructed them to build, I want to be there to support them."

"But you don't have to, and most people wouldn't give up a Saturday each month to do that. You could just be 'on call.' And you've also told me how you put your friends' priorities ahead of yours even when you're in a moment of need. Granted, I think you should have absolutely shared your feelings with them, but the truth is you tend to factor other people's well-being into your decision-making. I don't know what's more maternal than that."

I inhaled, steadying my mind to maintain composure. I didn't want my voice to quiver. "Thank you." I held my breath and closed my eyes. I wouldn't let the tears escape. "I know I'm being irrational, but I can't keep these thoughts from consuming me. The scary thing is I can no longer distinguish if I really want a child or if I'm fighting to not fail."

"Okay, let's go over why you want a child again."

I had memorized the list I had crafted over the years. As if I were reciting the Pledge of Allegiance, I said, "I have tremendous capacity to love, and I want to give that love to a child. I have financial resources to provide a child with a very comfortable life. I want to devote my life so fully and unconditionally to someone else's betterment. I want to create a healthy family unit."

"And?"

"And I can do all of these things without having my own child." I paused. "But you know I don't want to adopt. Not that anything is wrong with it, but it's not the path I see for me. I want to create life." My sister and I had discussed adoption when I first told her my desire to pursue IUI. She shared that if she had a third child she would adopt because there was a lot of need in the world, but that's easy to say when you already have biological children. I understood her altruism and the need to get kids out of the system. However, I saw adoption as a Band-Aid solution to larger societal problems.

"When you said, 'Three tries and done,' it was based on the data. You didn't want to let this 'consume you,' as you said. Do you think this is now consuming you?"

I bit my lips and then pushed out all the air in my lungs. "Yes." Anticipating her next question, I continued, "And I'd say it's the failure. I can't accept failure. And I know there was a time that I equated divorce to failure, but eventually, I could see that staying married would have been even more a failure to myself. But, but there's no paradigm shift to reframe how I feel about failing to conceive. My body failed me. It's biologically flawed. It just doesn't function, and this feels like some sort of cosmic punishment. It's like the universe is saying I'm not worthy enough to pass on genetic material."

"Allyn, you are a very rational person. You're one of the most logical people I know, so I'm surprised to hear this."

I shrugged. "Even logical people can succumb to emotional irrationality. In reality, having a child is irrational for anyone in the modern world, but it's still expected and encouraged."

"Have you been hiking?"

"It's been about a month. A lot of trails are closed. I've thought about hiking on Lookout Mountain. It's literally a couple of blocks from my house. Given it's a national park, it'd be illegal to access, but I considered it." I refrained from divulging how I couldn't cross the Greenway to make it to the mountain.

"Have you been journaling?"

"Ugh, no! My brain cannot focus enough to string together a single, coherent sentence."

"Let's have that as a homework item. Get back to journaling. Who cares if your sentences are coherent?"

I cared. I had journaled since elementary school. Over the years, I took breaks, sometimes for weeks or months or even years, but I'd eventually find my way back to inking out my emotions, creating a tapestry I enjoyed revisiting: laughing at my six-year-old worries; humming encore songs to the ticket stubs and wristbands tucked in a pocket; touching velvety, papery petals pressed between pages; and crying over long-forgotten heartbreaks. I wrote with abandon, chronicling my days as hero and villain.

"Okay. I can commit to that."

"And have you booked your hiking trip?" she asked, giving me a well-deserved kick in the ass, considering I possessed all the coping skills to navigate this.

A few months after my divorce, I had hiked the Inca Trail. It was a sensory experience: savoring alpaca, causa, ceviche, and pisco sour; high-altitude sun warming my face on a cool day; condors dancing across cloudless skies; journaling by headlight and gazing up to see the Milky Way; the energizing scent of coca tea in the morning; music blasting from the radios of trail porters and our combined laughter when I danced as they barreled past me. As soon as I returned from that trip, I started planning Huayhuash, another Andean trail. But Huayhuash had to wait while I prioritized crossing the peaks and valleys of Patagonia, the Swiss Alps, and the Himalayas.

When I started my fertility journey, I anticipated that I might not get pregnant, that I might spiral. I planned to hike the Huayhuash Circuit as a sort of consolation prize. Sorry, you're not going to cry out during childbirth, but how about crying out from lack of oxygen as you spend two weeks crossing 16,000-foot passes? With my spiraling, with the pandemic, with trail closures, Huayhuash had slipped from my mind.

"I haven't, but I can commit to booking the trip."

"Are you sure?" she asked, a cocktail of skepticism and surprise spiking her voice.

"Yes. It'll be a good distraction. And something to plan toward."

We ended the call without my sharing that my drinking had exponentially increased or how I was flirting with IVF. Admitting I was spiraling was enough for one call without opening up old wounds about my drinking, much less why I couldn't walk away from pregnancy.

With a glass of malbec in my hand, I opened the spread-sheet that housed my travel itineraries and hiking plans. Each travel itinerary had its own tab, color-coded by conti-nent. I had designated red for South America. I tabbed to the first of three red tabs, titled "Huayhuash," and navi-gated to the table with tour operator details. I sent an email, inquiring about joining a circuit or option for a private tour for an August departure date.

Within twenty-four hours, the tour operators re-sponded that they were not taking any new bookings be-cause the borders had closed. They advised for me to inquire again once the borders re-opened.

I remained hopeful that the pandemic would blow over soon. I requested two weeks of PTO in August and devel-oped a hiking plan to train for Huayhuash:

1. Distance – LeConte, Carver's Gap
2. Elevation gain/mile – Mount Cammerer, Cheoah Bald, Black Mountain Crest, Mount Sterling
3. High altitude – Weekend in Colorado

If preparing for Huayhuash can't extinguish my maternal desires, then that will be the surest sign I should pursue IVF.

1.5 VIRGIN FALLS

I turned right onto Scotts Gulf Road and gripped my steering wheel. My tires crunched two miles of gravel before I pulled into the Virgin Falls Pocket Wilderness parking lot. Two other cars were already parked. It was the last Saturday of April and also the first Saturday that Tennessee state parks had reopened since the shutdown. While the sun stirred from his slumber, I geared up, applying Urban Decay's Psycho lipstick, lacing up my boots, buckling my waist strap, checking my shoulder straps, and buckling my sternum strap. I smiled. My favorite kind of hug.

Me: *At Virgin Falls trailhead. Should be back in car 5 hrs tops.*

Mel: *[heart eyes emoji] I wish I could be there. At my age, I just need to take all the precautions*

Me: *I understand. I need the Smokies to reopen!! We'll see each other soon.*

Mel: *I hope so cuz I'm losing my shit*

I set my phone to airplane mode and crossed the parking lot to recapture my magic on one of the most unique trails in Tennessee. The trail paralleled a trickle of a drainage basin, meandering through a forest before descending to Big Laurel Creek. The creek performed vanishing acts on boulders clustered in the middle of its path—now you see me; now you don't. A tree on the other side of the creek bore the trail blaze. An overhead cable spanned the creek, signaling the way forward. In the summer, the creek disappeared, allowing dry passage, but today, one slip would result in a baptism and a bumpy ride downstream, accompanied by a bruised body and ego. I gulped. I hated water crossings.

Two years ago, Mel and I had nearly drowned whitewater kayaking the Class II rapids of the Hiwassee River. It was all fun and games until we toppled over a four-foot drop and found ourselves fighting, at risk of flush drowning. The experience shook us because it was a river people floated on, tying together rafts and cracking open beers. I still hadn't conquered my discomfort at the sound of wild, turbulent water.

The creek stood between me and the rest of the trail, and "Abracadabra!" wasn't an option. No matter how many times I trekked this trail, I always needed to dig deep and find the courage to cross. My stomach flipped, and my heart banged against my chest. I wiped my hands dry on my thighs and then reached overhead. I faced upstream, wrapped my hands around the cable crossing, and sidestepped across Big Laurel Creek. My body resembled a scissor opening and closing. I hummed a tune to deafen the rapids' roar. When both of my boots were back on solid ground, I wiped cold sweat from my forehead and tapped the trail blaze. I flew past the fifteen-foot cascading Big Laurel Falls, where the trail sharply descended. A rope aiding hikers down the descent rested on the ground; it hadn't been here last year. The descent was tricky to do without poles, but a skilled hiker could manage. I forewent the rope, descended, and veered to my left to behold the beauty of Big Laurel Falls.

I never did any proper research, but I figured there were at least a hundred waterfalls in the Southeast named Laurel Falls. I had visited three, but none were a forty-foot drop like this. I hopped down the moss-covered boulder field in front of the waterfall then kept left of the falls till I disappeared behind them, entering a cave. Inside the cave, I turned around to face the falls, hypnotized by the sun that lit the waterfall before the cave swallowed it whole and echoed its cries. Unlike other Laurel Falls, this one pooled, forming a stream that flowed backward into the cave, where it eventually disappeared, only to reappear above-ground at Virgin Falls, the crown jewel of the area.

I stood, meditating to the water falling and flowing back into the cave. My eyes were fixed on the campground on the waterfall's dry side. I'd never been much of a camper, but I longed to camp there with a special someone. The special someone used to be my ex-husband, then Ryan, and then my hypothetical child, but those were all dead ends. *Maybe I'll do it alone. Maybe I'll come to do everything alone.*

Two men startled me out of my thoughts. They walked toward me from someplace darker and deeper in the cave. We smiled as a greeting. I picked up my pack and departed the cave. It was time to press on. From Big Laurel Falls, the trail climbed gradually before intersecting with a trail sign:

Loop Trail
Sheep Cave →
Virgin Falls 0.8 →
Virgin Falls 0.5 ←

I turned left, chasing the waterfall's faint, white noise until it roared. I passed a makeshift campground, and there it was—Virgin Falls, a stream escaping from a cave and then free-falling 110 feet before disappearing into another cave at the bottom of the sink.

I basked in the tree-filtered sunlight, soaking in the budding leaves while I listened to the heartbeat of the forest. In that moment, life didn't seem nearly as bad. As many times as I have visited Virgin Falls, my most memorable trip was a few years back. It was three weeks after my divorce, and the first time I hiked alone.

I had reached Virgin Falls and beamed at achieving my first solo miles. A rainbow crossed the waterfall, and I needed to capture every angle. The water volume was the most I had witnessed in my half decade of hiking the trail. I snapped photos of the falls with my newly purchased DSLR, a divorce present, as if I were a beret-wearing photographer on a fashion shoot, directing my model to make love to the camera.

A woman's voice posed a question. Or, I assumed it was a question by the way she uptalked. Her voice was only a decibel louder than the falls. I whipped my head around, curious who had interrupted my photo shoot. Three women gathered. I first studied the woman whose height was closest to mine. I'd guess she was two inches shorter than me by both height and waist. Her University of Kentucky ballcap hid most of her silver-blonde hair. Her glasses covered mascaraed eyelashes topped with a blue shimmer. She appeared old enough to be my mother but not old enough to be my grandmother. The woman to her left was middle-aged, average height, with more love to give around her stomach and thighs. Her exasperated face matched her hair color. Accompanying them was a tall, middle-aged, bronzed woman with a wooden hiking staff, adorned with metal badges. Her long braid draped over her shoulder. She appeared to be one of the few White people in the area who had a legitimate claim to Cherokee ancestry.

"Excuse me? I didn't quite hear you," I said, projecting my voice above the thunderous falls.

"Are you here alone?" the petite woman asked.

"Yes."

"Do you come out here much?" she asked.

"Not too often, but I've been here a few times. This view never gets old."

"Oh, it's my first time out here. I saw some Facebook photos, and I knew I just had to come, and" — she motioned to her companions — "they offered to take me, and boy, this sure is amazing."

"Are you all from Kentucky?" I asked, eyeing her ballcap.

"I am, but these two are from the Smoky Mountains area. I retired to Sevierville after my husband passed. It was always our plan to retire there. We just loved the Smokies. My husband and I would spend our anniversaries hiking there, and we just knew we had to retire there. Unfortunately he didn't make it, but I knew he'd want me to still fulfill our dream, so I quit my office job, sold our house, packed up the dogs, and moved. Right after I moved in, I had to evacuate because of the fires. Can you imagine? It was scary. I just moved my life and didn't know if I was going to lose everything all over again. Once that fiasco was done, it hit me that I was alone. I didn't know anybody. I always hiked with him. So I joined a hiking Facebook group because I don't hike alone, and that's how the 865 community adopted me, and how I met these girls. They're like famous hikers. I'm surprised they want to hike with a slowpoke like me, but boy, I'm glad they do. By the way, my name's Melinda, but my friends call me Mel. You from around here?" The crow's feet framing her blue eyes crinkled deeper into a smile.

I blinked a few times, shifting my brain from brief hiker banter to full-on conversation mode in order to absorb the deluge of words and formulate a response. "No. I live in Chattanooga." Figuring she wasn't familiar with Tennessee geography, I added, "It's about two and a half hours from here and an hour and a half south of Knoxville."

"And your name?" she said.

"I'm Allyn. Everyone calls me Allyn."

"Alan?" she asked, wrinkling her forehead.

"Yeah, but it's spelled *A-l-l-y-n*."

"Do you hike a lot?" Mel asked.

"Yes, a good bit. You?"

"Now that I live in the Smokies, yeah. Almost everyone there is working on completing their 900, but I don't have any interest in that. I just want to hike the pretty trails and one day stay overnight at LeConte Lodge." She smiled at the falls. "Man, this sure is pretty."

"The 900? What's that?" I asked.

"Oh, the 900-miler club is for people who have hiked all the trails in the Great Smoky Mountains National Park. There aren't actually nine hundred miles of trails anymore since the park closed some, but they still call it the 900 since you have to backtrack and hike a lot of the same trails to collect new ones, so all in all you still hike about nine hundred miles even if it's not nine hundred *unique* miles." She thumbed toward the tall woman with the hiking staff. "Sarah's completed the 900."

"Congratulations," I yelled to Sarah.

She stared at the falls, unaware of the human activity around her. I followed her gaze to study the waterfall and debated if I should re-seek solitude.

"And Hannah's working on hers," Mel said.

"It'll take me a decade to finish, but I'll finish it," Hannah said. "You can follow my journey on YouTube."

"Do you always hike alone?" Mel asked.

"Well, no." I eyed her and her companions, assessing how truthful I wanted to be. "I'm recently—divorced, and this is my first hike alone." It was also my first time identifying as divorced aloud. No stones from the heavens pelted me.

"You should check out the Smoky Mountains Hikers on Facebook. You can find all of us on there," Mel said.

I shook my head. "I don't do social media. No Facebook. No Instagram. No Twitter. No nothing, Miss Melinda."

"Oh, you can call me Mel."

I nodded but figured she'd have to give me permission a few more times to break my cultural conditioning of giving older Southern women a token of respect. Funny how I never extended that habit to non-Southerners.

"Who do you share all your pretty photos with?" Mel asked, eyeing my camera.

"They're for me. I email some to friends. People I know in real life," I said.

"Well, I sure would love to see them, Allyn. Can I give you my number?" Mel asked.

I stored her number in my phone, figuring I could delete it later. Sarah took a small trail to the front of the falls and snapped photos with her phone.

"So, how do you pick your trails without social media?" Hannah asked.

"I guess the old-fashioned way. Meeting people on trails. Researching parks. Reading trail reports."

"That just seems weird to me," Hannah said.

I shrugged. "It feels weird to spend my time passively consuming a highlight reel of someone else's curated life. Sure, the promise of connectivity and convenience is nice, but at what price? I'd rather live my life than consume someone else's."

"I hear you, but I just don't think I could give it up," Hannah said.

"Allyn, we have some friends hosting a cheesecake hike the last Saturday of April. You should come if you are free," Mel said.

I scrunched my face. What else didn't I know about Smoky Mountains hiking. "A cheesecake hike?"

"Yeah, we're going to bring cheesecake up to Cliff Tops," Hannah said.

"Cliff Tops?" I asked.

"Yeah, it's on top of LeConte," Mel said.

Finally, a reference I could ground. I had heard of LeConte. It was the last Smokies hike that my ex-husband and I had attempted together. We didn't make it past Alum Cave. "That sounds so absurd, but hey, if I'm free, why not?"

"We should take a photo, so I can post it to my page," Hannah said.

"I don't mind taking a photo of all of you," I said.

"Don't be ridiculous," Mel said. "You have to be *in* the photo."

And as ridiculous as it sounded to take photos with strangers, I didn't protest. We huddled together and took our first selfie.

The last Saturday in April, my heart and lungs thanked me for taking a well-deserved breather at the trail intersection with Rainbow Falls. My vision blurred while reading the trail sign:

Rainbow Falls Trail
LeConte Lodge → 0.1
← Bullhead Trail 0.4
← Cherokee Orchard 6.5
Alum Cave Trail
← Alum Cave Bluffs 2.7
← Arch Rock 3.6
← Newfound Gap Road 4.9

I lowered my backpack to the ground. It was heavier than normal, weighed down with a frozen cheesecake wrapped in foil. Other than a few stops to take photos with people on the trail, we had hiked nonstop since our last break at the Alum Cave Bluffs. The cool air dried the sweat on my skin. We collectively shivered and reached into our backpacks to layer up.

"What do you think of the hike so far, Allyn?" Hannah asked.

"It's really beautiful. I can't believe I've never been here before. I'm really excited to see the lodge."

And I was. On the rare occasions when my ex-husband and I would go to the Smokies, we had hiked to Charlies Bunion, Clingmans Dome from the parking lot, and our un-successful Rocky Top and LeConte summits. I considered myself a serious hiker, exploring the Cumberland Moun-tains of Middle Tennessee, but as my quads screamed in pain that day, I acknowledged that I had overestimated my hiking abilities. I had never hiked an elevation gain of over 3,000 feet in a single day, and I hardly knew what switch-backs were or why they were needed. I didn't know if my lungs, legs, or back were in the most pain. I had wanted to take at least five breaks before the other women were ready for one. I was out of my league but itching to experience more.

"Hey, can one of you record me walking on the path as we arrive at the lodge?" Hannah asked.

"You and your YouTube channel. Can't we just enjoy the hike?" Mel said.

"Well, some of us are trying to secure marketing deals and sponsorships so that we too can quit the hamster wheel," Hannah said, nodding to Sarah.

Sarah laughed. "You do know it's still work, right? I can't just lie around on days I have to be on the trail."

"I don't mind taking the video," I said.

"Be careful, Allyn. It's a slippery slope. Next thing you know, she'll recruit you to join her on the 900," Mel said.

Even though I found the 865 community intriguing, I hesitated to jump from my ex-husband's sphere to theirs. I wanted to find my own footing. To be alone but not lonely.

Hannah walked the conifer-shaded path ahead while I recorded her. The buzz of distant conversations carried on the wind and grew louder as our boots' rubber soles stomped on the broken shale trail. We passed a few log cabins with rocking chair porches and hooked a left at a wide stair that descended into the complex. We had arrived at LeConte Lodge.

The grounds teemed with people. The stairs continued to descend past many more log cabins. They terminated at the grayed-wood, shackle-sided dining hall, where a sign noting the date and elevation hung above double doors:

LeConte Lodge
Elevation 6,593 April 29, 2017
Dining Room

We queued to take photos in front of the dining hall, commemorating the day. Then the women hollered and waved at various people. Weaving around hikers, we arrived at the official lodge building, climbed the wooden stairs, waved to a few people seated in rocking chairs on the deck, opened the screeching screen door, and were sucked into the hive.

People of all ages, sizes, and smells swarmed the lodge. And, yes, everyone was a trekker. There were no roads to LeConte. It wasn't a Mount Mitchell, a Mount Washington, or a Mount Evans with winding, paved roads spewing out passengers for ten-minute photo opportunities with a summit sign. To arrive at LeConte, one must hike. Even the llamas hike, but helicopter pilots got a pass.

A couple of bookcases, brimming with books and board games, stood against walls adorned with sepia photographs and a chalkboard chronicling the weather on the mountain. Kerosene lanterns sat on a few tables of varying sizes and shapes that dotted the space. A shadowboxed Tennessee state flag hung at one end of the lodge, watching over us. Most hikers stood in small huddles, though some sat in rocking chairs, and some lined up, like us, to sign the guest book. Others queued in front of a counter to check into a cabin or to buy mountain memorabilia. I read how other hikers signed the guest book before contributing to the legacy:

Name	Notes	# of Visits
Sarah	These boots were made for walking	55
Hannah	Watch my trip report @hannahhikes900	12
Mel	Another gorgeous day making mountain memories	24
Allyn	Kicked my ass but I loved it!	1

We then queued to buy our Mount LeConte T-shirts broadcasting the words, "I hiked it" with the year. The shirts were sold only at the lodge, advertising our prowess to the greater world.

After we acquired our merch, I lost sight of the three women. I strained my neck trying to find them, like I was searching for Waldo. Giving up, I scanned the lodge for a spot to perch and observe the 865 hiking community. I spied an empty spot along the wall. Carrying my pack by its top loop, I sidestepped and shuffled my way through many small groups to other side of the room. I nestled my pack in between my boots and dug inside for a protein bar. I people-watched, too overwhelmed, overstimulated, and out of my depth to engage in any of the conversation snippets about trails, 900 progress, or vlogging.

Halfway through the protein bar, I spotted Sarah. A group encircled her, savoring every word she spoke. She caught my gaze and waved. The group turned its head, following her interruption. I waved back, nodded, and smiled. She continued speaking to her congregation and laughed. They laughed in return like some sort of laugh track.

A few people moseyed over to my quiet space and introduced themselves. Word was spreading that I was "Allyn (no Facebook)," the new woman who hiked with Sarah at Virgin Falls. They asked me for a few selfies. I obliged and then pondered my new celebrity status. It was as if I ranked in the D-list of the 865 community because I had zero degrees of separation to the highest possible tier of the hiker hierarchy—a currency higher than half the room.

We eventually ate our cheesecake at Cliff Tops and returned to the Alum Cave trailhead.

For the remainder of the year, we all collected. Hannah collected trails for her 900. Sarah collected content throughout the Southeast for her sponsor. Mel collected me, and I collected a love for the Smoky Mountains.

And now, years later, on this last Saturday in April, a couple arrived at Virgin Falls, interrupting my memories. I lifted my pack onto my back and set off for the trailhead. I was accustomed to trails becoming busier as the day progressed, but the level of trail traffic that day was unprecedented. It rivaled Atlanta's Spaghetti Junction at rush hour. I stopped counting trekkers when I reached the hundredth person. In all my years visiting that trail, I had never counted more than what I estimated to be thirty people.

Pandemic trekkers. It was easy to differentiate them from real trekkers. Their clothing, their gear, their gaze, their lack of trail etiquette—take your pick. They didn't obey the right of way; they unleashed their dogs, whose shit lined the trail; they walked off trail, trampling flora; they blasted music from portable speakers. I arrived at the parking lot, which was now full.

As I drove out to the highway, vehicles lined the gravel road for up to a mile from the trailhead. My haven for solitude, my destination for recovery and healing—my respite—had been overrun.

1.6 CLIFF TOPS

Tightly spaced billboards beckoned me to Dollywood; Ripley's; dinner theaters like Stampede, Hatfield and McCoy, and Pirates Voyage; ziplines; canopy walks; river rafting; water parks; helicopter tours; and outlet stores. I exited I-40 and drove through endless mini golf and go-kart courses and trinket shops, where, if I wanted, I could print my name on a penny. Mel lived nearby, but I wouldn't get to see her. At a stoplight, I scrolled through our last text exchange.

Me: *I read the park is partially reopening Saturday. Free for a hike this weekend? I want to do Boulevard b/c it's my last trail to collect to LeConte.*

Mel: *Hey, girlfriend. Wish I could but I have to work that weekend. It's been crazy busy*

Me: *Really? Busy? I didn't know you were back at work.*

Mel: *Yeah, I made more money being furloughed but I'm old and need the insurance benefits. We're short-staffed and our guest numbers are the highest we've seen for this time of year. I'll be working more than hiking this summer*

Me: *[Wow emoji]*

Mel: *Yeah, the Smokies are like the only place in America people can go and feel normal. But don't worry. I still have time off blocked for our July overnight @ LeConte [Fingers crossed emoji]*

Since moving to the Smokies, Mel worked as a marketing rep for a major Smoky Mountains tourist attraction to supplement her retirement income. I sometimes wondered if her desire to work stemmed more from not wanting to face an empty home. Sure, she had her dogs, whom she treated like the children she never had, but dogs can't fill the void of a lost partner.

Buildings gave way to trees, and soon I turned onto US-441, the main artery of Great Smoky Mountains National Park and the primary reason the Smokies were the most visited national park in the United States. When the state of Tennessee transferred land to the federal government, the deed restricted the tolling of US-441, rendering the Smokies one of the few national parks in the States that can never charge an entry fee. That, coupled with the park's proximity to major cities and tourist attractions, all contributed to the Smokies' popularity. And then Tennessee politics, not in favor of mandates on free enterprise, had created a space where businesses reopened without coronavirus restrictions, and, as Mel said, Americans were flocking there to feel normal.

A large, portable traffic sign flashed messages in orange, block letters:

ALUM CAVE TRAIL CLOSED

While the Smokies had reopened, it was a partial reopening with the most popular trails and LeConte Lodge remaining closed. A few minutes later, I drove by the Alum Cave trailhead. Orange cones barricaded the parking lot entrance.

Before day could wipe the sleep from his eyes, I pulled into the nearly empty Newfound Gap parking lot, one of the largest and busiest lots in the park. It straddled the state line and offered the chance for anyone to exit their car and walk on the Appalachian Trail. It was here that I had first walked on the AT, when my ex-husband and I had attempted to hike to Charlies Bunion on a hot and humid August day over a decade ago.

I planned to take the AT for a few miles and then veer left on Boulevard Trail, hiking rolling hills for seven and a half miles to reach Cliff Tops. While Alum Cave was the shortest and easiest of the five trails to LeConte, Boulevard was the longest. I'd hang out a bit and then take the same route back for a total mileage of about seventeen miles. It was going to be a long day.

Me: *Starting Boulevard to LeConte. Targeting checking back in 8 hrs. I know you're working, but would you be free for dinner?*

Mel: *I wish, but some bigwigs are in town, so it's an all day and evening event for me*

Me: *I miss you.*

Mel: *I miss you too girlfriend [hug emoji]*

I applied lipstick and fitted my backpack. I looped bear spray on my waist strap. Despite my experience and preparedness, my stomach flipped with new trail jitters.

I breathed in the crisp, cool air and marched toward the Appalachian Trail. That section of the AT's grade was so gentle that at times it seemed flat, so I made excellent time and arrived at the trail intersection of the Appalachian and Boulevard trails ahead of schedule:

The Boulevard Trail

← The Jumpoff Trail 0.3
← Mt. LeConte 5.3

Appalachian Trail

Icewater Spring Shelter 0.2 →
Charlies Bunion 1.3 →
← Newfound Gap 2.7

When my ex-husband and I first attempted Charlies Bunion, this trail intersection broke me. Exasperated, I couldn't fathom hiking another mile and then four back. Back then, I had no perception of how long a mile was, so we turned around. That was a lifetime ago. But last year when I was on this section of the AT with The Marine, I was all too aware of how long a mile was.

When my coworker first introduced us, I had offered to take The Marine on a hike, but out of respect for my limited free time and my prioritization of Ryan, I never got around to it. But after my relationship with Ryan ended, I fulfilled my promise. I contacted The Marine and presented him the option of hiking closer to Chattanooga or the Smokies. He chose the Smokies.

I drove us because I had plenty of frequent-driver miles from Chattanooga to the Smokies, and his car was in the shop. The entire drive up, he talked about his impressions of the South, leaving me exhausted before the hike even began.

The Marine and I geared up in the Newfound Gap parking lot.

"Do you want me to hike in front?" I asked while I was buckling and tightening my backpack straps.

"Yeah, I've never been here," he said as he slipped on a small, sand-colored, military-style backpack. He was an entrepreneur and a recent transplant by way of Seattle, a former Marine, and another minority on the mountain who snowboarded, hiked, and biked. But he didn't consider himself an outdoorsman because, as he would say, playing outside was part of a Pacific Northwesterner's DNA. Despite being ten years my senior, his body rivaled that of a bootcamp-chiseled recruit.

"Okay, well, I know we've never hiked together, so I just want to go over a few things about my style," I said. "I'm happy to set a pace and stop for any breathers. Just let me know if my pace is okay or if you want to stop. Also, I'm okay if you want some distance between us. I don't need to see you, but I need to be able to hear you." He nodded. Given his love to chatter, I didn't think my last request would be hard to satisfy.

We let the forest swallow us. The wide trail allowed us to walk side by side. He looked up and sniffed the air the way an animal would when catching a scent.

"You okay?" I asked.

"The trees smell different here. These are baby trees." He held up his hand to show an inch of space between his forefinger and thumb.

"Well, yeah, I mean, this is Appalachia. While at one point these mountains stood as tall as the Himalayas, nowadays, the trees and mountains are smaller than the Cascades." I tittered. "Do you expect outside to smell the same everywhere?"

"No, Allyn. Don't be silly." He rolled his eyes, and we chuckled together.

"Well, I was just checking. You seem to have very negative opinions about Tennessee, especially Chattanoogans."

"Yeah, people here don't really do anything. They just sit around and eat. Back home, everyone is active," he said.

A bead of sweat broke free on my forehead. Despite him asking me to take the lead, his longer gait pressured me to pick up my pace. I couldn't keep his pace the entire hike, but I wasn't gasping for air yet.

"But I live in Chattanooga, and most things I do are outside," I said.

He smacked. "But you're different."

"I beg to differ. I was as city as they come, and I became an outdoor lover after I moved to Chattanooga. Most people I know here are triathletes. Chattanooga was made for running, cycling, paddling, climbing. People are outside everywhere."

"Well, I haven't seen it, but besides that, there's so much wrong in Chattanooga." He cleared his throat.

I pursed my lips and pushed out air to regulate my heart rate. "Look. I'm a transplant like you, and I struggled when I first moved to Chatt, but I assure you, it's a hell of a lot better now." I moved my neck gaiter from my neck to my hairline, dabbing my sweaty forehead in the process. "But I am curious what you think is wrong." My heart pounded, and my thighs itched. I resisted the urge to lie down on the trail, scratching them like a dog with mange.

"Chattanooga is racist," he deadpanned.

I stopped and faced him. "Whoa, seriously? You really think that? I feel it's one of the least racist cities in the South." I reached for my Nalgene and chugged water.

"The White people treat me like I'm invisible. Just the other day"—he twisted his backpack to his chest and pulled out a bag of trail mix—"I was at the auto store, standing in line, waiting to be helped. A White man came in after me and just walked right in front of me as if I didn't exist." He poured a handful of the mix into his hand and popped it into his mouth.

I scrunched my face. "Hmmm. That's pretty fucked up."

"Happens all the time here. And, man, Lookout is the worst!"

"Seriously?" I clutched my heart. "That's like my back-yard playground. Everyone in Chatt is so nice to me. They open doors, carry things to my car, call me ma'am—"

"But look at you. People don't know you're Black."

I cocked my head and sucked my teeth. "It's obvious I'm not White." I didn't want to invalidate his experiences as a darker-skinned Black man. He was right. Black people knew I was Black or at least had Black "in me," as I would often hear, but everyone else made their own hypotheses. I couldn't relate to this part of his Black experience.

I stowed my water bottle away and resumed hiking. He followed, challenging my pace with every step.

"Anyway, yeah, the people on Lookout are racist. I was in a store up there, and this old, White lady refused to speak to me. And peep this, I got right in her face and was like—" He stopped. I stopped and turned to look at him. He moved his face less than six inches from mine, bobbing his head to the syllables. "Good afternoon, how are you?"

I chuckled. "Hmm, I'm not doubting you. I just never experienced anything that ... overt." I searched my memory bank for Chattanooga racism. My thoughts landed on my neighborhood. My restored home had appraised far below what my Realtor and I had expected; when questioned, my Realtor said that if the home shifted one block west, its value would skyrocket. One block west was Whiter. Then after moving in, I observed that my hipster neighbors across the street never spoke to me or to any other Black neighbors. I swallowed down the bitterness that while not overt, the racism still existed.

"I know there's a good bit of racism against Mexicans because"—I altered my voice, emulating Tennessee twang—"they took all the good jobs that pay over sixteen dollars an hour." My voice returned to normal. "And the farther you get from the city center, Confederate flags do fly, but in my experience, I feel discriminated against as a woman more than any sort of racism. But I'm aware it happens. I mean, you seem miserable here. Do you see yourself staying in Chatt?"

We resumed hiking.

"For now. Once my business takes off, no." He hacked up phlegm and spat it out.

"Are you okay?"

"Yeah. I'm starting a new cleanse, so my body is just ridding itself of toxins."

I frowned. My eyes darted around in search of an answer to his nonsense. "Are you sure it's not allergies? They say we have some of the worst allergies in the nation."

"Don't get me started on that. Everyone here says they have allergies. If people just changed their diet and exercised, they wouldn't have allergies. I'm telling you, Allyn, vegan is the way to go."

I twisted my mouth. "I'm not sure it works that way. I never had allergies until I moved here. I exercise plenty, and while I'm not vegan, I have a pretty balanced diet."

He stopped. I turned to catch his gaze. He cut his eyes at me and scrunched his lips. He resumed hiking again.

"What?!" I said. "I'm not trying to defend the poor choices people make, but pollen is pollen. Certainly, there are overweight people in the Greater Seattle area, and let's be honest, if food tasted as good there as here, they'd all be overweight, too."

We continued our climb. Leaves rustled. Birds chirped. How I missed the sound of human silence. Anyone who hiked knew the importance of hike chemistry. Trail preference, distance, elevation, pacing, breaks, and conversation are crucial inputs. All I could think was, *Shit, we haven't made it there yet. We still have the hike and the car ride back. Fuck me.*

He interrupted my serenity. "Since your divorce, have you ever had issues with intimacy?" His tone had shed anger, exposing a buried hurt.

"Intimacy?" I asked, for clarity's sake. I bit my lips. My cheeks flushed, hoping that I intrigued him.

"Yeah, like emotional openness with relationships," he said.

"Well, I've only been in one relationship after my divorce."

"How long have you been divorced?" He guzzled water from a plastic bottle.

Still climbing the trail, I looked up as if there were a calculator above me, displaying the results of my mental math. "Almost three years."

"I've been divorced nearly a decade."

"Hmm. Well, no, I don't have issues being emotionally open. It might take me a while to trust, but once I let someone in my inner circle, I'm pretty fucking open. Why do you ask?"

"I struggle with it. I just don't trust women's intentions. I feel women always have some angle."

"That's no way to live. Sounds like your divorce did a number on you."

"She was attracted to the military lifestyle. She didn't want me." He crunched his empty water bottle.

I glanced back over my shoulder, curious about his facial expression. Despite the seriousness of the conversation, he wore a blank expression as he stuffed the plastic bottle into his rucksack. Before he glanced up to catch me checking on him, I turned to face the direction we had yet to travel. "You do realize that not all women are your ex-wife. It seems you have a lot you still need to let go of so you can move on as a person."

"Yeah, I write a bit to help process."

"Wow. A polymath! That's impressive." With college, with my career, with my choice in partners, I was unaccustomed to multifaceted men. "Is there anything you don't do? What do you write?"

"Mostly plays," he said.

"Oh yeah, really?"

"Yeah, the last play I wrote was about a Black man who unexpectedly found himself in an interracial relationship."

I stopped. I slung my pack down to the ground, reached for my water, and allowed the water to tickle my throat. "I don't mean to pry, but was your ex-wife White?" I wiped my mouth with the back of my hand and put the empty bottle back in the mesh insert on my pack.

"No, I'm not attracted to White women, but when you think about the world, it makes the most sense for a Black man to be with a White woman." He pulled a small plastic bag of edamame from a pocket on his pack and shoved a handful of beans into his mouth.

I hiccupped. "Huh? By what logic?"

"We're the most oppressed people by the White man. We both suffer the same abuse."

I knitted my brows and hoisted my pack on my back. "And Black women don't?" I marched forward, not wanting to prolong our time on the trail.

"Hell no! Black women have benefited from the protection of the White man's status for centuries, affording her and her offspring a better lifestyle."

I rolled my eyes. "How do you figure?"

"Well, in times of slavery, her children would be protected, assigned better jobs, and sometimes adopted and freed—"

"Dude, that was rape. There was no choice to lie with a White man."

"Okay, well, the protections are still there when Black women choose to be with White men now. A White man has economic and therefore political advantages in this world that his family benefits from. A Black woman with a White man is no better than a concubine."

Hotep speak. I dared not look back because if he saw my face, neither of us would make it back unscathed. My breath caught in my throat. My eyes widened not only in disbelief but also in disappointment. The same thought raced in my head. *He called me a concubine!* Granted, he had no clue my ex-husband and ex-boyfriend were White, but the casualness of his conviction infuriated me. *Is he fucking with me? He's not laughing or smiling. What makes him think I would agree? Or is he trying to be confrontational? Concubine, my ass! Maybe my ex-husband and Ryan were the concubines benefitting from* my *economic advantage. The advantage that I earned by working my ass off in school and playing all the political and corporate games, the games that afforded me financial independence.* Nothing productive could come from getting into an argument over race with another four miles of trail and a three-hour car ride back, so I remained silent on the subject. Seething.

Maybe he sensed my anger, or maybe I blocked out his voice, but for the next half hour, only our footsteps conversed. We turned left at the well-worn sign:

Charlies Bunion
Closely Control Children

After a few paces, the vista opened up to 180-degree views of the Smoky Mountains. The landscape didn't afford space to lounge and sit. Hikers stood with their backpacks nestled between their legs or dared to climb out to a few rocky outcrops to sit and rest their weary legs.

"So, what do you think of all this?" I asked The Marine.

"It's nice out here. I'm going to climb out on that rock." He pointed to the rocky promontory that the 865 hiking community called "the tourist bunion" because the real bunion was unmarked and farther up the AT. "And meditate, if that's okay with you."

While I watched him connect to the mountains I loved, I disconnected from whatever intrigue I held for him. His judgment, his anger, his bias was too much for me to bear. And could I blame the hate that coursed through his body? He was a Black man trying to make something of himself in a world that devalued, dismissed, and commodified him; the same world I navigated by bottling myself up and behaving as expected.

But as expected according to whom?

Years later, I still pondered that question: Who am I behaving for? I turned left on the Boulevard Trail, tackling new ground. I breathed out my nerves, pushing out the uncertainty that had crept in.

Compared to other Smokies trails, Boulevard was less maintained and less traveled. Every so often, a downed tree blocked the trail. Some I easily passed, walking off trail around tree roots or stepping over fallen trunks. Others I couldn't walk around or step over but could go under. So I'd remove my pack, set it on the ground, and push it to the other side before I limboed to freedom. Okay, well, it wasn't quite a limbo, but I contorted my body close to the ground. Other trees afforded no option to walk around, step over, or go under. They left me with no good option to move forward other than hoisting my body atop the trunk, hugging it as best I could, then inching my body over the trunk, and finally lowering myself back on solid ground.

Pockets of people passed me heading in the opposite direction. We did the familiar hiker acknowledgments of a wave, a smile, a small phrase about how gorgeous a day it was, or a simple, "Enjoy your hike." With every leaf rustle,

I whipped my head, scanning for bears or men—my biggest trail threats. The grade increased. Per my trail research, I figured I was on the final push to LeConte, near the chain section. My pace slowed. My heart rate quickened. Sweat wept from my temples. Ahead, I spied a chain bolted to the side of the mountain. I quickened my pace.

A landslide had cleared trees from the slope, opening up the trail to unobstructed views, which was a treat on a trail that otherwise snaked beneath the canopy's protection. I leaned back on the mountain and snapped a few photos. I then tucked my phone away and placed my left hand atop the chain for safety in case I misstepped and needed to take hold. Ten seconds later, trees re-enclosed the trail. I stopped to chug water and marveled at the artistry of trail building.

I pressed on, passing the actual summit of Mount Le-Conte, which was marked only by a pile of stacked rocks just off the trail. After a few more paces, I passed LeConte Lodge. All its entry points were cordoned off with yellow tape as if it were a crime scene. The quiet was startling.

Unable to detour at the lodge to sign the guest book and buy a T-shirt, I took the spur to Cliff Tops, the final destination for the cheesecake hike a few years earlier. Given Alum Cave, the shortest and easiest trail, was closed, I didn't expect many hikers at Cliff Tops; however, when I arrived, four separate parties shared the space: two sets of couples, a lone backpacker, and a family of four.

The younger couple snapped selfies. The backpacker sunbathed with a bucket cap over his face. The older couple sat near rhododendrons, feasting on a family-size bag of cheddar-and-sour cream potato chips. The family perched atop the fins of Cliff Tops, spaced out, commandeering the best seats. It was the equivalent of manspreading on the mountain.

There was no space for me to sit and maintain social distancing, so I dropped my pack to the ground and pulled out trail mix to munch on while standing. I turned to the older couple. "You definitely could eat an entire bag of chips after that hike up. What route did you take?"

"Rainbow," the woman answered. Her accent screamed Eastern Tennessee. "You?"

"Boulevard. Whereabouts are you from?" I asked.

"Maryville. You?" she asked.

"I live in Chattanooga, but I come up somewhat regularly."

"Yeah, we're happy to see the park reopen. We were going a bit crazy. We hope it doesn't close again, and maybe more trails'll open up," the woman said.

"Oh, I know what you mean. If things don't get out of control, it should stay open. Are you going back Rainbow or Bullhead?"

"We haven't decided yet," the man said. "It's all downhill, and that's what counts."

We laughed. Unfortunately, hiking Boulevard back to the parking lot wouldn't be all downhill. My legs were going to kill me.

I glanced west to the mountains. The young couple had left. The backpacker lay motionless. The patriarch of the family faced east toward me and the older couple while his family faced the view. His Red Sox ballcap seemed recently plucked from a store shelf.

He munched on baby carrots. I couldn't decide which version of Wallace Shawn he resembled more: *Clueless*'s Mr. Hall or *The Princess Bride*'s Vizzini.

"What trail did you take up?" I asked the father. I estimated his son and daughter couldn't have been more than ten.

"Alum."

"I thought Alum Cave was closed," I said.

"No, the trail is open," the faux Wallace Shawn said.

My jaw twitched. I glanced back at the Maryville couple. My eyes darted from the woman to the man and back to the woman. The woman spoke so that only her companion and I could hear. "The trail is closed. I'm pretty sure they're doing trail maintenance, but they don't know no better."

I turned back to the impostor. "That's odd because the website definitely states that the trail is closed. You didn't see any signs when you entered the park stating that Alum Cave Trail was closed or any orange traffic cones blocking the parking lot?"

"Guess the website isn't updated. No, we didn't see any closure notices. No signs. No barriers." He spoke with a slight lisp just like Wallace Shawn.

His teeth snapped a carrot in two. The matter was settled. Definitely the Vizzini version.

I bit the inside of my cheek, raised my chin, and squinted my eyes. I wasn't shocked. The Smokies catered to all, and unfortunately, those who didn't consider the park a home abused it like a rental. Dogs on trails. Littering. Holding up traffic on trails to take multiple photos. Provoking bears. Tourists. Morons. Tourons.

My eyes darted to the Maryville couple, who both shook their heads. The woman shrugged and let her hands collapse into her lap. I could no longer bottle up my frustrations and behave as expected. I untamed my heart and embraced my inner Julia Sugarbaker.

"You're lying. Maybe you think it's okay to lie to a complete stranger. Maybe because I'm a woman you think I'm inconsequential and a *white* lie is okay. Maybe you think I'm a stupid Southerner who would believe anything. Maybe you have a job where whatever you say goes. Well, not here. Not on LeConte. Not in the Smokies. Not in Tennessee." I narrowed my eyes. "You're just a modern-day carpetbagger, and maybe where you come from your behavior is accepted, but here"—I pointed to the ground—"here in the South, you're being disrespectful, and I'm not going to stand for it."

The backpacker removed the bucket hat that shielded his face. He sat up with wide eyes.

I continued, "Alum Cave is closed. The website stated it. Your wife likely questioned you when you drove by that big-ass traffic sign flashing 'Alum Cave Trail Closed' in orange letters. Your children probably felt a pang of guilt when you moved aside the orange traffic cones to park at the trailhead."

His wife and children turned to study me, and when I met their stare, they averted their eyes to the ground. The faux Wallace Shawn glared at me. I tilted my head and glowered at him, daring him to say something. Adrenaline coursed through my veins. Its power was intoxicating. I didn't have to look back at the Maryville couple to know they supported me. I was our spokesperson, and this was our turf.

He said, "Sorry."

I exhaled. I hadn't realized I had been holding my breath. The backpacker gave me a nod. I looked back at the Maryville couple. Their hands covered their mouths, suppressing laughter.

I shrugged and smiled, unsure of what had overcome me to cause my outburst. I had always found a way to keep the peace, but this lashing out felt therapeutic. Time after time, men were unapologetically themselves, so why must I be sugar and spice and everything nice? Why must I contain and control? My stomach somersaulted with conflicting feelings of shame and strength. I didn't want to stick around any longer. "Happy hiking," I called out as I lifted my pack and left Cliff Tops, retracing my steps back to Boulevard.

At mile twelve, my legs had fatigued. My tank was on E. Exhausted. Empty. Exposed. Emotional. I trudged along until I spotted the intersection with the Appalachian Trail. My pace quickened until I stopped at the trail sign. I watched people coming and going. Short, tall, old, bald, women with nails like daggers, flip-flops, saris, faces red as beets. The AT had transformed to Hartsfield-Jackson. I could plop down and people-watch all day.

An opening appeared, and I merged into traffic. This was always a busy section of the trail, but what I observed was unprecedented.

I unbuckled and twisted my pack to the front of my body and pulled out my face mask. I secured it onto my face and slipped my arm under my pack's strap and fastened back in, passing a group every other minute. They posed for photos in the middle of the trail, carried their Pomeranians, and blasted music from Bluetooth speakers.

With a mile to go to the Newfound Gap parking lot, a thin, middle-aged man wearing white Bermuda shorts and a pink polo sat with extended legs in the middle of the trail. Not off to the side. Smack dab in the middle. He held a crushed, empty water bottle. He had no pack. He looked up me as if I were a trail savior.

"How much farther to go?" He panted.

"To go where?"

He furrowed his brow.

"You're facing northbound on the Appalachian Trail. Are you going to Maine?" I asked.

In normal times, I would have made the logical assumption because hiking in the Smokies requires a degree of patience, but my patience was in short order that day. He wouldn't make it another half mile, much less hike to Maine. There's a level of responsibility in hiking, and he didn't have it. While I wasn't as prepared as I should have been when I first hiked there, I at least had sufficient water, supplies, and knew my destination, even if I didn't know how to judge distances.

"No, not Maine. The viewpoint!" He pointed north on the trail and then slapped his hand to his thigh. It was less of a slap and more his hand succumbing to gravity.

"I'm going to assume you mean Charlies Bunion." I swallowed the last drop of my water.

"Is that where you came from?" he asked.

"No, I went to LeConte. You're definitely not going to LeConte. Most people here aren't going there. Nearly everyone is likely headed to Charlies Bunion."

"How far is Charlies Bunion?"

"I think you're only one mile in. You've got about three more to go and then four miles to get back to the parking lot."

"Shit! Is there at least seating there?"

I raised my eyebrows. "Seating?"

"Yeah, like any benches?"

I scrunched my face and shook my head. "Oh, no. There are no benches. It's actually a very narrow space and is standing room only. Sometimes overlooks have enough space for you to sit on rocks and grass and eat, but Charlies Bunion is not that place."

"I wonder if I can make it," he said, pushing himself to standing and dusting the dirt from his shorts.

"I'm going to be honest with you. I think you should turn around. It's not going to get easier. You have no more water. It's super crowded. Come another time." I normally offered encouragement to other hikers to give them a confidence boost to carry on, but to lie to him would make me culpable for his casualty.

I didn't wait for his response or to see if he continued northbound or turned around. I kept moving, needing to regain my solitude. My heart ached as I counted the flock on my final push to my car. It was as if the world had discovered my sanctuary.

With modern conveniences shuttered, man had rediscovered the great outdoors, and the pandemic hiker had been born. People were unable to cope with enjoying their own company, the company of their family, the company of the internet, the reality of their capitalistic comfort. These people had no respect for nature, rules, or others' safety. They were vapid American followers. As much as they strived to be special or unique, posting photos to their socials, their faceless bodies all blended together. They were the screen sheep. Screen junkies. Bowing their heads to false idols.

All that I held sacred was slipping away from me.

No empty spaces remained in the parking lot. License plates hailed from Ohio, Illinois, Indiana, New York, New Jersey, Florida, Pennsylvania, and many more. It didn't have fifty-state representation, but it was damn near close. Vehicles stalked parking spaces, ready to pounce at any sign of people walking back to their cars.

Back in my car, as soon as I shifted into reverse, two cars lasered in on my spot. They were going to war. My stomach churned. I mouthed a silent prayer that the parks would remain open for the sake of my Huayhuash training and for that second bedroom that still haunted me.

1.7 MOUNT CAMMERER

"Hi, Allyn. Is this still a good time?" my therapist asked.

"Yeah," I said as I walked away from my desk for my monthly appointment.

"First off, I want to ask, how is your family? I know things are bad in New Orleans."

"Yeah, fortunately, they're all fine. I'm not allowed to go home until this all blows over. It felt really weird not having a crawfish boil with them on Good Friday. How's your family?"

"Everyone's good. Thank you for asking. So, what's been on your mind?" she asked.

I began pacing my bungalow, avoiding the closed bedroom door at the end of the hallway. "Well, I'm thankful the outdoors are opening up again. I'm really hoping more parts of the Smokies and other places open up so that I can really amp up my training."

"How's your hike trip looking?"

I inhaled and then blew out a large breath through puffed cheeks. "I'm getting a little concerned. There's no commercial flights operating, so I'd have to cross the border via land, and even then, the tour operators might not resume tours."

"How does that make you feel?"

"Like my plan B might need a plan B. But I'm just not ready to invest a lot into that. I'm keeping hope alive. August is still a few months away."

"How's work going?"

"Nothing's out of control. Everyone's kind of settled into a permanent work-from-home setup."

I glanced over at my desk in my dining room. "Truthfully, it feels odd not having to travel at all for work." Prepandemic, I'd flown every few weeks to spend time with my team.

"And you're journaling?"

I bit my lower lip. My journal remained tucked in my nightstand drawer. I had wanted to resume journaling when I could report a positive pregnancy test. "I can't say I have."

"I really want to encourage you to start journaling again. You mentioned it helps you to review your entries for answers and closure."

I shook my head. "I don't know if I'm seeking closure."

"Tell me what you mean by that."

I walked to my bedroom and stood in front of my cheval mirror. I stretched my shirt over my taut tummy. "I'm thinking about pursuing IVF. I know it'd be taxing, but I'm a tough broad." I held my breath, anticipating her reaction. I moved the phone away from my face, worried the call had dropped, but the call seconds ticked upward. "Hello?"

"I'm a bit surprised. When you started on your fertility journey, you were very against invasive procedures. What changed?"

"I, I just feel strongly about creating and providing a life full of love for someone that came from me. I want that bond. How I feel today is that I need to exhaust all possibilities."

"Last time we talked, you mentioned 'fighting to not fail.' When you envision yourself on this IVF path, does that feeling of 'fighting to not fail' go away?"

"No." I rubbed the back of my neck.

"Talk to me about that."

"Ehh." I searched my ceiling for an answer that did not reveal itself.

"We talked about failure a lot during your separation and divorce. Back then, you talked about failure as how others perceive you. Are you meaning that now?"

I laughed. "No. A single Black mother is the last thing America wants. Our paternalistic society still favors married heterosexual couples procreating. It's expected. As soon as I was married, I was constantly asked when I would have kids. Never *if*. But Heaven forbid a same-sex couple or a single woman wants a child. The level of scrutiny is unreal—like suddenly I'm interrogated as to why I want a child, as if women's desire to have children is rooted in a man! And then I'm assaulted with questions about my financial and emotional security. I mean, everyone else is why I've kept my fertility journey really close to my chest—why only my sister, Lenny, and Ryan know.

"So, no, my concept of failure is not external. We all have our internal compass of what success means to us. And for me, success means creating a family unit. And I've always envisioned it being this deep, biological bond. You could say that all my life's decisions have led me to this path: college, job, home. Family comes next. But I do question if I'm on 'goal autopilot.'"

"So, tell me how your vision of success—as you say, 'creating a family unit'—originated."

I looked up at my plaster ceiling. My eyes fixed on a small crack that snaked across the room. "I'd have to give that some thought."

"Seems like a good thing to journal about."

I laughed. "Good one."

"We're just about out of time, but I do have a question."

"Okay," I said.

"Have you resumed drinking?"

I sucked my teeth. "Yes."

"I want to remind you that heavy drinking is defined as more than three drinks a day or more than seven drinks a week for a woman."

I glanced at the three bottles remaining in my bar cabinet. My history with alcohol wasn't a secret to my therapist. My mother called me a functional alcoholic, but I had never branded myself such. I could stop drinking on a dime and have no desire to resume for months. "I feel there should be a sliding scale for people from New Orleans, but I hear you loud and clear."

By the end of May, the Smokies had reopened all trails. Given outdoor spaces were some of humanity's only outlets, I prepared for pandemonium.

Me: *Hiking to Mt. Cammerer today. Should be off trail by 2 pm.*

Mel didn't respond. I figured she was getting ready for work.

I drove to the Cosby entrance of the park, hoping the location of the trek, north of the heart of the park, would translate to fewer crowds.

Cammerer was an iconic hike with its stone, octagonal fire tower and panoramic views, but I was lukewarm about it. The panorama paled in comparison to others in the Smokies, but I went for the ass-kicking, 3,000-foot ascent. While the Low Gap Trail wasn't technically harder than trekking Bote Mountain to Rocky Top, I struggled more with its climb. Some trails were more of a mindfuck than others.

I parked near the Cosby Campground. Only a few cars rested in the lot. I figured the lot would be full once I returned. I geared up and set off on the trail.

The breeze flapped tree leaves. I gazed up. *How old are these trees? I don't know what kind they are. I never bother with learning those trail details for myself, though I enjoy hiking with the people who can recite their Latin and common names along with any herbal remedies. The trees had to be old enough to behold the land takeover from Cherokee to American federal government. Would they survive to witness America's seemingly inevitable collapse? What stories would they tell? Do they remember me, or do all humans look alike to them?*

I charged up Low Gap Trail, clocking a three-miles-per-hour pace. I turned off the AT, taking the spur to the fire tower. The climb wasn't as bad as I had expected. No leg pain. Not many trekkers. It was all rather uneventful. When I arrived at the tower, rustling noises escaped from its depths. I pushed the door open and peeked inside.

A solo female backpacker hunched over a pack, resting at her feet. Her gear was well-worn and designed for a man. She wore a tattered tank top and jeans cut off at the knees. It wasn't typical backpacker attire.

"Hey, I just wanted you to know I was here. I didn't want to startle you," I said.

She stood up and smiled. "Hey, come on in. This place is pretty amazing, huh?"

I entered the tower. Time had not been kind to her. Her weathered skin resembled a well-loved, leather baseball glove. Her decayed teeth bore the signs of lack of dental care and former drug use. Years of smoke breaks had gifted her crevasses, radiating from around her mouth, but her eyes sparkled, and she smelled of sweet peas and citrus.

"Yeah, it's a nice, clear day," I said.

"Are you overnighting?" she asked, eyeing my pack.

"Oh no. I just carry a heavier daypack than most. I'm doing an out and back. You?"

"This is my third day out. I plan to be off trail tomorrow. I really want to complete the Smokies section of the AT, so this was a test to see if I could do it."

"That's about seventy miles, right?" I had no aspirations to overnight anything on the AT, but being a peripheral member of the 865 hiker community meant I was familiar with certain facts and figures.

"Seventy-one-point-four." She emphasized the *one-point-four*.

"Oh, I can't deny that one-point-four miles. I know one-point-four miles can completely crush you."

She laughed. "Yeah, first day 'bout killed me, but the second day got better. And well"—she shrugged—"I'm alive and here today. Each day gets better."

My eyes welled with tears. I didn't breathe them away. I didn't look in a different direction. I didn't run out of the fire tower. I didn't fight it. One tear released and then another. My shoulders shuddered in rhythm to my chopped breath, and then I cried a monsoon.

"Sweetie, you okay?" she asked.

Her words struck me. Despite all the pain and waves of worthlessness, despite being stuck, despite not knowing if I should give up on my dream, despite going through the motions, hoping I'd shake my waking nightmare, I was alive and here—in a fire tower in the Smokies, with a stranger, releasing all my perceptions of shame and guilt.

I swiped my tears aside with my thumbs. In between sobs, I said, "Yeah, I know I don't look okay, but yeah, I'm okay. Alive and here." I smiled and tasted the snot my upper lip captured.

She nodded her head. "I get it."

And for some reason, I knew she did. She moved toward me but then hesitated. I think she wanted to hug me. The pandemic had stripped away pieces of our humanity.

"Do you come out here much?" I asked and then wiped my nose on my shirtsleeve.

"This is my first time out to this part of the park."

"Get out! Seriously?" I blotted my face with my neck gaiter.

"Yeah, I've always wanted to do something like this, but my kids came first."

I nodded.

"Now they're grown, and I can finally do all the things I wanted."

My therapist and I talked at length about how many women sacrifice their passions and pause their lives to be moms. How do you have a career, be the mom you want to be, much less are expected to be, and fulfill your personal dreams? I had spent months crafting how I could strike a balance. Being a mom would alter my life, but it wouldn't define me. I wouldn't feel guilty for leaving my child behind while I continued to travel and trek. Children needed to see that parents taking time for themselves was healthy and made them better parents. For years, I had financially prepared. I had mentally prepared. I had a plan, I had executed it—yet I still ended up with heartbreak.

But I was alive and here. I was alive and here.

"When do you think you'll set off to do the seventy-one-point-four miles?" I asked, emphasizing the *one-point-four*.

"Maybe next year. I'd have to get the time off work." She rifled through her pack. "Crap. Do you know if rain's in the forecast tomorrow?"

"I don't think so. I guess a pop-up shower is likely, but the temperature will be dropping."

"It was cold last night. I dunno if I brought enough layers." She placed her hands on her hips and surveyed her pack.

I rummaged through my pack and pulled out a few HotHands left over from my Machu Picchu trip. "Take these."

"Seriously?" Her caterpillar eyebrows joined together.

"Yeah, I haven't used them in two years. I'm sure they'll expire soon. You'll be thankful for them tonight." *How could I have known, when I'd accepted the HotHands from that English mother and daughter on a mountain in Perú, that they'd end up here?*

"Thank you. I appreciate it. God bless."

We both walked the outer perimeter of the tower, separately but together. We had a shared understanding. I lifted my pack, waved goodbye, and left. I never caught her name, but it really didn't matter. She broke through to me in ways my friends, my therapist, and my past self hadn't. Couldn't. I needed the words, the comfort of a stranger to know that everything was going to be okay. For the first time since my last negative pregnancy test, I believed it.

I set off southbound on the AT, beaming ear to ear for no reason other than the fact that I was grateful to be alive and in the mountains. *I can't recall the last time I smiled like this.* And then, my right boot caught on a tree root, and I fell over like a tree. Timber! My left knee took the brunt of the fall. As I was splayed out on the ground, my tongue traced my teeth, tasting and feeling for anything amiss. Metallic taste of blood? No. Missing or loose teeth? No.

I lay for a moment before bursting into laughter at my misfortune—the pain of the past months, the death of a dream I believed was my life's ambition. I released it all. I laughed until my abs spasmed and cramped, until the pain in my stomach was unbearable, until my chest tightened, until I gasped for air, and until I let go of the loss of a life that never was.

That evening, I lit a stick of palo santo and smudged my home. Free of my failure, I took the first step of my next chapter—I bought and shipped three more sperm vials.

1.8 MOUNT ROGERS

I turned my blinker off as I exited I-81 North at Whitetop Road. The road wound through a residential area. Grassy, sloping lots dwarfed brick ranches, farmhouses, and the odd mid-century modern. Where did these people work? The local government? Was a factory nearby? Any sort of industry? While outdoor tourism was abundant in the area, I didn't think the demand was high enough to support the population. Business owners? If I remembered when I got home, I'd Google it.

Every third property boasted Trump paraphernalia: flags, decals on vehicles, billboard-size signs staked in yards. While this was expected of a rural, Southern area, it didn't diminish my discomfort. What was the point of plastering political signs on property when the majority of your neighbors shared your sentiments? No one was questioning anyone's allegiance here, so why the fervent support? Was it a show of unity, or was it to irk visitors like me? Was it a warning for gentrifiers to colonize elsewhere? A territory marking or boundary setting? Advertisements for other likeminded people to settle there?

As I continued to drive, a washed-out sign stylized like a comic strip, staked on a church's lawn, caught my eye:

Man: Lord, send us someone to cure cancer, AIDS, etc.
Lord: I already did, but you aborted him.

I squinted my eyes and clenched my teeth. If only I could be pregnant to have that choice.

After thirty minutes of driving through rural Virginia, I reached Grayson Highlands State Park. This area was often described as the Virginian version of the Swiss Alps. I honor-paid for a day pass and parked near Massie Gap. Gray storm clouds menaced low in the sky.

I geared up and then spun around, searching for the Appalachian Trail. Several trailheads circled the large field, but the signature white AT blaze stamped none. I crossed Massie Gap's grassy field, where I spotted what looked like a check-in station, hoping I could find a trail map there.

A covered bulletin board stood at the entrance to a livestock gate. As I studied the trail map encased in plexiglass, my brows knitted, and I bit the inside of my cheek. I couldn't deduce my location on the map. I searched for Mount Rogers and attempted to trace the trails diverging from it, but the map didn't make sense. I couldn't get my bearings. I should've better studied the trails in advance. I pulled out my cell phone and zoomed in on my location, hoping trail lines would appear. None did. I pulled up the screenshots I had taken of trip reports, scanning for some text indicating the best way to get to Mount Rogers. Nothing. I studied the map a while longer and figured I had wasted enough time. I needed to commit to a trail and then reassess at a trail intersection.

I entered the livestock gate to trek on the Rhododendron Trail because it was one of the trails that intersected with the AT, and Mount Rogers was on the AT. The rocky and exposed trail quickly gained in elevation. After some time, I approached a square, wooden fence post. Reflective aluminum strips screwed to the post listed trail details. Something about the trail intersection's two-dimensional signpost struck me as strange:

🥾🐎	🥾
Horse Trail North ↑	Appalachian Trail ↑
Appalachian Trail ←→	Horse Trail North ←→
Virginia Highlands Horse Trail 0.5 mi ↑	Massie Gap 0.6 mi←
Thomas Knob Shelter (AT Southbound) 2.9 mi ←	Thomas Knob Shelter (AT Southbound) 2.9 mi ↑
Wise Shelter (AT Northbound) 1.9 mi →	Overnight Backpackers Lot 0.6 mi ←
Appalachian Spur Trail 0.4 mi →	Rhododendron Trail 0.16 mi ←

Below the trail names, a colored square or diamond indicated its difficulty rating, similar to ski runs. I viewed the post from different angles, attempting to make sense of it. Why not erect a Switzerland-style trail sign with signage oriented in the direction of the trail? I spotted another trail sign across the path and walked toward it:

> AT Trail Northbound →
> Scales 5 mi.
> Old Orchard Shelter 8.1 mi.
>
> ← AT Trail Southbound
> Mt. Rogers 3.8 mi.
> Rhododendron Gap 2.1 mi.
> Thomas Knob Shelter 2.9 mi.

I could make sense of that one. I needed to hike southbound on the AT to reach Mount Rogers.

The AT climbed to an expansive view. Low, dark clouds clung to mountain peaks. I picked up my pace, hoping I could finish the hike before the weather soured. At the next livestock gate, I avoided a collision with an older, gray-haired but balding backpacker whose knee cried blood.

"Are you all right?" I asked.

"Yeah, why are you asking?"

"Well, there's blood streaming down your leg. I have a first aid kit if you need help."

He looked down at his leg. "Oh, I took a tumble on some rocks. My legs aren't what they used to be. I assure you it looks worse than it feels. I didn't even notice it."

"Oh, so a bit of scrambling ahead?" I'd read that there were some scrambles, but I figured they were nothing to worry about.

"Yeah, but you're young and pretty. You'll be fine."

I chuckled at his old-man trail flirting. As if Mother Nature cared if I were pretty. "Thank you. So, are you thru-hiking?"

"Not really. Well, not with any sort of goal or purpose. I simply enjoy the AT. I spent last night at the shelter. Have you seen any ponies down here yet?"

"No, but I hope I see them. I've read so much about them. I'll be bummed if I don't see any. It's my first time out here."

Since Mel and I had become hike companions, we had endured tourists inundating the Smokies. We were always looking for other peak-season hike options that were near but not in the park. Through the 865 community, she had learned about Grayson Highlands and its wild ponies. I didn't believe her until I performed my own research. And while it would've been nice to hike with her, I had grown to enjoy solo hiking since my divorce. My need to be on trail surpassed anyone else's availability, and with each solo step I offered to the trails, the deeper I craved to be outside somewhere alone in my thoughts.

"Ah, there's a few hanging around the shelter. They were trying to get my food and were licking salt from my skin. Don't linger behind them. They *will* kick."

I frowned.

"If you don't want to be bothered, just keep moving, and they'll leave you alone. Where are you headed?"

"To Mount Rogers and back. I appreciate the tip on the ponies. I should get going in case the weather worsens." I glanced at the fickle sky. "I hope you have a good rest of your hike." I resumed my hike uphill.

"Don't lock the bears in the bear box!" he hollered as the distance between us grew.

I laughed, turned in his direction, and cupped my mouth. "I won't!"

I boulder-hopped along the trail, then hiked and then boulder-hopped some more, until I reached a craggy mound that stood six feet tall. I studied it for foot- and fin-gerholds. I cursed my petite frame. I thrust my body onto the hard, rhyolite mound as if it were a sticky wall and hoisted myself up. It wasn't my most graceful moment.

I continued until I reached another craggy mound I had to climb. This trail was more like a New England scramble than a Southeastern one. Mel would not like this.

A trail sign marked an unexpected trail split. I turned to study it:

> Wilburn Ridge TR.
> _____
> ↑Appalachian TR. 1

The trail sign confused me. *The previous confusing sign didn't denote a Wilburn Ridge Trail. And is the "1" next to the Appalachian Trail a mile, an hour, or what? Should I remain on the white-blazed Appalachian Trail, which I know will take me to Mount Rogers, or take the blue-blazed Wilburn Ridge Trail?* I pulled out my phone, checking if Google Maps would load the trails. Nope. I consulted the trip reports I had saved on my phone. One mentioned that Wilburn was another route to get to Mount Rogers. *The safest option would be to stick to what I know and stay on the AT.*

I followed the white blazes. The trail continued as a series of rocky mounds, followed by grassy balds, followed by more rocky mounds, all exposed to the sky. The wind pushed dark gray clouds from view. I tilted my head to the sun and smiled. Ahead, a trail sign stood at the entrance to a rhododendron tunnel with masses of lavender-pink catawbiense bouquets blooming in all directions. Many couples have paid good money for their wedding bowers to imitate only a fraction of what was before me:

> ↑ Appalachian TR South Bound
> _____
> ↑ Mount Rogers Spur TR. 1.5
> ↑ Elk Garden 5.7

This sign confirmed the numbers reflected mileage. Five hundred was carved on the back of the sign, marking the AT's mileage. Depending on a hiker's perspective, it was five hundred to go or five hundred behind you. Exiting the tunnel, the trail opened up to 180-degree views.

I stumbled off trail, exploring the large bald. I passed a bear box and giggled, remembering the older hiker's friendly advice. I wanted to sit, watch the clouds sloth, and offer my cheek for the sun to kiss. I dropped my backpack onto the ground and settled next to it. White, tufted clouds crawled across the sky. I wrestled my journal and pen from my pack and rapped my pen against my teeth.

Per my therapist's suggestion, I pondered the origins of how I equated having a family with success. I had friends who were childfree whom I deemed successful, so why did I feel I needed to create a child to mark success? And would I keep at this pursuit until I hit menopause? If so, then what? Would I freeze my eggs and consider a surrogate? Could I afford that? Or at that point would I adopt, quit, or accept the Universe's will? I chewed on my pen's clicker.

My sister had the model life. She had gone to college. She taught Louisiana history to awkward middle schoolers. She married her mother-approved college sweetheart, and then they adopted a yellow Labrador, bought a house in the suburbs without the picket fence, and birthed a son a couple of years later, followed by a daughter. She was happy. While she, too, was frustrated with our overbearing mother, our mother's feedback to her amounted to where to best place dishes in her kitchen cabinets. My sister was living the American Dream. She worked hard. She did all the things we were taught to do, and she was rewarded for it. She started new traditions with her husband and children.

I went from sister to spectator, and I was uncertain if this change was due to my physical distance or embracing a side of me that she didn't understand. She shared with me how eager she was to one day become a grandmother — whenever her children established good careers and found good partners. Because that's what we do, and that's why people flock from all over the world to come to America. We provide equal opportunities for everyone to build safe lives and prosperous families.

I wrote:

But as a Black American woman who has spent my entire collegiate and professional career in White and Asian male-dominated spaces, I know equal opportunity is a myth.

And if equal opportunity is a myth, how can the American dream be achievable for everyone?

And despite doing everything I was told: go to college, contribute to society, get married ... I am

Empty.

It's not that I am not proud of all I've done. It's not that I am not grateful for those who struggled before me, making my path possible, but ...

Where is my reward? Where is my happiness?

I hurt, and I'm struggling to understand my worth.

Voices carried on the breeze. I packed away my journal and hoisted my pack on my back and returned to the AT, where I spotted five ponies grazing on the trail. I cleared my throat, announcing my presence. While chewing, they raised their heads in my direction. We locked eyes. They lowered their heads to tear away at more roughage. I pulled out my phone and snapped photos of them. Walking closer to them, they didn't budge from the trail, so I stepped off it to walk around them. They didn't try to nip my backpack or lick my skin. I didn't touch them. We both respected each other's presence.

I passed the Thomas Knob Shelter. The spur trail to reach Mount Rogers — the highest point in Virginia and the tallest state peak east of the Mississippi without a paved road to its summit — was ahead to the right. I arrived at the viewless summit amid a conversation between a middle-aged couple seated on a boulder and a similarly aged man with a slight yet athletic build, standing across from them, who wore a Georgia Tech T-shirt and wire-framed glasses.

The man and woman were recounting a trip they had recently taken to the Badlands. "I can't wait to share pictures with my students and teach them about the Sioux," the woman, who seemed a few years older than me, shared.

I grimaced at her use of the colonized word *Sioux*. "Did you drive or fly out?" I asked.

"We flew," she answered. "With limited time off, we couldn't have driven there and back."

"How was the air travel experience?" Given that Perú's border remained closed, I hadn't booked tickets for Huayhuash or Colorado for my higher-altitude training hikes.

"Honestly, it was really good. We felt super safe," the man seated next to her said.

"That's so refreshing to hear, and it's really cool that you'll be able to share your experience of the Lakota, Dakota, and Nakota peoples with your students. I'm pretty confident they prefer to be called that and not the derogatory name that their enemy gave them. It may seem minor, but words have power." *Horrible mom. Nonmaternal. Inconsistent.* I smiled to ease any tension that might build.

She squinted her eyes and snapped her neck back. "Have you been there?"

I shook my head. "No. I've not been to that part of the country at all. I'd love to visit though and see places a bit farther west. Yellowstone has been on my list for years. I even have this entire trip mapped out to visit the Grand Tetons, Yellowstone, and Glacier. One day, right?"

"I was a ranger at Glacier," the man with the Georgia Tech shirt shared.

The couple and I exclaimed shock, awe, and praise. The three resumed their conversation about teaching. I lowered my pack, gulped down some water, and explored the summit, looking for the three geodetic markers that a trip report described. I spotted one and snapped a photo. Their conversation died down, and I returned to the group.

"When did you get out?" I asked the man wearing the Georgia Tech shirt. While most people wearing U(sic)GA paraphernalia never attended the school, donning GT merchandise was a right reserved for students and alumni.

His eyes widened and smiled, recognizing my verb choice. One doesn't graduate from Georgia Tech. You *get out*, as if you survived an academic imprisonment. He said, "1996, M.E."

"Ah, so you didn't take drownproofing."

"No, but I really would've loved that. What about you? When did you get out?"

"2004, ChemE."

"Drownproofing?" the man seated on the boulder asked.

GT Shirt and I exchanged glances, sussing out who would explain drownproofing to the couple. I tilted my head in his direction, yielding to his explanation.

"A required course for graduation that taught students how to survive various water situations. It was intense, like tying your hands behind your back. The military adopted this into their training. Tech discontinued the class in the late eighties."

The couple nodded.

"Have you found the geodetic markers? I've read this summit has three." I changed the topic, keeping me and the Georgia Tech alumnus from sinking into further nostalgia.

"No, we haven't," the woman said as she raised her leg, peering under where she sat. The couple stood up, lifted their gear, and spied around the boulder.

The GT alumnus and I walked around the summit, trying to locate the markings. I showed him the one I had spotted earlier, and we found another one, then returned to our packs. The couple found the last one on the boulder where they had been sitting. The alumnus and I studied the markings, unable to conclude if all three were the same or if there was a subtle difference we weren't discerning.

The couple strapped into their packs. I glanced over at my fellow alumnus, expecting him to also gear up as I assumed they had hiked in together, but he was unconcerned.

I moved my pack atop the boulder and pulled out a few snacks. He pulled out a tuna packet and began eating it with a stick he found lying on the ground.

"I actually have utensils in my pack if you want some," I said with a full mouth of nuts.

He looked down at his choice of fork. "It is a bit crass to use a stick, huh?"

"I'm not judging, but if you'd prefer a spork, I have one."

"I'm used to sticks." He smiled. His white teeth contrasted against his olive skin, bronzed from the sun.

"My name's Allyn."

"Ben."

He reached his hand toward me, and I shook it without hesitation. Then my heart skipped a beat, realizing he was the first person I had touched since the pandemic lockdown.

"Do you come out here often?" I reached into my pack, retrieving my own jalapeño tuna packet and a bamboo spork.

"Not too often. I live about four hours east of here, but I'm out here camping for the week, doing day hikes. I was on the Virginia Creeper yesterday."

I gasped. "Oh, I read about that. I'd like to do that one day, and the Triple Crown, but I'm trying to avoid super-popular places for a bit."

"Do you live near here?"

"Chattanooga. It's about a four- to five-hour drive. So, the weather's been good?"

"Yeah, it's been nice all week really. My daughters are with their mom, and I just thought it'd be nice to get away and decompress before school starts."

My eyes darted to his left hand. *He isn't wearing a ring, but many men don't wear rings. Is he single and co-parenting? Married? Separated? Why do I care? And a Georgia Tech grad who used to be a park ranger? How does that happen?* "Ah, are you a teacher? When does school start?"

"Yes, I teach middle school history."

I raised my eyebrows. I wasn't expecting history. Science, math, computers, sure, but history was a curveball. I cleared my face of expression before he noticed.

He continued, "I don't even know. The dates keep changing. No one knows what's going on. The guidelines seem arbitrary. For instance, the football team can practice but not the basketball team and not the cheerleaders. I coach the basketball team. It's been frustrating."

"Yeah, that really doesn't make a whole lot of sense, but it *is* the South. Football is a religion." I shoveled tuna into my mouth and swallowed. "I think it's amazing that you've been out here solo camping."

"You camp?"

"Oh no, but it's been weighing on my mind. I don't know why I haven't done it. I don't know. It seems a bit … involved." And scary to do alone as a woman. A fear that had stuck from my mother's many worries — only a zipper separating my unconscious self from the world.

"It can be, but you can borrow gear before investing to see if you like it, but what am I talking about? You've already figured it all out. You're an engineer." He chuckled. God, his smile was gorgeous.

"Well, yes, I have an engineering degree, but like you, I don't practice it anymore. I'm a product owner now."

"What's that?" he asked. He threw his stick utensil into the forest and packed up his trash.

"It's a role in software development. My job is to know and anticipate what my customers want. Then I prioritize their wants and needs and write the requirements that a team of software engineers use to build functionality for them." I covered my face with my hands. My fingers smoothed my eyebrows as I swept my hands from my face. "God, I'm so burned out."

"Yeah, I did the engineering thing for a bit. It's great money. It can also pave the way for great travel. I have a buddy who lived in Asia for a few years because his job took him there. But I don't know how much he really enjoyed Asia because he worked insane hours. His family enjoyed it, though." He laughed. "I've been teaching for almost a decade now. I haven't looked back."

His gaze landed beyond my shoulder. There was nothing behind me but trees. He was lost in thought, as was I. I breathed in the crisp, clean, fir-scented air. A bird's song carried on the wind.

"I don't think I'm going to make it to Huayhuash," I said, staring at my boots.

"*Way*-what?"

"I was planning to do this trek in Perú. It's called the Huayhuash Circuit, but the border situation hasn't changed. Flying international is very tricky now. The restrictions are constantly changing. I could fly down to South America, figure out a way to cross the border, into Perú, quarantine for a couple weeks, and then hike, but it's risky. What if I can't get back home?"

"The mountains aren't going anywhere," he said. "Well, that's not as true as it once was, but I think you have a few years before things drastically change."

"I don't know. I've got to do something with my time off. I'm not one of those people who take time off and sit around the house." I pulled my legs into my chest, hugging them.

"You travel abroad a lot?"

"Well, in recent years, I'd take a couple of trips a year. I'm not opposed to staying domestic. I've just always prioritized international travel because I figure a day will come when I can't make long plane rides, and that's when I can explore more of the US."

"You seem like you don't mind driving. Maybe a road trip and then some hiking?"

"Yeah, that could be an option." I chuckled. "Years ago, I built this spreadsheet to track my travel. I have a section dedicated to national parks. I've already visited a few in Washington, California, and Colorado, but I still haven't explored the Western interior. I have that Yellowstone, Tetons, Glacier itinerary, but I'm afraid grizzlies would be too much of a risk for a solo traveler."

"Yeah, grizzlies are dangerous. No one to go with you?"

I studied his face, trying to gauge his question's intent, interest or innocent inquiry? I wouldn't mind traveling with *him*, but I dared not be so bold to say anything. "Well, my friends who hike can't really afford to travel, can't take time off, or they live on a different continent. And my friends who can afford to travel wouldn't consider hiking enjoyable. So, I tend to just hike and travel alone a lot."

He darted a quick look at me then rubbed his chin.

I released my legs, allowing them to dangle. I undid my topknot and coiled one of my curls around my right pointer finger. "When were you a park ranger?"

"Right after college. I was looking to do something different. The park service was at one of those job fairs."

I nodded and freed my finger from its Chinese finger trap.

He continued, "They were very forthcoming that you don't make any money doing that work. You do it for the experience. I wasn't ready to start a big engineering job, so I signed up. It was a great year. I had a grizzly bear encounter once. A few of us rangers had an off day and set off on a hike near Many Glacier Hotel—"

I pictured it. A four-storied Swiss-style chalet butting up to Swiftcurrent Lake. How many photos had I studied of it while I was crafting my Yellowstone itinerary?

"And these guests on a boat were frantically waving at us. They saw a grizzly bear behind us. We were trapped between the bear and the lake."

"What did you do?" I asked, gathering my hair and re-doing the topknot.

"The boat came to the shore and picked us up! My year there was amazing. After that, I worked a real engineering job and felt dissatisfied. Each day I worked, a part of me died. Then, I landed in the education system, and it's been fantastic."

We packed up and started hiking out together. He talked a bit about Scales and a few other spots I should check out if I returned to Grayson.

"Hey, do you mind taking a photo of me?" he asked.

"No. I mean, sure, I'll take your photo."

He pulled out a point-and-shoot from the early 2000s, packaged in a plastic sandwich bag.

I laughed. "Is this even digital?"

"Yeah, it's digital. It's sad, isn't it?" He frowned before his face broke into a wide megawatt smile.

I doubled over laughing. My stomach hurt from the muscles tensing when I inhaled. I wiped away a few tears. "I mean, yes, it's definitely sad that you pulled this out and wouldn't just use your phone."

"Oh, my phone doesn't take pictures."

I tilted my head back and snorted. "What!?"

"I'm showing my age, huh?"

I wanted to run over to him, cup his face, and kiss him. He was adorable. "I wouldn't say it's an age thing. My grandparents have smartphones. It's definitely a rarity to come across someone like you, but I find it endearing. I think it's great that your life doesn't demand those things of you. I mean, I don't do social media. People think I'm weird for that, but I wouldn't have it any other way."

I took a few photos of him.

"Want me to take some of you?" he asked.

I contemplated. "Sure, I rarely ever have photos of me on the trail other than selfies." I handed him my smartphone. "Do you know how to operate that?" I grinned at him.

He laughed but stared at it, pondering.

"It literally works the same way as your camera. Just press this dot here."

After he took a few photos, we hiked out together.

"You should come back and stay the night. The stargazing is phenomenal here," he said.

"I can tell this place is magical. It reminds me of Carver's Gap and Max Patch, but it's far more rocky."

As the spur trail intersected with the AT, we turned left. South of the Thomas Knob Shelter, we stopped to marvel at the view. I never tired of breathing mountain air and imprinting the scenery into my soul.

I snapped a flurry of photos while Ben lingered. Was he waiting on me to finish, or was he planning his exit? He intrigued me. He was quirky but confident. How had he overcome societal pressures and denounced engineering for teaching in his prime earning years? Was he financially secure? What middle-aged man came out here to camp by himself? He seemed super content. Super at peace. Super relaxed. Was he married? What were his daughters like?

My face flushed, and a cold sweat broke out over my entire body. I turned my back from the view and faced him. I bit my lip, picturing what life with Ben could be like.

Swapping Georgia Tech stories. Plotting camping trips. His hand brushing against my cheek. His lips pressing against mine. His hands cupping my neck, pulling me into his warm, firm body. His hardness pushing against my abdomen. Him pulling my hair. My body yielding to him. Our bodies tangled into one.

Dormant desires awakened. I didn't want his sperm deposit. I wanted his passion.

My skin prickled. I licked my lips and then smiled.

He smiled back and then squinted. "Have you done any desert hiking?"

"No, I've been to deserts but no hiking," I said.

"You should check out Zion. It's close to Vegas if you don't want to drive there. No grizzly threat. Also, it should be safe from any wildfires."

"That's where The Narrows are, right?" My heartbeat quickened as imagery flooded my brain of trekkers hiking upstream between vertical canyon walls.

"Yeah, that's pretty iconic, but there's so much more than that. I remember when I went, I felt like the landscape was so foreign. I figure if you can't go abroad, why not go somewhere domestic that feels very different than anything you ever experienced?"

"I'll have to look into it then." I bit my lip again.

Our eyes locked, and neither of us looked away. *Should I say something? Should I find a clever way to ask if he's married? Should I ask for his number? Should I ask him to hike out with me, or for him to show me his camp?*

"Well, I guess I'll let you have some solitude," Ben said.

I studied the tall grass that hid my boots. "It was really great meeting you, Ben." I looked back at him. "I hope all goes well with the school year. And your family."

"Thanks, Allyn. You too." He nodded and walked away.

I hiked out, passing ponies and cattle. When the breeze carried human noises, I held my breath, straining to pick up notes of Ben's voice so that I could find a reason to cross his path. But I didn't see him again.

Ben gave me a lot to ponder on my four-and-a-half-hour drive back home. Once I unpacked and bathed, I poured myself a glass of malbec and snuggled under my baby alpaca blanket. I longed to have a man next to me.

Me: *Hey! Long time no talk. How's life been?*

Ryan: *Going a bit stir crazy*

Me: *I know what you mean.*

With a simple ask, I was confident he'd be over in a flash, but did I want to reopen that door? *There's a reason we broke up.* I scrolled up our message thread, rereading the hurt from the Hail Mary day and reliving how he'd used me for physical pleasure. *Am I capable of using him?*

Me: *Hey. You up for a small hike?*

Ryan: *What's your definition of small?*

I chuckled. The man who used to boulder and who had completed two Ironman competitions didn't have the mental endurance for a slower-paced ten-mile hike.

Me: *Three miles tops. Thinking Cummins Falls. Never been, and you know how I feel about hiking in water.*

Ryan: *Maybe*

Me: *Calfkiller Brewing is on the way to the trailhead. We could stop there on the way back.*

Ryan: *I'm in. Tell me when.*

I messaged him the date and then uploaded photos to my newly created dating profile.

1.9 CUMMINS FALLS

My phone buzzed. I locked my laptop and answered the call. My therapist opened with a familiar question, "Hi Allyn. What's been on your mind?"

I shoved aside the thoughts from my last work meeting and opened the tiny notepad next to my laptop. I read the chronological list of everything that had occurred in the last month since we talked:

1. *Hiking*
2. *Travel plan change*
3. *IVF insurance authorization*
4. *Date with Owen at the Tellus Science Museum*

We wouldn't have time to cover it all. I began walking the corners of my home. "Well, you'd be proud of me. Work got a bit crazy, so I took some time off and did some hikes a bit farther away."

"How's the hike trip coming along?" she asked.

"A change of plans. Given the borders are still closed, I'm going to go to Zion."

"You seem to be in a much better place."

"Well, I feel like me again," I said.

"What do you mean?"

"I have my goals. I'm working toward something. I'm seeing results."

"But what about after Zion?" my therapist asked.

"What do you mean?"

"I'm concerned you're keeping yourself busy to distract from the fact that IUI didn't work. I'm worried you're delaying your loss."

"About that. I decided to move forward with IVF."

I heard a page turn. I wondered if she called me from her office, or if she were home in her pajamas. "What made you change your mind?"

I thought of the AT thru-hikers who fought to stay on the trail despite shelters closing, despite exhausted food supplies, despite the great outdoors shutting down. I thought of the woman at the Mount Cammerer fire tower and how she had waited for decades before embarking on her journey. "It's not time for me to give up."

"Okay. Well, I'm sure you know this, but the reality is that IVF can take a while to work—if it works. And while I do hope it works quickly for you, I want to ensure you're prepared for more ups and downs."

I nodded as if she could see me.

She continued, "Last time, we talked about your vision of success is creating a family unit. Did you spend any time thinking about that?"

"I did, but I can't say there was this pivotal or aha moment."

"Hmm, do you think some of that could have come from your parents?"

I sighed and then shrugged. "I suppose it's very possible."

"Talk to me about how you think they might have influenced that."

I huffed. "Well, coming from a family history of divorce, I'm sure it's led me to crave something that is mine. Paperwork is fleeting, but you can't run from blood. My dad ran from four wives, but he didn't run from me and my sister.

"It's crazy to think he's been deceased longer than he was present in my life, so other than blood ties, I don't know how much he's influenced me." I tittered. "My mother would say I got that alcohol gene from him. Maybe she's right. I figure we both drank to forget. Him, Vietnam. Me—just general malaise with life. The only advice I remember him giving was steering my sister and me to be with more white-collar types. And for him, white-collar types meant light-skinned men. But, my mother, well—" I resumed pacing, avoiding the vacant second bedroom as was now my routine—"she pulled her life together following her divorce, went back to school and eventually became a nurse educator. From a young age, she instilled in me and my sister that we should be independent, never depend on a man. So I poured myself into school to get financial freedom. I graduated top of my class, went to a super-competitive college, pursued a STEM career like she wanted me to do. I have done really well in my job and own my home. I have never once asked her or anybody else for help.

"But despite all that, all I hear are criticisms. There's always something I should stop doing altogether and something else I should do better. And since the divorce, all I hear is her not liking me being alone, which is code for 'single.' And when I was with Ryan, she said he wasn't as good as my ex-husband. And when I was with my ex-husband, he didn't make enough money until our final year together, and as she says, I lost him, and then he made babies with someone else. She says I'm not putting myself in the right situations to meet the right guy. And that I'm not getting any younger. But why does it matter? And what's the right damn guy anyway?

"All I've ever wanted to hear is, 'I'm proud of you.' But despite everything I've accomplished, nothing is good enough." I grabbed the carnelian sphere that sat next to my laptop and surveyed its Mars-like colors. I wished I had the strength to face my mother and say the words Sarah told the Goblin King in *Labyrinth*, "You have no power over me," but instead, I blurted to my therapist, "So, yeah, I'm tired of feeling like a fucking failure." I sighed. *What did my therapist even ask me that triggered my trip down Trauma Lane?*

"Do you think you can have this conversation with your mom?"

I scoffed. "She'd likely accuse me of being an entitled millennial, blaming all my problems on my parents. I don't see her actually understanding."

"Well, maybe you can write her a letter. You don't have to send it, but maybe start there for homework?"

I approached Ryan's Honda Element with an uneasy familiarity. It had been a little over four months since we had last seen each other—for my Hail Mary—and roughly a month and a half since I invited him on this hike. It had been a struggle coordinating our schedules, avoiding bad weather, and navigating the new Cummins Falls reservation system. We had texted, but we kept it light. I couldn't deduce if he was keeping his distance out of respect for my need for space, or if our friendship had been forever altered.

I opened the passenger door. Some Grateful Dead song poured out, joining my neighborhood's Saturday chorus of chirping birds, lawn mowers, and muffled conversations from the Greenway. I swayed and bobbed to the beat in a mocking manner as I settled into my seat and then routed us to Cummins Falls. "How've you been?" I asked.

"A bit better. I'm picking up a chocolate Lab mix next week. Did you know that you have to make appointments to adopt pets now?"

I shook my head.

"Every dog I tried to schedule an appointment with at the shelter was already adopted, so I started contacting rescue organizations."

It had been about a year and a half since his fourteen-year-old beagle had died. When we were together, I blamed our relationship stalling on the amount of time he'd had to dedicate to care for his dog, but once his dog had been discharged to Jesus and there was still no advancement, it was clear something else lurked.

"Who knew there was also a dog shortage? You'll have to show me photos."

"He's beautiful, but what have you been up to? I was happy to hear from you. I wanted to reach out, but—"

"But I made it clear I needed space." And I had. I was livid with him for his action or rather inaction, but I also knew how easy it would be to let him comfort me. Having a few laughs would enthrall me into believing whatever promises he'd make. To be sold on the dream that maybe he was ready to father my child. I had shaky boundaries with him, so falling back into old habits, however comforting, was hazardous. "I had been hike-training for Huayhuash."

"Really?" He checked his mirrors before changing lanes. "You're finally going to go?"

"That was the plan, but the border situations weren't improving, so I'm going to Zion instead." I searched his face for recognition. "It's in Southern Utah."

We talked about alcohol appreciation, cancelled concerts, streamed shows, and work woes. There wasn't a quiet moment. Our laughter continued to serve as the soundtrack of our relationship. It brought us together. It enabled me to see beyond the parts of him I didn't like. *But I have to remember that laughter isn't enough for me to stay.*

Before I realized it, we had time-warped to Middle Tennessee, home to the state's best waterfalls. He circled the large gravel lot a few times before finding a space to park. We both changed from our Chacos to tennis shoes. Given we would be wading for the majority of the hike, we didn't want to risk rocks or sticks penetrating our skin, and boots would get too water-logged. We walked through sticky air that pressed down on us like a weighted blanket, then queued to show our gorge access tickets. When the park reopened following the COVID shutdown, it had implemented a reservation system. Only 150 nonrefundable tickets were issued per day as a way to mitigate overcrowding in the gorge.

Rangers grouped us with other parties to watch a safety video about flash floods, instructing what to do in the event we were stuck in the gorge. In recent years, a few deaths had occurred due to flash floods. Since then, the park had implemented several safety measures, including closing the park in the event of inclement weather, strategically placed life jackets, and the mandatory safety video.

We descended into the gorge, where another ranger verified we had tickets before we entered the shallow waters of Blackburn Fork River, a cool welcome to our sweat-soaked skin and clothes.

We followed a sandy bank until it disappeared underwater. Then we crossed the ankle- to calf-deep river to walk on a rocky bank until it also ended. We continued zigzagging from bank to bank on our journey to the falls, where the water never rose above our knees. Other trekkers chose to wade their entire route in the water.

Ahead, I spotted a group of Black hikers: three women and two men. They appeared to be a few years younger than me, likely students at Tennessee Tech, given the purple paraphernalia they wore. They were coming back from the falls. My eyes grew wide. Barely above a whisper, I said, "Yes, my people are out! My people. My people." Exuberant, I clenched my hand in a fist and pumped it by my side. When we passed, we acknowledged each other with The Nod.

I don't know how many times I've been told, "Black people don't hike," "You do White people stuff," or have been called weird for my love of the outdoors. My favorite retort was that Black people were some of this country's original thru-hikers, finding their way to freedom on the Underground Railroad.

Even though my mother and I shared a collective memory, we often disagreed about race. She'd grown up in the era of paper bag tests with segregated Catholic schools and neighborhoods. While I was always aware of my color, my magnet schooling and diverse, middle-class neighborhood didn't bake race into my identity. I didn't let race define me even though it was often how others did.

My mother hated that I hiked, and when the threat of pulling my Black card didn't work, she fearmongered with stories of murders on the trail, scary men, and the dangers of being a woman alone, as if I were some Victorian woman who required a chaperone to leave home.

But fears, even outlandish ones, stem from some truth. Bad things happened to Black people in the woods. Shit, *still* happen. For a long time, we were excluded from outdoor spaces, and when we weren't excluded, we were segregated to inferior parts, so childhoods telling stories by the campfire, swimming in a lake, and finding fellowship among the fauna and flora wasn't normalized for us. And over half a century of ~~equal~~ legal rights to access later, we still weren't getting out. So, whenever I saw People of Color embracing our right to access, flourishing outside, I celebrated.

Ryan chuckled and asked, "Do you feel safer now that 'your people' are here?"

"What are you talking about? You're 'my people' too." I play-punched his tricep.

"Oh my God, are you talking about your Irish ancestry?"

"Of course. Look at the freckles on my nose and cheeks." I pointed out the freckles that only appeared with sun exposure. "This curly hair." I pulled one of my corkscrew curls straight and then released it, so it could bounce back into a spiral. "My mother's DNA testing proved it's in 'me bones.' I'm likely more Irish than you." Years ago, my mother hopped on the ancestry craze. The equal parts Benin and French ancestry didn't surprise us, but the 20 percent Irish did.

We doubled over in laughter.

"But seriously, I'm happy to see more minorities out. While it never deterred me, I think it makes other people more comfortable to try out the outdoors because, for some, there's a certain discomfort in being outside in majority-White spaces."

"Speaking of racial tension outdoors, have you been following that news story about the Black man who was birding in Central Park and the crazy White lady with her dog?" Ryan asked.

"I'm aware of the story." I studied my feet, which trudged through the shallow water.

"I mean, it was wild how she went from being the aggressor to calling the police, pretending to be the victim. And I can't believe she did all of that on video."

"*Your* people have been acting crazy for years. But no one believes *us* until it's on video, and even then, there's skepticism. I mean"—I paused and twisted my mouth—"when I first heard about the story, it reminded me of you." I glanced at him.

He scrunched his face. "Me? I don't get it."

"Father's Day."

That holiday carried a weight between us, and when he heard my response, his shoulders slumped in defeat. "I had a feeling you'd might say that."

"Well, what happened to him could've happened to me, but you couldn't even comprehend it."

My head throbbed. I blinked the blurriness away. The Netflix home screen was on. I turned my head to the other side of the sofa, taking in the empty wine and beer bottles and a vape pen cluttering my coffee table. We had consumed more than was our custom, and deep down, I figured it was our way to cope with the day celebrating our entombed fathers. An approaching dawn filtered through the windows, casting a gray-green hue in the room.

Ryan slept on. I shook his leg.

"Hey, let's go to bed," I said. My voice croaked from dehydration.

He nodded and stood to his feet like Frankenstein's monster. We shuffled to my bedroom and slipped under a crisp top sheet. We arranged ourselves in our familiar positions, with him nestling behind me as my big spoon. His hand grabbed my breast.

"I'm really not in the mood. I just want to sleep," I said.

"But it's been so long. You're never home. You can go back to sleep after."

"You know I never do," I said.

He kissed my shoulder.

I closed my eyes, hoping to return to slumber, but I couldn't. He wedged his hand between my thighs. I removed it and scooted away. "Babe, I really want to sleep."

His body chased after mine. "Come on, I missed you. You're always away for work." He nuzzled my nape. "You can sleep after."

I clenched my teeth and rolled onto my back, yielding to his demands. His hands made quick work of my panties, and then he climbed atop me. I star-fished in protest, but I don't think he was bothered by it. A few minutes later, he squirted onto my stomach and rolled off me.

"I love you," he said.

I didn't have it in me to say it back. I got up to clean myself. By the time I returned to bed, his snores drowned out the songbirds. I grabbed my phone and pulled free a corner of sheet tangled around his body to cover mine. My tongue rolled over my sugar-coated teeth. Too depleted to get back up and brush my teeth, I scrolled through the tabloids and proper news sites, seething in silence.

When did this stop being fun? As with most things, there wasn't a singular, defining event, but there was a shift after he had completed last fall's Ironman. The goal-oriented, driven, disciplined man I had fallen in love was a veneer that had splintered, exposing a core of aimlessness and complacency. Had Ironman given his life purpose, and that's it, he peaked, or was he slipping into the clutches of depression?

Why didn't I leave? It's not like we were legally tied. We didn't have comingled assets. No vows before God. I hated that he wore the same hoodie six days a week, only removing it for workouts, sex, showers, and laundry. I hated that he drank in excess. I hated that he complained about his job but took no action to change his situation. I hated that he had a geriatric dog tethering him to his house. I hated his house, layered with crumbs, dust bunnies, and the sticky spills of mystery. I treated his bathrooms like a public toilet, with their sinks choking on hair and toilet bowls stained with moldy streaks resembling mascara tears.

But he made me laugh until I cried, until my stomach twisted and flipped, until I couldn't breathe, because according to him, his job wasn't done until I smiled.

His body stirred. With eyes closed, he stretched and yawned. "Where's my Father's Day gift?"

I ignored him.

"Where's my Father's Day gift?"

A vein bulged on my forehead. The gall! The man who knew from day one that I wanted to be a mother. The man I *asked* to be my child's father. The man who had dangled the carrot of fatherhood for the last six months but refused to try to conceive with me. The man who refused to wear a condom after I stopped popping birth control pills. The man who stuck by my side as I shopped for donors. "You're not a father, so you don't get a gift." My thumbs resumed massaging my phone screen.

"Where's my Father's Day gift?" He rolled over to face me, grinning.

I didn't bother looking at him. "Stop it. You've asked three times now. Stop fucking asking! You're not a father."

"Geez. Sorry." He sulked as if he couldn't understand why I was annoyed. Aggressor turned victim. He reached over to hug me. "You know I didn't mean to upset you."

I glared at him.

"Come on. Don't do that, Allyn."

Fighting back tears, my nose stung. I returned my gaze to my phone. "You don't want to be a father. That's why I'm shopping for donors."

"I never said I didn't want to be a father. It's just—"

"It's just nothing. You don't want to donate your sperm, but you're going to stick by your girlfriend while she chooses to be impregnated by some other guy. Are you going to leave once the baby comes, or will you stick around to earn a Father's Day gift?"

"I'm sorry, Allyn. I'm not going to leave. I just wish you would have waited before you moved forward with donors."

I scoffed as I scrolled through a detailed account of another Hollywood breakup.

"What do you want me to do? Lie about not being ready?" he said. "Then you'd hate me for lying. I'm in a no-win situation here. Besides, I'm not going anywhere. I'll be—what's that phrase you say—I'll be on you like white on rice." He then crawled on top of me and tickled my sides.

I squirmed, laughed, and fought his body, which was more than twice my weight. He sprang off me and onto the floor in a prayer position.

"What would you like to eat for breakfast, milady?" He kissed my hand.

"I'm so tired of eating out. Maybe your eggs benedict? I think I have all the ingredients, but maybe not arugula."

"I can go to the store. Anything for you." He kissed my hand again.

My cheeks burned. I cracked a shy smile to hide the frustration that lit my face. He'd do anything. Anything but impregnate me.

While he brushed his teeth, I made myself a cup of tea and put on a pot of coffee for him. I walked to my glass front door and raised the Roman shade, assessing the shenanigans outside.

My hipster neighbor's red husky was wandering the street again. I shook my head, cupping my teacup to quell the quiver of rage that had started to build.

I jumped when Ryan's arms blanketed me in his warmth. He bent his head and kissed my neck. A feeling of grubbiness swept over me when I inhaled his minty breath.

"What's wrong now?" he asked, trying to match my gaze.

"I just cannot with them. I'm done walking their dog back to their yard and locking their gate. It's so irresponsible. They're bad dog owners. From now on, I'm going to call McKamey. I'll let the animal shelter keep a record of their neglect. If you're going to have a dog, be a responsible owner."

"Why don't you just have a conversation with them?" he asked.

"A conversation?" I placed my cup on the small entry-way table.

"Yeah, like, 'Hey, I noticed your dog roaming the streets and around in my yard lately. Could you lock your gate so that your dog doesn't wander the street?'"

"This has been going on for months. It's not a 'lately.'"

"I don't understand why you'd have to escalate this to authorities without a simple conversation."

I rolled my eyes, still studying the husky's movements. "So, let me get this straight. You want me to approach the neighbors who haven't acknowledged my existence in the one and half years I have lived across the street from them? The neighbors who speak to you every time you visit but can't even be bothered to wave or acknowledge me?"

"I'm just suggesting that you be the bigger person."

I freed my body from his arms and faced him, eyes narrowed and arms crossed. "Oh, so even though I've been doing them a solid by saving their dog's life by walking him to safety every time they leave their gate unlocked or open; even though they're the ones who are breaking the law by having their dog unleashed and wandering the street unattended; even though I'm the one who has been picking up their dog shit in my yard for months; even though you take my side when I suggest holding my Black neighbors accountable for not mowing their yards or partying until one in the morning" —I changed my voice, emulating a saccharine, jocund, 1930s Hollywood depiction of the feebleminded house slave—"fo' the good White neighbahs 'cross the street, I shouldn't hold 'em account'ble fo' neglecting they dog's safety? I need to be the biggah person and talk to folk who don't even a'knowledge me? Ain't that right, mistuh?"

His mouth gaped like a fish, searching for oxygen.

I paused. Ryan made me smile and laugh like no other, but he didn't respect me. And if he didn't respect me, no matter what he said, he couldn't love me. How would he recover from this argument? An apology, a hug, and a tickle weren't going to cut it this time.

"Seriously, Allyn? I don't get how you jumped to that. You're being dramatic."

Dramatic. Unreasonable. Emotional. Unstable. Overacting. "You're not going to invalidate me in my own house. They" —I motioned both of my hands in the direction of my hipster neighbors' house—"have issues with Black people. You can't deny that. But you expect me to have a civil conversation with them about their shortcomings? Their failings to their chattel?" I counted my points on my fingers. "I'm the bigger person at work. I'm the bigger person whenever your friends say suspect-ass shit. I'm the bigger person in so many White spaces because I have to live in your world, but you don't have to live in mine."

My voice stole the quiver from my arms. "But this is my home, my property, and I will not have you—a guest in my house, by the way—tell *me* to be the bigger person. Fuck being the bigger person. I'm right. And you" —I pointed to him—"should support me."

"I do support you, but this has nothing to do with race. It's about being neighborly."

I clenched my teeth. My hands balled into fists. "Get out."

"Seriously?"

"Get the fuck out."

Without saying a word, he about-faced, went into the kitchen, opened the refrigerator, and grabbed his craft beer cans. He stormed through the rooms that held a century of quarrels and tromped to the front door. Before he could place his free hand on the door handle, I jutted my hand into his path, stopping him.

"What?" he asked.

I swallowed as my eyes pierced him with my disappointment and the wrath of my collective memory. "My key."

I turned my head toward the rooms of memories, offering him my cheek. I refused to watch him fumble through his pockets as he fished for the one thing keeping me from my freedom. My hand flinched when he dropped the key into my palm. My fingers closed over its hard coolness.

A chime beeped when he opened the front door. The screen door swooshed open and then closed. I didn't turn my head from the silent rooms of secrets to watch him get in his SUV and drive off. I stood shell-shocked, paralyzed to the spot, too angry to cry, too strong to collapse, until a few minutes later when the smell of coffee turned my stomach. I closed the door and then poured the coffee down the drain.

The next day, I was back on a plane for work. I extended my time, staying the weekend to hike in the White Mountains of New Hampshire. For the first time in months, I could breathe. Frustration turned to hope. I missed Ryan, but not in the way I expected—I didn't miss a boyfriend but rather our companionship.

When I returned home, I called him, explaining how I missed our banter and how I hoped we would remain friends. He agreed.

And he opened up to me as a friend in ways he never had as a boyfriend. As a boyfriend, he didn't know how to convey how depressed he was after his dog died without facing my judgment. And he explained his exhaustion in his quest to make me happy. He signed up for therapy, he quit therapy, he bitched about work, he refused to find a new job, he drank more. He shared all of it; I was there for every day of it, and I could handle it as his friend, but not as his girlfriend. And while he spiraled, I moved forward, more certain than ever that a donor was the right path for me.

Now we sat on a large boulder and watched people swim, play, and sunbathe next to the seventy-five-foot Cummins Falls. I spotted the life preservers and prayed the skies wouldn't darken.

"Honestly, I wish you would date. You have a lot of great qualities. You've been such a good friend to me. I've noticed vast improvements in your"—I air-quoted—"'wokeness.'" Then I rolled my eyes at the word.

He laughed. "I'm not interested in dating." He leaned back onto his elbows. "Are you dating?"

I felt his eyes on my face. I picked at a nick in the boulder. "Yes." I glanced at him.

His face flushed. "Is there anyone you like?"

I had chatted with a few guys but only had one official date at the Tellus Science Museum—it still consumed me. "No. I'm thinking of stopping."

"Well, since I have all these great qualities and you don't like anyone, why wouldn't you want to be with me?"

I breathed out a laugh. "I just feel like we're on different trajectories. There's a lot of history of you not understanding who I am and supporting … what's most important to me." I stopped picking at the boulder and rubbed my throat. "I don't think I've given up on being a mom."

"More fertility treatments?"

"Well, yeah, I'm not tying up my dream in a romantic partnership again. Sorry, not sorry."

He spread his hands in surrender. "Look, I'm Team Allyn. And while I don't have this burning desire to be a dad, I want to be with you, and if that means we have a baby, then let's have a baby."

My neck snapped back in shock. *Is he now saying the words I've been longing to hear? Is he lonely from the pandemic? Is he more mature now? Did he date a couple of bad eggs and realize how good he had it with me? Do I even care why?* "Wow, seriously?"

"Yes. What do you think?"

"Honestly, I'm shocked. This is so unexpected." I had wanted this for months, so why wasn't I screaming yes? Why wasn't I already peeling my clothes off?

"I thought you'd immediately say yes."

I studied the people under the waterfall. "I'm not saying no, but I've just been wrapping my brain around starting IVF."

"Hey," he said, commanding my attention.

I turned my head to face him. Our eyes locked.

He smiled. "You don't need to do that anymore."

I tore my eyes away from his and redirected my focus on the waterfall. But was he right? I hadn't gotten pregnant with my ex-husband, even if we hadn't tried to conceive for very long. I hadn't gotten pregnant with three rounds of IUI. Medically, I wouldn't be deemed infertile until three more months of unsuccessful attempts. Maybe I needed aggressive intervention. Was Ryan CMV negative? My ovaries were aging, and Ryan was ten years older than my donor. Older sperm posed risks like Down's, low birth weight, cleft palate, schizophrenia, bipolar disorder, and seizures. Worry clouded my mind.

Ryan reached his arm toward me and pulled me in for a side hug. Maybe he could be the plan B to my plan B. I rested my head on his shoulder and released the thoughts that burdened me.

After a few seconds, I lifted my head. "Do you see that?" I nodded toward a large, saggy-skinned woman, digging her swimsuit out of her dimpled butt.

"Tennessee's finest." The corners of his mouth crept upward.

"Your people! You think she gets that from her Cherokee or her Scotch-Irish side?"

He laughed. His laugh made me laugh. We laughed until our stomachs knotted.

That evening, I unfastened my journal and flipped a few pages to the first available blank line. I scribbled the day's date.

A bit to catch up on. I don't want to rehash everything, but IUI didn't work. There's also this pandemic that has turned the world upside down. I was originally training to go to Huayhuash, but the border situations are iffy, so I'm going to go to Zion NP instead. I should be excited, but truthfully, I'm just going through the motions and ready for it to be over, so I can start the next chapter.

My insurance approved my IVF treatment. I'm scheduled to begin after Zion. But then today Ryan said he wants to get back together and try for a baby. I don't know if that's such a good idea.

He's made vast improvements in understanding diverse perspectives, but I don't know how much of that was self-driven from what happened between us versus everything going on in the world right now. Did he seek knowledge and different perspectives because he took to heart the things I've said or because it's now fashionable? And is he only wanting to be with me because he's lonely? Or horny? I'm unsure if he's taken proper steps to address his depression.

And I need to better understand his goals—if he even has any. Is he still just sitting around drinking? There's just a lot for me to figure out.

But I didn't say no, and that has to mean something, right?

1.10 LECONTE LODGE

Mel drove up US-441 and then doubled back, looking for a parking spot. Vehicles flanked both sides of the highway — some in approved gravel spaces; some half-kilter on embankments, crushing the flora; while others crossed the solid, white line, partially obstructing traffic. We parked a mile north of the Alum Cave trailhead around 10 a.m.

We never arrived at trailheads that late, but check-in at LeConte Lodge wasn't until noon. We geared up and set off for the mile-long walk to the trailhead.

"I wish I would've brought wine in a canteen like you," Mel said. "My nerves are shot." She accepted the swig that I offered.

I had booked unlimited wine service for our overnight. "I figure if we need more wine, we can pour it into our Nalgene bottles to have something for later, and then ask for more wine that we'll drink with dinner. We should be good with that because if we drink more than two liters of wine, we won't make it off the mountain tomorrow."

She cackled. "They can just roll us down the trail, girlfriend."

"Wouldn't that be a sight?"

We fell into our normal groove of silent conversation.

At the footbridge to Arch Rock, she asked, "Phew, can we take a break? My back is killing me."

"Absolutely, this is the heaviest my pack has ever been. You should be thankful you didn't bring wine."

We flung our backpacks to the ground and stretched our legs and backs.

"I'm so excited you got us an overnight at LeConte," Mel said. "I was worried it'd be cancelled because of the pandemic. I've been dreaming of doing this for decades. I hear the food is so good, especially breakfast. It's a shame we won't be able to eat in the dining hall. I hear that makes for a great experience."

The dining hall was closed to mitigate COVID risks. There would be no shared meals, no rocking-chair circles, no board games, no fireside tales from the trail. While we savored uncrowded trails, the lodge was a gathering place, a Smoky Mountains rite of passage.

"Yeah, I also read that the food is amazing, but we'll get cabin-side service—whatever that is. But I'm happy that I was able to do this for you. Really." And I was. On the first day I met her at Virgin Falls she had told me it was her dream to stay overnight at LeConte Lodge. She had explained how difficult it was to obtain reservations, and she was right. The lodge accepted bookings via phone or a random lottery drawing from an online application. On the opening day of bookings, eight months of vacancies would be gone. I applied for the online lottery, and on opening reservation day last October, I had used my work desk phone, my work cell phone, and my personal cell phone, dialing for a miracle. Three phones and thirty minutes later, a voice answered. My first two date choices were already booked, but I scored a reservation for my third date—the latest of the three and fortunately not cancelled due to the pandemic.

Around Inspiration Point, we stopped for another breather. I studied the dead flower heads that remained on the rhododendrons. "It's a shame we missed the Catawba rhododendron bloom. I've never managed to hike this trail or Carver's Gap in their peak."

"It's truly magical to see. My anniversary was in June, and we'd come to the Smokies every year on our anniversary week. For the first ten years, we never went to the park. We were just stupid tourists hanging out at the pool, playing golf, and eating out, and then one day, we actually drove to the park and hiked a trail and were hooked. You can see how we easily fell in love with this place."

"Wow, I never knew you were one of *those* people who went to the Smokies and never visited the park."

"Yeah, can you believe it?" Mel laughed. "But hiking here became the highlight of our year. It's why we wanted to retire here." She removed her ballcap and wiped sweat from her forehead.

"I've been to many places in this world, but there's something about this place that's home," I said.

We powered through the rest of the trail and arrived at the lodge. With the crime scene tape removed, people freely walked around the grounds, but it was quieter than I had expected, even with the limited service. The familiarity of the space coupled with our unfamiliarity with the changes behind the closed doors was like driving by your childhood home once it belonged to a new family. We climbed the deck steps to the lodge and read the door sign:

Capacity: Six people

We opened the screen door, peering inside to count. We were persons three and four. We masked up. The silence inside the lodge was deafening. Gone was the rowdy laughter of trekkers, the rocking chairs scraping the wood floors as they moved this way and that, the plastic clank of board-game pieces, and the flip of crisp pages in the guest book. It was devastatingly barren.

We signed the guest book. It was my sixth visit and Mel's twenty-eighth. We stood in line and bought our "I hiked it" T-shirts as a souvenir for our pilgrimage. Then we waited to be shown to our cabin. Our hostess emerged from the staff only area and handed us a key to Cabin Nine. She was petite and blonde and looked barely old enough for college.

"Are you excited for your overnight at the lodge?" our hostess asked at the start of our tour of the property.

"Yes," we answered. Overstretched smiles painted our faces, masking our uncertainty for the night ahead to all but the most Southern of eyes.

"We're so happy you're here with us. I know things are a bit different right now to maximize guest and staff safety, but you'll have a great time."

We walked by the dining hall. No one was gathered to take photos in front of the date and elevation sign.

"Guests staying with us can get unlimited coffee and hot chocolate until four o'clock. Then, our kitchen starts preparing for dinner. Dinner will be served at six via our *cabin-side service*." Our hostess elevated her voice as if cabin-side service were an upgraded amenity. "We'll have a runner bring you your meals. You two have unlimited alcohol. There's a separate crew that will come around to pour until seven."

Mel and I looked at each other with our brows furrowed. Through our years of silent trail conversation, I interpreted the look in her eyes, which matched my own thoughts: *Only an hour of unlimited wine?!*

The hostess pointed to a log building near the lodge. "Right over there is the bathroom for overnight guests only, and there are two pumps for water. The one you walked by up to the lodge, and" —she pointed in the opposite direction— "one over there. There's a sponge and basin in your cabin for bathing. The most important thing for you to remember is to lock all food items in the metal bins we have in the dining hall no later than eight."

"Because of the bears, right?" I asked.

"Actually, mice. We've not had them that bad this season."

"Mice?!" Mel scrunched her face in disgust. "I wish you hadn't said that."

"Yeah, mice are a bigger threat than bears at the lodge," the hostess said.

Mel and I exchanged frowns.

We all walked to the other side of the property to our cabin. It was dark inside, as if the walls were blackened with soot. A table and one chair sat on one side as if they had been punished. The bunk beds were adorned with orange wool blankets. Daylight fought to enter through two opposing windows, covered by white curtains.

"Do you know how to operate a kerosene lamp?" the hostess asked.

"Yes," Mel answered.

"Good. We ask that you turn it off when you are not in your cabin. Well, that's it. If you need anything, go to the dining hall or back to the lodge."

This wasn't the LeConte Lodge experience we had fantasized about, but fortunately both of us possessed the capability to salvage shitty situations. I waited until our hostess was out of earshot to say, "I did a lot of research on how to prepare for an overnight at the lodge, and not one person mentioned mice." I was upset.

"Yeah," Mel said in a hushed voice. "I don't know if I'll be able to sleep knowing that."

"Well, you can sleep on the top bunk, so the threat is reduced."

"Are you sure?"

"Yeah." I wanted her time at the lodge to be the best possible. This was her dream.

I unpacked my sage and smudged the cabin. Once the space was cleansed, we dragged the rocking chairs from the porch to a sunny, grassy spot in front of the cabin. She ignored the book in her lap while I ignored my journal. We tilted our heads back to absorb the sun.

"Even with my jacket on, I'm freezing. It's going to be cold tonight," Mel said.

"Yeah, I have a chill that I can't shake." I offered her another swig from my canteen.

She cradled the canteen before taking a sip of the malbec. "How did you come to know so much about wine?" she asked.

"Well, I don't think I know that much about wine, but it probably started with my dad. He preferred liquor and beer over wine, but his family made this sweet fruit wine. On holidays, all kids older than twelve were allowed a glass. I guess you could say it was a rite of passage. I learned how to make it, which made me enjoy it more. Other than the family wine, I didn't really drink it or expand my knowledge of wine until I studied abroad in Italy, where it was cheaper to drink than Coke. And now I've developed a palate. It's an expensive vice."

"I really like this malbec."

"Yeah, from a pure taste perspective, malbec isn't my favorite, but each sip reminds me of El Chaltén. Los Andes."

"How are things going with your big hike trip? That's coming up soon, right? What's it called? *Why*? *Way*-something?" She capped my canteen and then handed it to me.

I reached for it. "Huayhuash." I uncapped my canteen and took another swig, letting the red candy slide down my throat. "Because of the pandemic, that's not going to happen. Not anytime soon. I could likely get in the country but not out. And they have an indigenous population like we do, so the trail might be closed to protect them. It's just not my year."

"You can say that again."

"But I *am* still going somewhere. The end of this month, I'm driving out to Zion National Park."

"I've heard of it but don't remember how far it is from here."

"It's in Utah—about a three-day drive."

She blew out a breath through her lips. "You're going to drive to Utah?! I'm not surprised. Whatever gave you the idea to go there? Some hiker trip report?"

I laughed. "A few weeks back. I met this guy hiking up in the Virginia Highlands, and he suggested it."

Mel gripped the rocking chair's arms and leaned forward. "You're going with him? You're dating again?"

"Whoa, no! I'm not going with him even though if he offered, I would've considered it. We never exchanged contact info, though. As far as dating" —I took a longer swig— "I did online dating for a little bit, but that was kind of a bust."

Her eyes widened. "Online dating! Why, girlfriend, I never thought you'd do that, especially since you don't do social media."

"Obviously, I'd much rather meet people in person because my philosophy is there's already a common framework putting the two of us in the same setting, but the pandemic is limiting." I drummed my fingers against my canteen. "At best, I leave my neighborhood once a week to hike. The odds aren't in my favor waiting on some organic connection. Hikes, gas stations, grocery and package deliveries are my organic opportunities these days."

"So you're not dating now?"

I grimaced. "I gave up online dating, but I'm kind of back together with Ryan now."

A laugh erupted from a cabin closer to the lodge. We turned our heads to identify the source. Mel folded her hands across her stomach. "Even after your breakup, you two had a lot of love for each other, so I'm not too surprised this happened."

"But everything feels different this time," I said, studying my feet.

"Different good?"

I shook my head. "Our chemistry is off. I don't know if this feeling is going to pass or not. I used to love sex with him, and now it feels like I'm acting. I just can't get into it. He's nice, but he doesn't excite me anymore."

"Maybe you've hit that point in the relationship where love is more about respect and sacrifice."

"That could be it, but there are times when I lie next to him feeling suffocated. And I wonder if this is how my ex-husband felt about me."

"Oh, Allyn. I never met your ex-husband, but based on what you told me, you're not him. You're not a quitter. You're compassionate and strong. You always find a solution for anything, and I mean *anything*."

"That's just it." I sighed. "Mel, I haven't shared everything with you." I gulped down the last swallows in my canteen. My hand wanted to motion the cross before I confessed the secrets I had been sheltering from damn near everyone. "I've been on and off trying to conceive for the last few years, including when I was married. I never got pregnant with my ex. Ryan refused, so I went down the donor route, but that didn't work. And now, Ryan and I are trying, and maybe I'm only with him because I'm not quitting on my baby plans. Like, maybe my heart has already quit him. I don't know. I care for him. I do. He treats me so well. Maybe I should just be thankful to have a man who loves me." I picked at a hangnail on my thumb. I'd do anything to not look at her face.

"Wow, Allyn. I had no clue you wanted a baby. Why didn't you think you could share this with me?"

Mel was an only child of a father who died young and a physically and emotionally abusive mother. Mel then married another only child and had a hysterectomy early in their marriage, ending their biological options. They never considered adoption and instead became dog parents and traveled like all Southerners do: to the mountains, which only meant the Smokies, and to the beach, which meant the Gulf, Myrtle Beach, or Hilton Head. Because she and her husband had more income, they sometimes vacationed in Mexico.

"Well, there's judgment—"

"Allyn, I would never judge you." She scooted her rocking chair closer. Her hand found mine, and she gave it a quick squeeze. "Do your mom and sister know?"

I finally looked at her face. "My sister knows I've been trying, but she doesn't really ask about it anymore. Her questions every month about if I am or not pregnant were too much anyway. It's heartbreaking enough getting my cycle, not to mention being asked about it by everyone who knows I'm trying. And my mother, well, no, she doesn't know anything. You know I try to keep our conversations light because I can't stomach her constant criticisms of my life choices. I haven't told her about getting back with Ryan or even Zion yet. She'd have a lot to say about both."

I nibbled on my thumbnail to plug my monologue of entitlement. For one thing, Mel wasn't my therapist. For another, complaining about a mother who went from homemaker to nurse educator and pushed both her girls to pursue education to achieve financial independence seemed ridiculous in comparison to what she had dealt with growing up.

"Well, you know my history with my mother, so I'd never advocate for you to stay in a toxic situation, but from the things you shared, it does seem like your mom cares about you. You know, in your mom's and my generation, financial security was the most important thing. Many women married for that security. She probably doesn't know another way to show she cares about you."

I shrugged. "She's just hypercritical, and it just pushes me away."

"Well, if it does, it does. Forty years on, I still have a weird relationship with food because of my mom. It's not your job to carry her insecurities and scars. You have to live your life for you, not anyone else. You're a strong cookie, girlfriend. You'll know. Trust your gut. You'll know if it's time to walk away from her. Just like you already know what to do with Ryan."

But do I already know with Ryan? I smiled away my discomfort with trusting my gut. My forefinger rubbed the jagged edge of my thumbnail. Despite Mel's support, despite Lenny's confidence in me, neither appreciated the doubts I harbored and how my mother, Ryan, and my fertility clouded my ability to see a path forward. "I really love that I'm here with you right now despite things just being"—I looked around at the other guests dining outside at their cabins—"unexpected."

"I love that I'm having this weird moment with you, too, girlfriend. Sure, I always dreamed I'd be here with my husband, but it's better that I'm with you. You know, I have just fallen in love with you. I'm always telling folks how witty and smart and beautiful you are, and I'm just in awe of all the things you do. You're so brave, you're so adventurous, you don't take shit from anybody! I think of you as my daughter. If I could have kids, I'd want them like you."

I teared up and leaned over to hug her. As I enveloped her in my down-wrapped arms, I acknowledged that my tears weren't of happiness but of longing. I couldn't deny that I ached to hear those words from my own mother and be smothered in her arms.

Ten minutes to sunset, twenty or so of us gathered at Cliff Tops. Families. Lovers. Friends. The fiery orange sun toasted our faces in his final descent. Bringer of life. Bringer of death. We were spectators to his daily performance of painting the sky blues, pinks, yellows, and purples. We snapped photos. We sat in silence. We had hushed conversations in small huddles. I stared at the horizon, watching the sun disappear. I sighed. The air instantly chilled, and I was overcome with a sadness. I looked over at Mel. Her head tilted toward where the sun had been; her eyes were closed, and a small, soft smile spread on her lips. Was she thinking of her husband's absence from that moment, or was she happy to finally realize a dream? Regardless, in that moment, I wanted to be her smile.

With our headlamps lighting the trail, we trekked back to our cabin and slept a sleep only those with alcohol-fired bellies and wearied backs and legs know.

Bill Withers's "Lovely Day" played at 5:30 a.m. I slid out of bed and changed into my clothes from the day prior.

"Are you wanting to catch sunrise at Myrtle Point?" I asked, shaking Mel awake.

"I'm so tired. I dunno. Are you going?"

"Yeah, this is likely my only opportunity as I don't see me hiking up LeConte in darkness to catch a sunrise. I'm not *that* hardcore."

"You're right, but do you think we'll have a view?" She struggled, opening her right eye like she were one of those blinking dolls with a stuck eyelid.

"We'll never know if we don't go."

She climbed down from the top bunk. Her silver-blonde pixie hair stood on end as if she had stuck her finger in a socket. After she dressed, I led the way to Myrtle Point.

When we arrived, there were a few people already there. The sky was overcast. We would see no sunrise.

"Mel, is that you?" a voice called.

I whipped around as Sarah and Hannah walked toward us.

"What are you doing here?" Mel asked.

"Well, you posted on Facebook that you were staying overnight with Allyn, and we thought we'd do a reunion of sorts," Hannah answered. "We couldn't make it up yesterday, so ta-da, here we are!"

We all took turns hugging each other.

Turning to Mel, I asked, "Did you know about this?"

"No, this is a surprise for me, too, girlfriend. If I would've known, I would've brushed my hair and teeth." We laughed.

The four of us stood in silence, watching the gray, obscured sunrise, knowing what was there even if we couldn't bear witness to it. And while my mother and sister refused to understand, these stray women I'd collected along the way shared the same ethos as I did. I couldn't detangle the love we had for each other from our love of the land. And I was okay with that messiness because we were a family of sorts.

PART 2:

DISTANCE, DISCORD, AND DISCOMFORT

2.1 CROSSROADS OF AMERICA

As I crossed the electrolyte tablets off my Zion packing list, my phone buzzed. Lenny's photo flashed on the phone's screen. I answered the call.

"Hey, chick! Big drive today!" she said.

"Yeah, I'm doing one final packing check and then will load my car."

"I'm scheduled to be stateside early November, and if all goes well with quarantine, we should get together for Thanksgiving, unless you're going home."

"I'm not going home. I'm still not allowed, but—I might have plans."

"Really? Is there someone new you haven't told me about?" Her voice raised a few pitches, imploring me to spill the details. I imagined that if we were together, her eyes would be growing tall and her lips would be curling up in the corners.

"Ehh, no. Ryan." I winced.

"Are you fucking kidding me? You're back with him now?"

"Yes. No. Maybe. Yes? He invited me to his family's Thanksgiving, and you know how well I get on with his mom." I walked to my dining room, where I had staged all my gear, and began cross-checking items.

"I don't approve. He does nothing for you."

"This is why I didn't say anything to you. I know how much you don't like him." Feeling a bit defensive, I added on a slight exaggeration. "For the record, my friend Mel is thrilled that we're back together. She says the way he looks at me is straight out of a romcom."

Lenny sucked her teeth. "Romcom? More like a part four of a horror franchise. She's a post-divorce friend. They don't know you like I know you."

There was a bitter truth to her words. "Oh my God, Len. I just don't know if Ryan's and my story is over yet."

"I know it's been a minute. How's the sex?"

"Not at all like it used to be. It's like I'm going through the motions, hoping to reignite something, but what if the passion's gone forever? Maybe I have some mental block that's keeping me from getting over everything that happened last summer. Like, does he really respect my point of view now? I don't know, but I don't want to go back to dating."

"And you're still moving forward with IVF, right?"

"Yes, but I haven't told him yet. I'll deal with that when I get back."

"I truly don't understand why you decided to be with him again."

"I still love him. He's attentive, and he's finally willing to get me pregnant. Len, it wasn't all bad. We had happy moments."

"The opportune word is 'moments.' I don't want my friend sort of happy. I want her to thrive. Are you sure you don't see a way forward with Owen?"

Owen was one of the men I had met online dating. I groaned. "You just like Owen because (*a*) he's military, and (*b*) he's Black."

"Well, he's disciplined, and there is something to be said about already understanding each other's culture and inside jokes."

"I get it. I'm very attracted to Black men, but—" I tucked an errant curl behind my ear. "My environment and passions are working against me. Given we went to a PWC, I live in a town that only has a 30 percent Black population, and I don't do activities typically associated with 'the community,'" — I air-quoted — "the odds aren't in my favor. I'm open to all love connections and would be thrilled if one happened to be Black. You have to give me credit for trying, though." I chuckled. "You remember The Marine, right? That ended before I could even fantasize a start. And besides, Owen doesn't deserve a second chance after the shit he said."

"But Ryan does?" she asked.

I sighed. "It's different with Ryan."

"Is it, though? Seems to me you're willing to help one along his journey but throwing the other one away because he's flawed. Think about it."

I saluted. "Aye, aye, Captain. Look, I need to hop off here and load my car if I want to arrive at the hotel before sunset."

"'Kay. Message me later. This conversation isn't over."

I finished my inventory check of gear and food. The plan was to prepare all of my meals and only stop at hotels and gas stations. I still hadn't entered enclosed, public spaces, and I didn't want to expose myself to people, which could throw my hike and IVF plans into jeopardy.

Rain pelted my jacket and gear when I packed my car for my drive at half past five. I started my ignition. My headlights strained to light the path ahead, but they revealed my trash can sitting at the curb. I opened my car door and slogged across my yard to wheel it back to my house. A mow line divided my trimmed zoysia and my next-door neighbor's growing collection of spurge, nutsedge, and crabgrass. *When was their yard last cut?* With the summer rains, it didn't take many days to transform a yard to a jungle. I tipped my trash can on its side, dumping the soured rainwater onto the street. *When did I last see my neighbors? If their yard is still wild when I return, I'll mow it. Who knows when their slumlord will get around to it?*

I plopped down in my driver's seat and peeled off my jacket. I stared at my phone, gripped in my hand. I frowned and unlocked it. My fingers pecked at the screen.

Me: *Starting drive now. Today's destination: Topeka, KS.*

I sent the message to Lenny, Mel, Ryan, my sister, my mother, and a few coworkers. I turned off the group messaging option. I loathed when group messages morphed into a conversation between two people, rendering the remainder spectators. I placed my phone in my cup holder, then drove off my crushed gravel parking pad at 6 a.m., right on schedule. Topeka or bust!

Other than selecting trails, figuring out how to get to Zion required research. While flying was an option, I wasn't comfortable getting back on a plane no matter how many seats remained empty between passengers. There were two main driving routes I could take to Zion, I-70 or I-40. Both routes presented challenges:

1. The I-70 Challenge: Driving the Eisenhower Tunnel, which, at 11,013 feet, concerned me. While my car was recently serviced and it was a Toyota, there was no denying that there was a certain danger to driving an older, high-mileage car at an elevation that might cause engine or tire trouble.

    If my car made it past the Eisenhower Tunnel, I still had to contend with the Glenwood Canyon fire that had closed a section of I-70. If that section of I-70 remained closed, there would be about a four-hour detour because there weren't many routes over the Rockies. American westward migration had taught us that.

2. The I-40 Challenge: New Mexico mandated a fourteen-day quarantine order for an overnight stay. While I figured this would be hard to enforce, there was a risk that I could be reported. Without staying overnight in New Mexico, I would have to push myself to drive nearly 370 miles across the state and overnight in Arizona. The longest I had ever driven solo was eight hours, and since I wasn't able to legally stay the night in New Mexico, I was looking at an eleven-hour drive day. I didn't know if that was possible.

   Also, confounding the New Mexico overnight restriction was the larger question of whether I would be permitted to drive though Native reservations. COVID was decimating the Southwest tribes, and the restrictions were changing rapidly. If I couldn't drive through reservations, I was looking at a four- to five-hour detour, elongating an already long eleven-hour drive.

Despite the fire and the elevation challenge, I chose the I-70 route as it afforded more flexibility in being able to stop and stay overnight someplace. I figured the real challenge was my driving stamina.

I hoped the rain would not follow me. A heat wave was impacting Utah, but it seemed the temperatures would let up a bit during my days there. I drove away from the safety bubble of my hodgepodge of a neighborhood, turned left on Broad Street, drove over Lookout Mountain, where Lee

Highway turned into Cummins, and then turned left onto I-24. As I-24 briefly dipped down into Georgia, I fought my instinct to merge left onto I-59 South; this was not a trip home to Louisiana.

The time zone changed to Central. As I-24 climbed Monteagle Mountain, I zipped past motorists and truckers like a shiny red 328 Twin Turbo dodging old, pale blue VW Beetles. The first rays of light greeted me west of Nashville.

As I drove farther west of Nashville, I entered uncharted territory. I had never driven that section of interstate. Before I knew it, a sign greeted me:

Welcome to Kentucky
Unbridled Spirit

Google Maps said, "Welcome to Kentucky." An image flashed on my phone screen of a woman holding a champagne glass. She wore a pink dress and a Derby-sized hat. After a few seconds, she disappeared.

Somewhere along the way, the rain stopped. I traversed mile upon mile of rolling, green hills. A billboard advertised the National Quilt Museum. As I drove to the northern reaches of Paducah, I zipped by a red sign with white, reflective letters:

YOU ARE NOT ALONE.

The website and phone number to the National Suicide Prevention Lifeline were printed below. Crossing the Paducah Bridge, I reflected on the irony of a suicide prevention sign posted on the same river that escaped slaves had crossed to achieve freedom. *What a difference the passage of time has on a place. But death and freedom are similar; they are both escapes from pain.*

And I was escaping.

Escaping the confined sanctuary that was my home, escaping the bubble of my gentrifying neighborhood, escaping my neighboring mountains, escaping the haunt of losing something that had not yet begun. I knew not what was ahead, but I had to leave what I knew behind:

Welcome to Illinois
The Land of Lincoln

Hmm. But Lincoln was born in Kentucky. Speaking of the passage of time, will this sign one day read: "The Birthplace of Obama's Hope"? What the hell is in Illinois besides Chicago, anyway?

Farmland. Acre upon acre of crops. Cornfields as far as the eye can see. Corn that was more likely to end up in my gas tank than my stomach. It wasn't much different than South Georgia, except there was no cotton.

I picked up my phone and recorded an audio message.

Me: *Driving through Illinois. I've never seen so much corn in my life. I expected this from Kansas—but Illinois? Wow, fields for miles.*

I sent it to the same group as earlier. My phone buzzed with responses. I read my mother's.

Mommie Dearest: *The prairie state*

I missed the disconnectedness of international travel. Whenever I was abroad, my friends and family held zero expectations for me to stay in communication. I refused to buy international cellular plans and SIM cards so that I wouldn't be tempted by an incoming work email. Despite disappearing in the Appalachian Mountains most weekends by myself, despite traveling across the Atlantic and Pacific by myself, despite summiting peaks in the Alps and

Andes with no one I knew, driving alone across the United States for a bit of national park hiking necessitated Twitter-like updates. My mother had made it clear that if she didn't hear from me, she would text and call until I answered, so I balanced my need for freedom and respect with her perceived concern for my safety. I wouldn't put it above my mother to call the law to find me if she didn't hear from me. Some battles weren't worth fighting.

I tore my eyes away from her text and refocused on the road. I-24 ended. I took I-57 North until it connected to I-64. My mind floated from thought to thought as one song on my playlist ended and the next began. I open-palmed my steering wheel thrice in frustration. "Damn it. I forgot my loaf of bread." I didn't want to enter a grocery store—I hadn't entered a grocery store since the pandemic started—but peanut butter and jelly sandwiches were the backbone of my meals. My mind raced, contemplating alternate solutions. What would be the cost for grocery delivery just for bread? Maybe I could pick one up at a gas station? I groaned at my forgetfulness.

Fifty miles east of Saint Louis, I scanned interstate signs for gas stations I recognized. I pulled off at Exit 50 and turned left. A few gas stations clustered on one side of the road, and I honed in on BP, turning left into its small, four-pump station. After I pumped gas, I sanitized my hands, masked up, and dashed inside to use the bathroom and search for bread.

The bell on the door jangled, announcing my entrance. I held my breath as long as possible; in my mind it reduced my risk. I looked up, scanning for a bathroom sign—down a short hall to the right. En route to the bathroom, I walked past an indoor gaming room. In front of a slot machine, an obese man sat on a tiny stool, reminding me of chocolate cupcake topped with a tall mound of strawberry icing oozing over the sides. The slot machine's lights danced on his transfixed face. He didn't recognize my movement. The two-stall bathroom was gas station clean. There was toilet paper, minimal odor, and only a drop of urine on the seat. A metal dispensary hung on the wall near the sink. While I was washing my hands, I surveyed its contents: tampons, condoms, and weed. What more could a woman need in life?

"Weed is legal in Illinois?" I asked out loud as if the dispenser would respond.

There were neither paper towels nor a mechanism to dry my hands. I touched the door handle with wet palms, then doused them with hand sanitizer, sanitized the hand sanitizer bottle, and then re-sanitized my hands.

I walked up and down the gas station aisles, searching for bread. Sweet snacks, savory snacks, energy drinks. Many items past their sell-by dates with layers of dust caked on the packaging. No bread.

The store clerk wasn't wearing a mask, nor were the other patrons entering and exiting. My pulse quickened. I bolted from the store. I hand-sanitized again before touching my car door handle and then drove away.

Back on the interstate, I merged onto I-70. Driving across the Stan Musial Veterans Memorial Bridge, the Gateway Arch came into view:

CITY LIMIT
St. Louis

Where was the state welcome sign? Did I miss it? My phone spoke. "Welcome to Missouri." I glanced at the screen. The Google Maps icon flashed and disappeared. Was it ice cream and cotton candy?

As the interstate cut through the city, I couldn't shake how the city resembled a post-apocalyptic ruin: Midcentury homes in disrepair. Boarded windows. Brown, gray, brown, gray. A city devoid of vibrancy. If this city was the gateway to the American West, it forebode dark, depressing days. It was a far cry from *Meet Me in St. Louis*—or was it? I gawked at the modern-day reality and not the twentieth century Hollywood version of a great American city. Given Saint Louis remained one of the most segregated cities in America, I struggled to consider it great but agreed it was very much American.

As I left Saint Louis, the sky grayed. Clouds hung low. Various billboards littered the interstate's rolling hills: Jungle Law; opioid help lines; anti-abortion ads aplenty with one quoting Reagan, "I've noticed that everyone who is for abortion has already been born"; and a slew of Trump ads.

I rolled my eyes. *When will the epoch of men dictating what I can and cannot do with my body end?* Living in a blue city in a red state, I'd heard the gamut of views, but the extreme opinions on both sides of the political spectrum concerned me. We were no longer listening to each other. It was all about winning. Self-interests prevailed. Conversations could no longer be had. Each side retreated to its own hate bubble. It was maddening. Had nineteenth-century Americans experienced the same divisiveness? Was there as much vitriol? Would there be another split in the Union?

For the first time in my life, I was ashamed to be an American. I was aware that my country had been founded on freedom principles, but it was never freedom for all.

Throughout our entire history, someone was always inferior, and something was always taken. Despite this culture of baseless superiority, I had truly believed that, by and large, people remained civil. But things were no longer civil. The larger population was petulant. People were angry, and anger without viable solutions was dangerous. And did they even understand why they were angry, or was it demented herd mentality?

Misinformation was rampant. People lashed out at threats—some for no good reason they could articulate, some because they were afraid of losing advantages afforded to them for centuries, some because they were being hunted and killed like game, and some because they were tired. America had always thrived on fear and hate, but the tremors from the last few years were becoming stronger and more unpredictable.

No government was perfect, but citizens weren't doing enough to educate themselves, to objectively look at data and make informed decisions to advance our nation forward. These were sad times. Was this how Europeans felt in the 1930s?

Driving through Missouri and seeing a Trump billboard every two to three miles was bleak. I had Trump-supporting friends I loved dearly, but it was getting harder to separate their fervor for him from the larger racial problems in America. Could they support Trump and *actually* support me as a person? Or was it another situation of, "Oh, you're not like *them*," or "You're different, Allyn."

Years ago, when a college friend married a Dutchman, I traveled to Amsterdam for her wedding and visited The Secret Annex, the attic where Anne Frank, her family, and the van Pels family hid for over two years. The tour ended in a room where videos played of present-day Jewish people recounting the impact Anne's journal and their heritage had on them. A thirty-something American woman shared that she and her brother would play a game in their youth, identifying which of their neighbors would be brave and hide them if the events of the 1930s and 1940s were to repeat themselves. Who would risk their own lives, their own freedoms, to protect them? I now wondered the same.

The weather matched my mood. I reduced my speed and ensured I signaled with my blinker for every lane change. For me, that stretch of Missouri was a sundown town, and I needed to get far, far away. My parents had never given me The Talk that most Black children experience, but my survival instincts took over. I felt more in danger driving on an interstate in my own country than I had on any of my international trips. Did I want to bring a child into a country falling apart?

I called my mother.

"Where are you?" she answered.

"Ehh, somewhere in Missouri. Let me see if I can see a mile marker."

"How's the drive? Are you tired?"

"No, I'm not tired. I've been driving for ... umm ... eight hours now ... a little longer than the time it takes me to get home. I'm settling in but a bit bored with the scenery. The day is dreary. I'm just over it all. Mark Twain would be outraged at what's become of this place."

"What do you mean?" she asked.

"Columbia!"

"Huh?"

"I just drove by a Columbia, Missouri, sign. Just rolling hills, crops, highly charged conservative advertisements."

A word I pronounced the British way. "I'm ready to be done with this state. I can't relate to this version of America."

The call dropped. Of course, I'd lose my signal in Bumfuck, Missouri. Ten minutes later, I regained signal. I had two new voicemails, and my mother had left a few text messages.

Mommie Dearest: *Are you okay?*

Mommie Dearest: *Left you a voicemail*

Mommie Dearest: *I think you lost signal. Call me.*

I dialed my mother back. "Hey, seems like I lost service."

"Looks like you're smack dab in the middle of the state. Yeah, Missouri seems like a place where the aliens would go abducting people," she said, more to herself than me.

"Oh my God, Mom! But who knows what happened in that dead zone. The aliens could've abducted me, done all sorts of experiments, dropped me back in my car cruising at eighty miles per hour, and I'd be none the wiser because my memories are wiped." I played into my mother's paranoia with fantastical stories to distract from the rotation of our more unpleasant conversational topics, such as my singleness and my need to spend hours outside, disconnected from the anchors of life. She didn't try to understand why exploring new places and trails was critical to my existence. She'd only ask why I didn't do normal things. Then our conversation would spiral into a debate about what was normal, and then I'd refuse to talk to her for weeks.

"I'd feel so much better if you were with someone. It's unnatural to just drive across the country by yourself like some kind of trucker."

"When that package arrives on your porch in forty-eight hours, I'm sure you don't care how it got there."

"You're right, but you're *my* daughter, and I wish you were with someone."

Southern subtleties. "Well, life just hasn't worked out for me like that." I held my breath, unsure if we'd continue on with my unnatural choices, much less if I'd blurt out that I was back with Ryan so that she could subject me instead to a discussion about how I shouldn't just be with someone but the right kind of someone.

"Where are you stopping for the night?"

I exhaled, relieved I didn't have to be her punching bag. "I booked a hotel right outside of Topeka." It sounded as if she were flipping the pages of an atlas, tracking my journey.

"Ah, okay. It's near the border. How far are you from there?"

I fumbled with my phone, assessing the Google Maps information. "Google says two and a half hours. There'll still be daylight when I get there. I'll ping you after I check into the hotel."

Off the phone and alone in my thoughts, my consciousness weaved in and out of recent social events as I obeyed traffic laws and leapfrogged cars. Sometimes it was too mentally taxing to reconcile all the injustices still occurring today. America was the rebranding master. Instead of slavery, now we had incarceration. Instead of Jim Crow, we had urban renewal, enabling gentrification. Lynchings remained unchanged.

An old-fashioned movie reel flashed in my head of the senseless Black deaths and wrongful incarcerations in my lifetime. My heart dropped. My stomach churned. Could I keep swallowing my disappointment and turning the other cheek? It was no secret that hate crimes had risen since the last presidential election. There was no lack of video evidence chronicling excessive force against People of Color. But the pandemic had been the catalyst necessary to transform those ingredients into a cause White people rallied behind. It was like someone had flipped on the light switch in the dark room of oppression, and White people became conscious and stoked the fire of cancel culture as if focusing on commercial branding, entertainment from decades prior, and past transgressions of famous people were doing anything to positively impact the lives of People of Color. There was a whole lot of doing something that was effectively doing nothing. And I worried Ryan was swept up in that movement and not growing to become a more well-rounded person.

Would Ryan make a personal sacrifice? Had he confronted his own biases? Would he agree for his children to forgo magnet and private schools to ensure education equality? Would he protect minority spaces and not whitewash them? Would he invest as much value and reverence in the intellectual minority as the athlete he cheered and betted on? Would he be strong enough to be the only voice holding his peers accountable when he observed bias? Would he realize that equality wasn't possible without equity? Would he celebrate a minority getting a job over him? Would he not make minorities work twice as hard? Would he stop seeing Black contributions as three-fifths of his?

When were people going to take real, effective action?

Being Black was beautiful but also a heavy burden I hadn't asked for.

This weight meant I often didn't have the luxury to simply be me. Others expect minorities to take a position on every issue every waking moment. It was as if my reactions were under a microscope. If I didn't walk around angry all the time, then it meant I didn't get the struggle and had to be re-educated and reprogrammed. It was as if my voice spoke for all Black people, as if we were one monolithic, singular consciousness like The Borg. Was it so inconceivable to think that Black opinions were as varied as our shades? No, I wasn't a spokesperson for the entire race. No, I wasn't always angry. No, I didn't myopically see the world as right and wrong. No, I didn't want to talk about how I felt. No, I didn't want to hear your opinions. No, I didn't want your apology.

It wasn't that I wanted to bury my head in the sand and pretend nothing was happening, but I wanted the space to not be overcome with daily thoughts of the bias, the division, the hate, the sudden consciousness, and the need for White people to seek validation. I needed an off day. Moments when I didn't have to think or feel or have an opinion or engage about it. I needed days when I wasn't defined by being Black because, as much as I was, I wasn't.

And that's why I fell fast for Owen.

2.2 WHILE I BREATHE, I HOPE

After I created my profile and uploaded my photos, I set my match parameters:
1. Location – 100 miles
2. Age range – 35 to 45
3. Ethnicity – Open to all

Within minutes of signing up for online dating, as many women must contend, the algorithm detected new blood in the pool, and the sharks circled my profile. Even though my friends had told me I'd get inundated with un-welcomed attention, nothing prepared me for the on-slaught of messages and likes. I battled my anxiety at being accessible to so many men.

Me: *OMG I don't think I can do this. Why did I do this?!?!*

Sister: *Huh*

Me: *So, I signed up for online dating.*

Sister: *[crying laughing emoji]*

Sister: *[it's fun to do bad things gif]*

Me: *I'm overwhelmed. There's too much shit to sift through. I want to at least respond to everyone who has reached out.*

Sister: What?! *Why? You don't owe them anything*

Me: *I get that, but if someone took the effort to reach out, I should at least respond even if it's a "Thanks but no thanks."*

Sister: *If you want, but it's really not necessary*

Me: *How would you know? You've been married 20 yrs! This didn't exist then!*

Sister: *Do you want me to help you?*

Me: *Like outsource my online dating screening to you?*

Sister: *Yeah, it could be fun*

I considered it, but I doubted my sister had the remotest idea what I was seeking. If I left it up to her, she'd try to match me with all sorts of gym types who wanted their women subservient and dolled up. I signed myself up for this mess, so I would see it through for a couple of months.

Me: *I'll put on my big girl panties and do it. I'll let you know if I change my mind.*

Sister: *K*

I had examined the profiles of men who wanted to match. "The Bible is my favorite book," "God must come first," and "I'm looking for my wife," were common statements. Did men truly believe that, or did they think that would reel in women?

I hadn't a clue what I wanted so much as what I didn't want. After a few days of no viable matches, I expanded my location radius to include Atlanta. More men. I scrolled through the inbox of likes. One profile after another. By the tenth profile, they had morphed into more or less three categories: Peter Pans looking for an adventure buddy, God-fearing hunters and fishermen looking to start a family, and fuckboys. No one grabbed my attention. I lowered my age range to twenty-eight. And then, Owen found me.

Owen was a thirty-year-old National Guardsman recently returned from a tour in Eastern Europe. His profile was balanced and well-written, but what drew me in was his megawatt smile. And it definitely helped that his body was delicious. Buzz cut, chocolate eyes, tall, broad shoulders, narrow waist—the perfect triangle. Other men must have hated him. And unlike most other Black men's profiles, there was no mention of religion or looking for his "queen" or food being the way to his heart or any Princestylized spellings or mention of wanting a family. I assumed that when men want a family, it meant spreading their own seed, and I wasn't waiting for another man. So I replied to Owen.

For two days, we wrote dissertations to each other. I was blown away by how articulate he was. He shared that his service helped him pay for night school. He aspired to practice estate planning. While he didn't share my love for nature, we bonded over astrology, Buddhism, tarot readings, Japan, and our crystal collections.

We exchanged numbers. He messaged me when he woke up, we video-chatted during our lunch breaks, and we talked before bed about anything and everything. Funny moments at work. The profundity of *Avatar: The Last Airbender* (the animated TV show). Our crazy uncles. Soon, I couldn't imagine a day without him. His texts replaced my want for wine. I wanted Owen.

After an intense two weeks of long-distance communication, we agreed to meet at the Tellus Science Museum. We were two blerds, walking beneath the shadows of dinosaurs and through halls brimming with minerals and gems, reading placards, and stealing glances at each other. And when Altair and Vega crossed the Planetarium's Celestial River for their annual reunion, he reached for my hand. Tingles traveled up my arm and shot across my breasts. My body hair stood on end. My lips parted. I panted. I repressed my urge to mount him, grab his face, and shove my tongue in his mouth. Every inch of my body wanted that man inside of me.

I pulled my hand away from his. I wiped my sweaty hand on my jeans, tucked a curl behind my ear, and reached for his hand. I tried to suppress images of sex but failed. Sex. Sex. Sex. Me straddling him. Him towering over me. My ankles locked into his spreader bar with his face wedged between my thighs. *It has to be him. He is the one to usher me back to my sexuality. Back to all the pieces of me that make me a woman.*

As soon as we exited the museum, he pulled me in for a hug. My head rested in the valley of his pecs. His hand pressed my head deeper into him. I wanted to be held like that forever. He released his grip on me. We removed our masks. Pandemic be damned, I wanted him to kiss me. I wanted to give into whatever he offered.

"Did you have a good time?" he asked.

I giggled like a schoolgirl and tucked a curl behind my ear. "Do you really have to ask?"

He smiled. "I just wanted to make sure."

I stared at the ground, blushing. Looking him in the eyes would've made my knees buckle. "Yeah, I definitely would like to see you again." I glanced up at him.

He fist-pumped. "Yes! Mission accomplished."

He raised his eyebrows twice in quick succession.

I laughed and then bit my bottom lip. He escorted me to my car. Our giggles, interrupted with "What?" and "Nothing," were the chorus we said atop the racing rhythm of my heartbeat.

"Call me when you get home?" he asked when I opened my car door. It was more of a demand than an ask.

"Yeah, I will." The words rolled out with ease as my stomach flipped and a bitter taste pooled in my mouth. I swallowed the disappointment of his demand. Despite his check-in request, I still wanted to be engulfed in his reassuring arms and kissed, but there was no kiss. Maybe he shared my sentiment that we couldn't stop at only a kiss. I got into my car, and he closed my car door. I prepared for my drive back north, buckling my seat belt and typing my address into my phone. When I looked up to check my mirrors before shifting my car into reverse, a figure caught my eye. Owen stood in front of my car. He jumped in the air and then clicked his heels. I gripped my steering wheel and doubled over in laughter.

Me to Owen: *Nice! [heart eyes emoji]*

With Owen, I could relax and be myself. While we fell outside the societal parameters of what people expected of Black Americans, to each other, we were normal. There were no pretexts. We nerded out. We had moments of pure giddiness. Why couldn't we be happy and Black despite the chaos surrounding us?

When I got home, I texted my friends about how great the date was, and then I gave him a call as he ~~requested~~ demanded.

"Hey, I'm home. How long have you been home?" I asked as I began pacing through the rooms of my home.

"Maybe thirty minutes."

"Cool. Yeah. I'm glad we met today."

"Ditto! When can I see you again? You know, I can drive up during the workweek."

"Oh no, I'm not ready for that. I—" Yes, I wanted him to fuck me. "I need us to take things slow. There's undeniable physical attraction, but I need to get to know you more as a person." And I needed him to be okay with my fertility pursuit, but that wasn't my top priority.

"I like that." He laughed.

"No, seriously. It's important for me to feel physically and emotionally connected to someone. So far, I feel we're so aligned, but I need to know more about you."

"I can respect that. Most women just want to fuck me. They aren't interested in getting to know me, so whatever you want to know, I'm an open book."

"I know I have a lot going for me, but you could be with a twenty-year-old. Are you wanting a Mrs. Robinson experience?"

"Well, you don't look your age, but I'm drawn to older women. I like you a lot, Allyn. You don't treat me like a child, and I'm not an object to you."

But throughout my days, all I thought about was him naked. Me naked. Sex. Sex. Sex. Was I another contributor to the fetishization of Black men? "I really like your energy." And I did, but his body seized my thoughts. I bit my lips.

"Ditto! I can be completely myself around you. Like listen to EDM and not worry about being judged. Or talk about my love for anime. I can express my emotions and not have to worry I'm not masculine enough. It's like I don't have to prove any Blackness to you, but you understand that, being biracial too."

"Whoa, whoa, I'm not biracial. I'm Black." I stopped in my tracks. "My profile even says that. Why did you think I was biracial?" I hadn't thought of him as biracial. I figured he was light because his coarser hair, wider nose, and full lips screamed Black to me.

"Well, your skin color."

"Oh, people from New Orleans just look like … me."

"Okay, well, you definitely look biracial. I had people in high school call me 'mulatto.'"

"What? That's fucked up. Seriously, you didn't have a problem with that? Which one of your parents is Black?"

"They both are."

I scrunched my face. "So why are you claiming to be biracial?"

"Well, because in my family tree, there was a White man—"

"Stop! Stop, right now. By that definition, everyone in America is biracial. You are *not* biracial. You are Black. Wow." Why would he would call himself biracial? Was he uncomfortable identifying as Black? Did he find it easier to navigate White spaces claiming to be biracial? Was it easier to date women being biracial rather than Black? "So, do you even date Black women?"

"Yeah, but you're as dark as I go."

My mouth hung open. "What?" I was confident that I had heard what he said, but I had to be certain.

"I don't date dark-skinned women."

I knew colorism existed, but I assumed it was a construct for older generations. My father would tell my sister and me, "You can date him, but you can't marry him," because creating a permanent tie with a darker-skinned person reduced our status as lighter-skinned women.

I was flabbergasted. I understood having a preference, but there was no damn good reason for colorism. The color hierarchy within the Southern Black community was sickening, and I was a benefactor of the discrimination. As a Southern, lighter-skinned woman, I had a currency. I was less sexualized, deemed more beautiful, more refined, and carried more clout than a darker-skinned woman. Light-skinned women were regarded as the best White alternative.

"I'm really shocked. I didn't expect this from you. I mean, your mom is Black. How can you think this way?" I resumed pacing.

"It's just a preference. Some men like blondes. I like lighter skin."

"But, but are you not attracted at all to darker women? Like, what if she was everything you wanted but had dark skin?"

There was a pause. "I couldn't be with her romantically. Physical attraction is important."

"I don't buy that. I don't date a lot of Black men, but it doesn't mean I'm unattracted to them. There are so many darker-skinned Black women who are drop-dead gorgeous."

"I disagree."

"Why?" I was pleading, more to myself than him. "I wanted you so much. Why?"

"I don't see how that is relevant to you," he said. "I want you, so how I feel about another woman shouldn't matter."

"Because I'm Black. Because I'm a woman. Because I'm a Black woman. Because I have darker-skinned friends. Because for you to not find darker-skinned women attractive means you aren't comfortable in your own Blackness. I love that our Blackness doesn't define our connection, but your colorism is a problem for me."

"Colorism? Again, I don't really get the problem for you."

"You're close-minded!" I blurted out. "I don't get how a man who embraces holistic healing and lives on the fringes of what is considered normal for Black people can be so judgmental."

"I'm not judgmental."

"Maybe judgmental isn't the right word. And—" I sighed. "Look, I can't really articulate all my thoughts, but to be with you is turning my back on what it is to be a Black woman."

"That's illogical."

"Call it whatever you want. I can't see you again." I groaned. "God, this sucks because I was really into you. My body so wanted you. I felt you embraced all of me. You never questioned or judged my Blackness. I was simply Allyn."

"Are you serious?"

"Yeah. As much as I want you, I can't."

"Ugh, come on, it's not that serious."

"Will you change your mind about darker skin?"

Silence engulfed the call. I counted to ten, hoping he'd say something to salvage the spark we had created.

"If you can't see how this speaks to your insecurities and makes you a less confident, attractive man, then yeah, it is that serious," I said.

"How about you just sleep on this?" he said, again demanding more than asking.

"No. Please don't tell me what to do."

"I'm not telling you. It's a suggestion. Take time to think about it. I think you're catastrophizing."

"Catastrophizing?" I asked. I stopped and peeked out of my glass front door. One-Eyed Willy was sunning on my porch stairs.

"Yeah, you're blowing this out of proportion."

"Don't minimalize how I feel. I'm not catastrophizing. I don't need time. Fuck, I wish things turned out differently."

"Allyn, don't do this."

"I'm not doing anything. I'm not asking you to change who you are, but I can't be with who you are." What if I had a darker-skinned daughter? Would his colorism make her feel less than? It's the question that burned in the back of my mind, but I dared not ask.

"This conversation is going nowhere," he said.

"Seems so," I said.

Because it's in those private moments—when no one is watching, when no one is listening, when no one is applauding, when you make a personal sacrifice to stand beside a marginalized group—that real change happens.

The following morning, I rolled over, unlocked my phone, and read through the messages I had received while I slept.

Owen: *Good morning. Sleep well? How are you?*

Me: *Morning. Yes. I'm well. Why are you messaging me? Yesterday happened. I didn't forget.*

Owen: *So it's over just like that, huh?*

Me: *Yes. And you know I'm not looking for a friend.*

Owen: *I know. I'm really sad about this. I figured it would blow over.*

Me: *It can't.*

I stared at our message thread, which was filled with recorded and written correspondence. I hoped a new message would appear. I clenched my teeth. A new message icon popped up on my status bar. I navigated away from me and Owen's message thread to the new message.

Ryan: *Check this out.*

He shared a *90 Day Fiancé* Reddit thread about Michael and Angela. We texted back and forth a few times before I blocked Owen and rolled out of bed, stunned all over again at the loss of something that never was.

The clouds broke as I hit Kansas City. The city shined and sparkled—the antithesis of Saint Louis. While Saint Louis suffered, Kansas City prospered. Our cities perfectly reflected our fucked-up society:

Welcome to Kansas

I read the sign as Google Maps said it. I glanced at my phone, spying a Dorothy icon. Ruby slippers sparkled and floated by her head. The speed limit increased to 80 mph. *Fuck yeah!* When I pulled into the hotel parking lot off I-470, I had logged over seven hundred miles. It was the farthest I had driven in one go, and I wasn't tired. I was confident about tomorrow's arduous drive, crossing the Continental Divide.

Me: *In hotel in Topeka. There's no place like home.*

I couldn't stomach paying for grocery delivery for a loaf of bread, so I drove to the grocery store that was a block from the hotel. My heart pounded. My mask steamed with my shallow breaths. The sliding doors opened, and I entered a grocery store for the first time in six months. Like our fable of how grocery scanners had amazed George H.W. Bush, my eyes darted, surveying the strangeness of a mundane experience. They settled on the arrows taped on the aisle floors, indicating the direction shopper traffic should flow.

I breathed as little as possible, as if my mask were connected to a limited supply of oxygen. I tried following the arrows taped on the ground but gave up and charted my own course. After scoring a loaf of wheat bread, I visited Chick-fil-A. I figured if I could take a risk entering a grocery store, then I could treat myself to the politest hate chicken in America.

Back at the hotel, I scarfed down the food, refilled my ice chest, and showered. I flipped through the TV channels until I stopped on *90 Day Fiancé*. The show was my lullaby and had beckoned me to sleep on many work trips. I scrolled through my messages until I reached my thread with Owen. I replayed audio and reread the passion while remembering the pain. Was Lenny right? Did I dismiss him too quickly? And did I forgive Ryan too easily?

My phone buzzed.

Ryan: *[Dorothy and Scarecrow easing down the yellow brick road gif]*

We texted bullshit gifs and memes back and forth until I fell asleep.

2.3 TO THE STARS THROUGH DIFFICULTIES

I blasted the defroster and turned the windshield wipers on low speed.

Me: *6 a.m. Boring drive day through the Plains. Then crossing the Rockies. Likely won't text much. Today's final destination—Grand Junction, CO.*

As I drove away from Topeka, I squinted, attempting to see through the fog blanketing the interstate while the predawn sky remained black. My oxidized headlights and fog lights couldn't cut through the dense clouds smothering the road. I yawned. My eyes were glued to what few pockets of asphalt appeared, scanning for the white lines outlining my path. I entertained my mind by inventing a game of only allowing myself to listen to British musicians.

My speakers blasted Prodigy, Bloc Party, Radiohead, Queen, Depeche Mode, The Spice Girls, Chemical Brothers, Massive Attack, Glass Animals, Elton John, The Cure, George Michael, Kate Bush, Adele, M.I.A., and Sade in an unskipped song succession. Did I even listen to non-British music?

The sun rose behind me, but the fog lingered. Dawn revealed hills. Kansas was *not* as flat as I always had believed, but it was unquestionably all earth and sky. There were many fields with large wind turbines erected in grassy seas of sunflowers. The turbines conjured some *War of the Worlds*–type event where they would come to life and attack humans. It also hit me how treeless the landscape was. I chuckled at the presence of an alpaca farm smack dab in the middle of the country, and my mouth salivated as I remembered how much I loved the taste of alpaca. I smiled passing a sign for Rock City. How did it compare to Chattanooga's Rock City?

While billboards had littered the interstate in Missouri, signs of human life spoke more softly here. The taming of the plains signaled the feeding of an unseen civilization. Save for a red tractor trailer, with "Trump" in blue text with white outline, no political fodder assaulted my eyes. Most of my drive through Kansas was sprinkled with declarations of love for Jesus and adverts for agricultural insurance.

I was in stitches with laughter as I closed in on a Kia Sorrento and read its bumper sticker:

When the world turns crazy, turn to Jesus

Lindsey Buckingham sang the first lines of "Go Your Own Way." Is Fleetwood Mac British? They were British, but then Lindsey and Stevie came into the mix. I disqualified them and skipped the song:

Welcome to Colorful Colorado

Google remained silent and flashed an icon of a man with ski goggles and a ski suit, as I time-traveled back an hour to Mountain Time. My hunched shoulders relaxed, and my grip loosened from the steering wheel. I was certain that land would forever weave in and out of my life.

"And so we meet again, Colorado," I said, pretending to be some sort of American frontier sheriff with a cigarette dangling from my mouth.

I had visited the state three times before. First, for a job interview when my ex-husband and I wanted to relocate out West. The IT industry was more mature out there, and we predicted more career growth for him. Outside of interviewing, we caught Depeche Mode's performance at Red Rocks and drove to Mount Evans's summit. I wasn't a hiker back then and thought I was badass on top of my first fourteener, but nothing materialized from our desire to move to that sleepy, outdoor haven nestled against the Front Range.

Eight years later, I was divorced and returning for my second visit. It was my Make-Allyn-Great-Again year, the one where I did whatever I needed to do to heal myself post-divorce. I traveled to hike the Rockies in preparation for Machu Picchu. The legalization of cannabis, craft breweries, relatively affordable housing, and industry diversification were calling cards to a different demographic that descended on the landlocked outdoor enthusiast's playground. On a hike with the Colorado Mountain Club, we laughed, noting that only three of the fifteen hikers had lived in Denver for more than ten years. No one was *from* Denver anymore. The city's charm had been choked out and replaced with the generic American hallmarks of chain restaurants, suburban sprawl, and uninspiring towers reaching for the clouds.

Denver was in the midst of another boom. Not all growth was bad. Not all growth was good.

My third visit to Denver was with Ryan. He had cheated on his Ironman training so that he could jam to Yonder Mountain String Band at Red Rocks. I wasn't interested in the band but wouldn't miss a chance to catch another Red Rocks performance. That long weekend was a hazy, boozy high, but from what I could recollect, it had been fun.

I turned my radio volume up, opened my sunroof, and soaked in the summer sunshine. Today was the make-or-break day on my road trip. I sped by tract-home subdivisions dotting the flatlands of Eastern Colorado, and then jagged peaks appeared in the distance like some kind of mirage. The Front Range. It was surreal to think that just yesterday I'd been in my Chattanooga safety bubble.

I had 225 horsepower, water, food, and a hunting knife. In the olden days, some might have called me a pioneer. I zipped by the white-tented Denver airport.

As I drove by Red Rocks, Yonder Mountain's cover of "Jolene" reverberated in my mind. I turned my radio volume down and tapped at my phone screen to place a call.

"Hey, how are you?" I said when Ryan picked up. I sang to the melody of the song, "I'm forty miles from Denver and wanted to ring before I got to higher-altitude driving."

"Yeah," he said, recognizing the tune and song title. "You're making good time."

"Actually, I'm only about twenty miles from Denver and heading westbound but just drove by Red Rocks and remembered you were shocked Yonder Mountain didn't play that song."

"I'm surprised you remembered that," he said with a chuckle. "I don't remember saying that, but then again, I was feeling it."

"Speaking of feeling it, is weed legal in Illinois?"

"Yeah, why are you asking?"

"Yesterday, I saw this wall dispenser in the gas station bathroom. It seemed very odd. I didn't know if it was actual weed *weed*."

"Versus fake weed?" He laughed. "Yeah, it's been legal there ever since 2019. Speaking of weed, you should buy some."

We were D.A.R.E. kids. What would Barbara Bush think of us?

My car stuttered a bit. I mashed down on the accelerator, and ten seconds later, the old Toyota lurched up the mountain. And I wasn't alone in the struggle to power up the passes. After my second climb, I altered my acceleration technique to minimize lag. I navigated the ascents better than many vehicles with Colorado license plates, but given how many ~~pioneers~~ transplants were in the state, that wasn't saying much. Maybe all my years of driving Missionary Ridge and White Oak Mountain had prepared me for crossing the Rockies.

I patted the dashboard. "You've got this."

Up a pass, down a pass, flat, up, down. I was nearing the Continental Divide. As much as I was ready for my tether to be cut, I yearned for something familiar. I closed my sunroof and reached for my phone.

"Hey, Mom. What are you up to?"

It was a stupid question to ask. She was likely worried about her spirited daughter taking off again. I wagered with myself how long it'd take for her to re-express how much she wished I was with someone. As much as she had taken pride in her transformation from a housewife to a financially independent, single mother, she still adhered to patriarchal norms, centering her narrative around men.

Growing up, I couldn't recall my mother not being in some sort of situationship. It was as if her life had no value without male presence. Despite raising independent, well-educated daughters, it was as if she expected us to put that all aside and be content as kept women. Her mantras over the years reverberated in my mind:

"Never turn down a man's offer to give you money."

"Never give back jewelry."

"Attraction can grow over time."

"Make him feel needed."

"Show off your body. It won't always look like that."

"Watch your figure."

"Older men can give you a better lifestyle."

"He may be fun to date, but never settle with him."

"How are you going to meet a normal guy if you're always alone in the woods?"

It was as if she had groomed my sister and me to manipulate men for financial gain. Maybe Mel was right that my mother couldn't see beyond financial security. And despite providing my own financial security, I would never measure up to what my mother wanted for me until I was more like my sister, securing a man who could provide for me and then provide her with grandbabies who would provide great-grandchildren. All made possible by my mother.

"Where are you now?" she asked.

"I'm west of Denver, past Red Rocks and hitting some major climbs up mountains now. I should be hitting the Eisenhower Tunnel soonish. I hope my car makes it." I paused to hear her silent panic.

"You should've taken a rental or gone with someone."

Ah, *someone* had re-entered the conversation. "I drive a Toyota. It gets regular maintenance. There's no reason I shouldn't trust it. Besides, it's the most reliable thing in my adult life."

"Yeah, yeah. Toyota or not, it's not safe for you to be out there alone."

I slipped back into teenager mode, rolling my eyes and groaning. "I have insurance. I have roadside assistance. I'm an engineer, for crying out loud. I am a highly trained problem solver. Being with someone doesn't guarantee my safety." I refrained from quoting statistics on intimate partner violence.

"Remind me where you're stopping tonight."

Does no one read my texts? "Grand Junction. It's pretty close to the Utah border. Crazy to think that in only two days I'll have traveled to the other side of the Continental Divide, and tomorrow I'll be in Zion!" A smile etched my face.

My mother mumbled names of Coloradan cities and towns. It was clear that she was following along with a map. "That's a lot of driving. You've been on the road eight hours. It's not good for the body to drive that long. Wouldn't you want someone with you to share the driving load? Aren't you tired?"

I wanted to say, "How many more times are you going to bring up my solo drive?" but I knew better than to open that can of worms. "Shockingly, no. The start of the day was a bit rough, but I have a lot of energy right now. I think I'm fueled by adrenaline. Maybe I missed my calling as a trucker."

She proceeded to give me updates about my sister's family. She knew I regularly spoke with my sister, so I gathered this was another tactic to nudge me in an intended direction. She then spoke of her single coworkers and asked me for the umpteenth time if I belonged to any local professional organizations. She reminded me that those could be opportunities to meet someone. And by someone, she meant the right someone—a man who could take care of me, a man of her choosing.

I cursed at myself for calling her. Why had I expected our conversation to go any differently? Why'd I think she would take an interest in my journey … ask me about what I planned to do out there? I could've called any of my friends, but I called her. Isn't the definition of insanity doing the same thing but expecting different results? My mother wasn't going to change no matter how much I quipped, protested, or presented her with logic, so what could I do to win her favor? Would she soften toward me if I could give her a grandbaby by any means necessary? Would she soften toward Ryan? If I never settled with a mother-approved man and didn't have children, would she ever accept me and share in my happiness? Or would we be having these same conversations when I was sixty?

The conversation meandered from her coworkers to her new neighbor and the amount of car traffic at the neighbor's house. I was half listening, so I couldn't discern if my mother suspected drugs or if she thought her neighbor was a hussy. I had my fill of my mother's passing judgment even though I was thankful it wasn't targeted at me. "Hey, Mom, traffic's picking up. I'm going to concentrate on the road."

"Okay. Call me when you get to the hotel."

There was no traffic, but I was done with her Southern subtleties. I continued to climb. As soon as I read the Eisenhower Tunnel sign, I was driving through it. The tunnel was longer than I imagined. I don't know why my mind thought it'd be similar in length to the blink-and-it's-over Chattanooga tunnels. I'd have died if I held my breath.

Somewhere inside the tunnel, I crossed the Continental Divide and officially drove out of Louisiana Purchase territory. My eyes squinted when the tunnel finally ended, and I returned to daylight. Brake dust perfumed the air. Traffic was backed up for miles in the eastbound direction. Meanwhile, my car careened downhill at speeds of 75 mph. I feathered the brakes, to not overheat them.

But the drive wasn't all downhill. My Camry and I were climbing again, passing by exits for Breckenridge. There were a few road cyclists. Cycling, climbing, snow sporting. A magnet for the outdoor enthusiast. If you could see past the influx of people, Colorado was captivating.

It was past noon. The sky darkened, and I stowed my sunglasses. Sparks of lightning overexposed the sky ahead. It was a classic Rocky Mountains afternoon thunderstorm. An important hiking rule out there was to descend to the tree line by noon to avoid thunderstorm threats. After more lightning, the sky couldn't contain its tears and deluged the roads. At times, the water gripped my tires and pulled them. I'd hover my foot over my brake pedal and nudge my steering wheel to regain control. More water pooled on the road, forming haphazard tracks. The water and I battled for control of my car. White-knuckle driving. Were my tires that bad? I checked my speedometer. I was driving 45 in a 65-mph zone. Thunder boomed all around. I had grown up with daily thunderstorms every summer, ones that rattled doors and windows, but at mountain elevations, a storm was like driving through a bowling pin deck.

After thirty minutes of monsoon-like conditions, either the storm stopped, or I had driven out of it. Water shed from the roads, and I rebuilt the confidence to resume normal speeds. I passed a sign for Vail. My shoulders swayed to my playlist. I opened my sunroof and put my sunglasses back on. I slalomed past cars until a long line of brake lights halted my momentum.

I was east of the Hanging Lake Tunnel, where the Glenwood Spring fires had been raging. Less than two weeks ago, that section of I-70 was shut down. I didn't have expectations for the interstate to be reopened, but twenty feet inside the tunnel, I was in a gridlock. I had no cell signal, but fortunately, I had enough gas to not panic.

People turned off their cars. Some got out and walked the tunnel. I skipped song after song, waiting for the chords of a British one. And then, chanting sounded followed by a breath of silence and those pulsing beats. I bobbed my head and raised my arms. *Fuck British Invasion.* I sang along to the opening English lines of T.O.P.'s "Doom Dada."

Break lights brightened the tunnel. Ignitions started. A smoldering mountain greeted me on the other side of the tunnel. The rocky and evergreen mountainous landscape gave way to something more like a desert painted with dusty browns and reds. Before I knew it, I was exiting the interstate.

Me: *Just arrived at hotel in Grand Junction, CO.*

The hotel parking lot was full of license plates from near and far: Georgia, Utah, Idaho, California, Montana, and Florida.

It was 7 p.m. Mountain Time. I had driven twelve hours, and unlike yesterday, I was tuckered out. My phone buzzed and buzzed. I scrolled through to see if any texts were of interest.

Ryan: *I miss you.*

I called him after I checked into the room.

"I've only been gone two days," I said. "It's not like we really do anything when we're together. You can sit, drink, and watch movies and be fine for a few more days without me, right?"

"I know we don't do anything, but isn't that nice? You're my favorite person to do nothing with."

"Ha, that's the strangest compliment I've ever received. But thank you, I think?" I pursed my lips into a half-smile. "So, did you do anything fun today?"

"Nothing fun, but you'd be proud of me."

"Yeah?"

"I cleaned up the place. Bathroom and all. I'm pretty sure it'd pass your inspection standards."

"Really? Wow, I am ... impressed."

"Yeah, when you get back, I want you to come over, let me cook you dinner. I've been researching recipes for alpine macaroni. I know you love that. And then we could keep practicing for a baby."

Sex. I wanted it, and Ryan used to deliver. We first met at a semi-subterranean bar with the spiral staircase off Houston Street. Every time he saw me there, he offered a drink. I declined. Even though I wasn't physically attracted to him, I loved the admiration and his voice. His Southern drawl held the promise of field dressing, moonshine, four-wheeling, college football, beer, barbecue, Faulkner, lifted trucks, swimming holes, smoking jackets, whiskey, bluegrass, ma'ams and sirs, jacket offerings, Hurston, dress jeans, campfires, trap music, prayers, hats off inside, and debates over whether banana pudding was best served warm or cold. That voice promised everything my ex-husband was not.

Ryan was an overqualified customer-service rep who had expressed no desire to professionally advance. And then one day, he hit me with the line, "I know I may not look like much, but I've just started training for Ironman. I assure you, if you buy low, you'll be able to sell high."

My head fell back in laughter. I allowed him to buy me a drink. We shut down the bar, and later that night, he gave me an orgasm deeper than anything I had experienced.

Is everything I want breathing on the other end of the call? Am I sure he wants me and not chasing experiences? Would he be a pillar of strength during my IVF, or would he derail my plans again? Shit, how am I going to tell him I'm still moving forward with IVF?

I peeled back the comforter and slipped underneath the top sheet. I found *90 Day Fiancé* and scrolled through messages on my phone. I reread the Owen thread. Maybe his preferences were rooted in our shared history, which had shaped his opinion about darker-skinned women. Did I shut him out too quickly, like Lenny said?

I unblocked Owen and composed a message.

Me: *Hey! Long time, no talk. How are you?*

I stared at the screen as if I expected an immediate response. Then, wishing I could unsend the message, I distracted myself by doing what I did best. Plan.

I Google-mapped directions to Zion so that I could download the route in the event of a spotty connection. It was a six-hour drive. I zoomed in on the route and observed the nearness of Arches National Park to the interstate. I was familiar with Arches. I had read *Desert Solitaire*, but Edward Abbey's colonial claim to that Southwestern land didn't inspire me to visit. I Googled the small park for a quick read about its trails. I then added Arches National Park as a stop on the way to Zion. It added about two hours onto my drive. I could:

1. Sleep in and make the six-hour drive to check into Zion Lodge at 4 p.m.; or
2. Wake up early, drive two hours to Arches, hike there, and then make the drive to Zion.

The choice was obvious. I downloaded the map and scrolled through my phone alerts. Other than a meme from Ryan, there was nothing. Maybe Owen had blocked me? Maybe he now had a girlfriend? Maybe he wanted nothing to do with me?

I set my phone alarm and clicked off the table light.

2.4 SHE FLIES WITH HER OWN WINGS

Bill Withers sang. I rolled over and turned my alarm off—
3:30 a.m. I didn't have time to diddle-daddle if I wanted to
catch sunrise at Delicate Arch, the most recognizable arch
in Utah and possibly the States. It would take an hour and
forty-five minutes to drive to the trailhead. Trail reports described a thirty-minute to an hour, mile-and-a-half hike
from the trailhead to the arch. I calculated that I had to be
on the road by four to not miss the 6:48 a.m. sunrise. I
sprang from bed and dressed in my hiking uniform: a
white, long-sleeve, button-down technical shirt, ruched
Kuhl hiking pants; my teal neck gaiter; and Urban Decay's
Psycho lipstick.

The black sky twinkled. My oxidized headlights, only good
for legal purposes, illuminated I-70 West five feet at a time,
highlighting curves a few seconds before I hit them. I refrained from using my brights. There was no point in seeing that far out; I had sufficient reaction time. I embraced
the dark and the certainty of the road, the stars, and me in
my car.

My phone spoke, "Welcome to Utah." I hadn't seen a
state welcome sign and had missed the state's Google icon.
The speed limit returned to 80 mph. When I hit 90, my
steering wheel vibrated in my hands while my car shook.
Not wanting car parts to break away like a missile launch,
I slowed down to 85.

Orion rose. His belt and arrow sparkled as he took aim
at a hidden bull. The final hour of night cloaked me in a
hug of calm. I smiled in her warmth.

Red taillights from a tractor trailer pierced the darkness ahead. As I passed it, the trailer sucked me toward it. I fought my steering wheel against the pressure vacuum. I broke free of its clutches and sped away. It wasn't long before the dark swallowed me again, and in that weird womb state, I cocooned in the nothingness reverberating in my mind.

Google Maps commanded me to exit the interstate to travel south on UT-191. After thirty minutes, I turned left for the Arches National Park entrance. The road climbed and twisted and climbed. Finally, I turned left into the trailhead parking lot. It was 50 percent full. I hung my national park card on the plastic rearview mirror hanger, and the usual new-hike jitters retuned. My stomach knotted. Anxiety pressed on my bladder. Saliva pooled in my mouth. *I've never hiked in a desert. Am I up for this? Will I look out of place?* I couldn't sit in my car forever, freaking out about the unknown, so I geared up. I took off my Chacos, put on socks, laced my boots, lifted my pack onto my back, buckled my waist strap, checked my shoulder straps, and buckled my sternum strap.

I checked my phone—6:15 a.m.—and messaged Mel my location. There was sufficient first light that a headlamp wasn't needed.

I strolled past a few warning signs, informing hikers to carry at least two liters of water, to wear a mask, and to stay on the marked trail. I suppressed my desire to take pictures of the landscape—I needed to haul ass to not miss sunrise at the Arch. After a quarter of a mile, I panted my way up a sandstone incline.

Despite all my preparation, I hadn't considered how trails were marked in a desert. Without tree blazes, without a worn path, without strategically placed logs and rocks, staying on-trail had its challenges. There was the occasional blaze on a rock, a solitary sign with an arrow, but there was also a good amount of walking around, assessing what appeared to be a trail and checking my digital trail map.

In last night's research, I had read about a viewpoint of an arch framing Delicate Arch on the route. I clambered up a few rock ledges, searching for this view with no luck. Time was slipping, so I charged toward my destination.

I reached Delicate Arch within minutes of sunrise. A pack of about fifteen people, their backs to the arch, photographed the peach sky. I turned toward the arch. The first rays of light warmed it from brown to apricot.

I climbed over a small ledge to get closer to the forty-six-foot-high arch. My quads tightened, and my knees locked, breaking my body from catapulting forward. I repositioned my weight and relaxed my legs. Despite the countless photos I had viewed of Delicate Arch, I had never appreciated that it sat on the lip of a large, sandstone bowl. It was like a massive, empty cereal bowl with an oversize, Lucky Charms rainbow marshmallow balanced on the edge. I slid my pack to the ground and fished for my camera. As I pulled my camera strap over my head, I surveyed people standing beneath the arch for photo ops. The arch dwarfed them. I snapped a few photos devoid of people. Sunsets here had to be spectacular.

My spine tingled, and my skin prickled. I vowed that I would return to watch a sunset.

I slung my pack onto my back. My calves fought gravity from pulling me down the sandstone drain. I walked to the left of the arch, climbed a ledge, and sat. As the sun climbed, it revealed the oranges and reds of a large ridge in the distance. Back East, we fevered for the yellows, oranges, and reds of fall, but I didn't have to wait for leaf-peeping season to get my color fix out here. The desert was as colorful as a farmers' market: peaches, apricots, carrots, heirloom tomatoes, Grainger tomatoes, yuzu, squash, yams, mangoes, pumpkins, apples, radishes, grapefruit, and plums. All colored striations layered like the most delicious doberge cake. My stomach grumbled. I pulled out a protein bar and munched the hunger away.

Group after group staged photos underneath the arch. Handstands. Peace signs. Arms reaching to the heavens. Jumping shots resulting in cracked phone screens. Instagrammers.

Many left after their social media shots. More people arrived fifteen minutes after sunrise; I hoped that they hadn't rushed to try to make it. Young and old came and went. Most stayed for ten minutes and left, satisfied with their photos. How many people did this Arch see? How much longer would this Arch stand? Would the masses still flock here once it collapsed? We humans are fickle. We're enamored by the beauty created from nature's destruction. Then we're distraught by its continued destruction. And then we forget its existence.

My teeth chattered. I pulled my puffy jacket from my pack and zipped it on.

My thoughts ambled to my life on the other side of the Continental Divide. Ryan just wanted me back so that we could do nothing together. My sister was likely too busy to even have noticed that I had already left for my trip. Mel likely had already texted me back, encouraging my exploration after she received my check-in message. My mother likely had already called and texted multiple times and would flip out upon learning that I once again drove alone in darkness to "just be outside," susceptible to every possible danger.

I retrieved my journal and pen.

Hi Mom,

It's just past sunrise at Delicate Arch. There's nothing like a stunning landscape to put life into perspective. I've worked really hard to be able to see this and all the other places I've traveled, and I couldn't have done it all without you pushing me. And for that, I'll always be thankful. I can't tell my story without you.

I hope when you tell the story of your life that you are proud of the fiercely independent daughters you have. If you are, will you let us know? It'd be nice to hear it from time to time. As you've stated many times, you worry about me—a mother's worry that will never go away no matter my age. While I can't expect you to stop worrying and trust you did your job, I am asking you to respect me as a fellow independent woman. I want to share pieces of me, but I can't stomach your judgment. Would you want someone criticizing every move you make? Can you just love me? Can you be happy for me even if this isn't the life you want for me? Because, Mom, I'm definitely living the life I want.

I rapped my pen against my teeth, rereading the note. While I would have loved to sit out there all day, I had to get to Zion. I signed my initials.

A.T.

I clicked my pen, closed my journal, and packed them away. I chewed the inside of my cheek as the photo queue grew.

"Do you want me to take your photo?" a man with silver-streaked, shoulder-length hair asked me.

"I appreciate the offer, but no. Do you want me to take yours?"

"Oh, no. No, thank you." We smiled at each other, knowing no photo could encapsulate what we were feeling. I stowed my camera and jacket back in my pack.

I rose and lifted my pack onto my back. Before I climbed over the bowl's lip, I glanced back at the arch and smiled. I then scrambled over the sandstone ledge and journeyed back to the trailhead. Masses of people marched to the arch. I surveyed the landscape, searching for that viewpoint of another arch framing Delicate Arch. To my left, I spotted a couple taking photos fifteen feet above the trail.

I cupped my mouth. "Is that the view of the Arch within the arch?"

The guy said, "Yes!"

I scanned for alternate paths to climb up. There were none. I twisted my mouth, surveying how to climb the fifteen-foot wall separating the trail from the viewpoint. This was double the height of a Grayson Highlands craggy mound. I searched for fingerholds, but the smooth sandstone had no identifiable path to climb.

I wiped my sweaty palms on my pants. I didn't have great upper body strength, and I didn't want to risk injury ahead of my big Zion hike.

"Do it!" the woman called down. "You're only here once."

I shrugged and then nodded. I unstrapped my backpack and hoisted it onto a narrow ledge about three feet above my head. I stared up the wall as a gymnast stares down the vault before running. I jumped and slammed my entire body on the sandstone, making contact with all my extremities, and pushed my body up to where my back-pack was. I flung it on my back and found finger- and foot-holds to climb the rest of the way up. The couple high-fived me once I reached them.

I wiped my hands on my pants and then smoothed out my shirt. I unzipped the small pouch on my waist strap and soaked my hands in hand sanitizer. "Whereabouts are you all from?"

"Upstate New York," the woman said. "We just gradu-ated from Cornell."

"Congratulations on your graduation!"

Her partner lowered the camera from his face. They glanced at each other; their faces beamed. They had not a worry, not a stress. This was a strange year to finish school and start jobs—if they could find one.

"Yeah, we had plans to travel to Egypt this year, but then the pandemic," he said.

"Oh, Egypt. I went, about"—I closed one eye and counted the years in my head—"ten years ago." In the Cairo Airport en route to Sharm El-Sheik, my ex-husband and I had predicted we would be like the older Chinese couple seated across from us. The old man would drop things, and the woman would pick them up and hand them to him. He would sniffle, and she'd reach in her purse and hand him a tissue. She'd pull out candies and offer them to him. He'd hand her the empty wrappers, which disap-peared into her bag. We only made it six years after that. It was a bittersweet memory. Have I lost the opportunity to be half of that old, Chinese couple, with the shared love, familiarity, respect, and reflections on a fulfilled life? Was that possible with Ryan?

The woman's eyes lit up. "Really? How was it?"

"It was amazing. So many temples. You will get templed out. Because it was the revolution year, tourism was down, so the merchants swarmed us. That was annoying, but to behold what ancient civilizations built … amazing. Kind of like this but different. I hope you get a chance to go there."

She looked at him and bit her lower lip. Sadness haunted her eyes. "Yeah, maybe next year."

"We got a bit templed out in Cambodia," he said.

"Oh, I love Cambodia!" I said.

"How does it compare temple-wise to Egypt?" he asked. He capped his lens and stored his camera in his bag.

"Eh, it's really hard to compare. Angkor Wat is very concentrated. I mean, there are temples outside of the main complex, but you have a heavy concentration of temples in one spot. But in Egypt, it's completely spread out. In Cambodia, it's very cool to see how nature is reclaiming its space. Both have amazing detail. In Egypt, you're blown away by the rich colors." I looked at the sky, now a hazy hue of blue. "Kind of like this landscape with the colorful sands, rock, and sky. I can't really pick one over another. They're both magical."

"You seem pretty well-traveled. Where are you from?" he asked.

"I currently live in Chattanooga." I pulled my camera from my bag and changed my aperture setting.

"What else are you planning to do here?" she asked.

"I have no plans other than make it to Zion tonight."

"Oh, we just came from there. You'll love it. How long will you be there?" she asked.

"Three full days. I have some hikes I want to do, and a spare day in case the weather sours," I said.

"Do you plan to stop by Bryce?" he said.

"I read it was near Zion, but I haven't planned on it." I snapped a few photos and then adjusted a few settings.

"If you can get your other hikes in, you should check it out. It's a small park with a few short hikes," she said.

I nodded. "I'll have to research it. Thanks for the suggestion."

"We should get going. Maybe we'll run into each other again," he said.

"Maybe." I shrugged. "I hope you two enjoy the rest of your trip and get to Egypt!"

"Thanks," she said. "By the way, I love your lipstick."

I smiled as they left. More people passed by beneath me, but only a few peered up and spotted me. Satisfied with my photos, I packed my camera, scooted down, and joined the major artery of traffic. As the sun climbed higher in the sky, I wiped a stray bead of sweat with my neck gaiter. I gathered my shirt by its collar and fanned my chest.

It wasn't even nine yet, but the threat of heat exhaustion and dehydration scared me. A few hikers carried umbrellas. With my phone, I snapped photos of the vast, enigmatic landscape. I was in awe of the simplicity and complexity of the light and shadows. A slight turn of the head or a passing cloud altered perspective, rendering each moment ephemeral. It was easy to understand how people romanticized the West.

"You can do it!" I said to an overweight man who was wiping his drenched forehead with a neck gaiter.

"The view is worth the climb," I said to the family wearing jeans.

"You've got this," I said to the couple without packs and water bottles.

When asked, I offered directions. I was accustomed to this, since my hiking uniform exuded park ranger vibes. The hike was short, so anyone attempting the trail would struggle through their discomfort and make it despite their unpreparedness.

Preparation. I teared up. According to my plan, I should've been on some high-altitude pass in the Peruvian Andes right now. Hell, but really, I should've been at least four months pregnant. Or rather with a doting husband and a child on the cusp of entering kindergarten. Shattered hopes and dreams. But who was to say that Ryan couldn't fulfill that dream? I had wanted nothing more than a pregnancy with him a few months back, so why was I still melancholy?

Back at my car, I routed to Double Arch. Surveying the Gaudi-esque landscape, I contemplated if he had drawn inspiration from the desert.

When I arrived, I shared the space with five others. I marveled at how water had created the winglike arches. After thirty minutes, droves of people descended on Double Arch. I stowed my camera and checked the time. It was only 9:30 a.m.

I walked to my car, dropped my pack in the passenger seat, took off my boots and socks, and slid my feet into my Chacos. I blasted the air conditioning and turned off airplane mode. I was surprised I had signal. As expected, I had multiple missed calls, voicemails, and quite a few texts from my mother.

Mommie Dearest: *Are you okay?*
Mommie Dearest: *Where are you?*

Mommie Dearest: *Call me.*

Mommie Dearest: *Have you made it to Zion?*

Mel: *[heart emoji] Enjoy your day. I can't wait to hear all about it. Take lots of photos!!! Let me know when you get to Zion!*

I composed a message to my mother. I didn't want her to worry.

Me: *I'm fine. Not in Zion yet. Taking my time to get there. Will message you when I arrive.*

I withheld details to save myself from further interrogations and criticisms.

While cooling down, I searched for Bryce Canyon on a trail app. The Cornell graduate was right; there were numerous easy, short trail options. I Google-mapped to a Bryce trailhead; I was only four hours away, and Bryce was an hour from Zion. I checked the weather in Bryce—sunny and clear. I considered my options:

1. Stick to the plan and drive to Zion. I'd get there before the lodge's check-in time, but often, early check-ins could be accommodated. Then, I'd have time to properly plan for Bryce for my extra day or return trip to this area.

2. Detour to Bryce and arrive in Zion a couple of hours before sunset. The weather might not be good on my spare day, and who knew when I could return to this area with my IVF plans? Arches had turned out to be a good detour.

I glanced at my pack in the passenger seat and bit my bottom lip. Without another thought, I downloaded the Queen's Garden trail map and routed to Bryce.

While waiting at the national park's traffic light to turn right onto US-191, I surveyed my surroundings. Moab was a few miles farther south. A slideshow of Jeep-crawling and mountain biking played in my mind. A horn honked, jolting me back to the now green traffic light. I turned right and retraced my drive up US-191. My head whipped left and right, absorbing what was now brought to light. I drove by a sign:

Canyonlands National Park

Should I turn left and detour? Stop for a peek? Were there any quick-hit hikes? What was the difficulty? Would I need to drive a bit to get to a trailhead? If I went there, I likely would need to ditch Bryce. I shook my head. I couldn't do it all. Too many uncertainties. I kept straight. Since I planned to return to Arches, I could tack Canyonlands onto my growing list: Glenwood Canyon, Arches, and Canyonlands.

Thirty minutes later, I merged onto I-70. My eyes grew tall when I read the next interstate sign:

Last rest stop for 110 miles

Holy shit! Would I have cell service? How long would it take for help to arrive if I needed it? I glanced at my miles-to-empty and gas gauges. I had plenty of gas to make it, but why risk it? I exited along with a caravan of cars behind me. I topped off my gas and entered Love's Travel Stop.

I had never been in a Love's, which I can only describe as a general store, restaurant, and hotel under one roof. Fresh loaves of bread sat on shelves. It was by far the cleanest gas station bathroom I had encountered on this trip. My hands lingered under the faucet, savoring the instant, warm tap water. Back at my car, I opened a bag of jalapeño ranch potato chips and settled into my drive.

I was no stranger to remote places. I had hiked the Tambopata rain forest, traversed unnamed peaks in Bhutan, and cruised up the Nile, feasting on the endless sands of Upper Egypt and its drowned cities, but Utah's remoteness startled me. There was nothing but an interstate cutting through isolation. No towering trees. No billboards. No American flags flying. No green signs announcing mileage to towns. Dust-laden mounds and grass dotted the expanse. A few exits snaked away from the interstate into further desolation. The road climbed and descended a few 8,000-foot passes. High desert. Lands where dinosaurs once roamed.

When I had pored over details to select the route to Zion, I had been so focused on the challenges getting there that I hadn't given thought to the landscapes I'd encounter along the way. Utah held everything and yet nothing. I nestled in my seat, contemplating the everything everyone expected of me and the happiness I hunted to banish my emptiness.

A female voice interrupted my trance. "In two miles, take Exit 48 to Utah 24."

"Exiting the interstate so soon?" I asked, expecting no reply.

After departing the certainty of the interstate, I crossed open ranges, where the occasional bloated cattle littered the shoulder, and crisscrossed my way through the vast and wild Fishlake National Forest.

I doubted Google Maps as it directed me east and then west. I was certain I entered Sevier County—named after the nearby river the Spanish missionaries called Río Severo and not the Tennessee explorer and founding father—at least twice. I checked my phone. It wasn't frozen.

I didn't have a paper map, and there weren't many vehicles on the road. I mulled backtracking to I-70. Where was I?

Even though I loved escaping on trails, my comfort decreased the longer I was away from interstates, signs, and mile markers. With each turn, I disappeared farther into the land of dusty rock and sand, leaving civilization as memory in my rearview mirror. Time could travel backward or forward twenty years, and this piece of America would be the same. Did the locals loathe having their isolation disturbed by road trippers like me? How did people survive out here? I passed a few ranches whose irrigation-created green fields splashed the landscape. Living out here had to take a tremendous amount of skill and tenacity.

Wasn't that the appeal of the West, though? To disconnect from the larger world, from civilization, and form a deeper connection to the land? To own? To build? To reinvent? To blend? To disappear? To turn inward? To get lost? To be found? Sure, there were remote, wooded areas back East, but the remnants of man were never far. Driving those Utah state roads forced me to accept life's fleetingness. Our individual existence was a small drop in the ocean of time. Was I making the most of my drop?

I turned left. I turned right. I turned left. There were no road signs save for elevation and county markers. I couldn't trace my way back to I-70 by memory. I fished gum from a bag in my passenger seat and chewed away my anxiety. Should I pull over on the side of the road and flag the next 4x4 truck that passed? Should I reroute?

"Turn right on Utah 62 West."

I glanced down at my phone. I moved my fore and middle fingers together to zoom out. Utah 62 headed south.

Zooming out more, I spotted Bryce. At least I was moving in the right direction. Why had Google taken me on this route? It seemed like I could've stayed on I-70 a bit longer and taken a more direct approach on US-89. Did Google's engineers force some drivers on circuitous routes to collect new data for the sake of app improvements?

I passed Sorenson's Ranch. As I neared the Otter Creek Reservoir, I encountered a few different dude ranches. I sang the "Hey Dude" theme song. Was ranch life rewarding or only a series of never-ending days of hard work with little reward? Was ranching as soul-sucking as corporate life, but without a benefits package? Were their drops more fulfilling? Was raising capital for ranching the same as a startup? The business end of ranch life fascinated and distracted me from my predicament.

"Turn left on Utah 22."

I drove through the small town of Antimony.

"Turn right on Johns Valley Road."

I turned onto a packed dirt road. Could this be right? I glanced at my phone. I no longer had service. Why the hell would Google route me onto a dirt road? Was this even a public road? What if there were major ruts? Could my Camry make it? Would I regain cellular signal if I needed to use roadside assistance? How long would I have to wait for help? I glanced at my phone, determining how long I'd be on this road. Thirty miles?! I had driven before on unpaved forest roads without cell service, but not for thirty miles in an alien landscape. My jaws chomped away at my now flavorless gum. I wiped sweat accumulating at my temples with the back of my hand. My shoulders nearly kissed my ears. I increased the fan speed on my air conditioning. I drank a swig of water, hoping to relieve my parched throat.

I assessed my options. I could:

1. Make a multipoint U-turn, drive back to where I had cell service, and figure out a different route to Bryce.
2. Turn around and skip Bryce today and visit on my spare day, when I had sufficient time to map and plan the route.
3. Press on for thirty more miles, not knowing what other Google Maps shenanigans lay ahead.

My fingers steadied the steering wheel. I surrendered myself to press on. I drove mile after mile, passing ranches. Twenty miles in, a road sign came into view:

Capitol Reef National Park

I didn't catch the mileage, but it wasn't far. At a bend in the road, a low-clearance sedan passed, traveling in the opposite direction. My shoulders relaxed in the comfort I wasn't traversing that road alone, and if that car could make it, so could I. Soon after, the dirt road turned to asphalt, and I rolled down my windows, inviting the summer breeze in.

When I parallel-parked near the Queen's Garden trailhead, my car's digital clock displayed 2 p.m. My lips fluttered. I pulled down my visor and flipped open the mirror cover. My tongue glided over my teeth, clearing away errant food particles. I smiled a goofy grin and laughed away my new trail worry. Despite my change in plan, everything was falling into place.

2.5 LIVE FREE OR DIE

I hoisted my pack onto my back. As I was buckling my waist strap, a mechanical hum stopped the birds' songs. A wave of heat pressed against my back, and I twisted my head to identify the source. A Jeep Wrangler pulled into the parking spot behind me.

Three men, who appeared to be around my age, exited the Jeep. Two were shirtless, and the third wore a loose-fitting T-shirt and cargo shorts. The shirtless men were the effortlessly thin type, but they weren't gym-toned. If they gorged on food or beer, they'd have a small belly. They oozed the confident and chill vibe worn by Californians. I found this equally pretentious, exciting, and intimidating. Their presence bothered me.

Who hikes at 8,000 feet on a sunny day without a shirt? A fucking Californian. Were they among the countless sheep who had discovered hiking during the pandemic, or had they recently finished some hardcore activity and considered this an après-hike? Were they sizing me up as I was them? Were they wondering who hikes in a desert in August with long shirts and pants? Did they think I was another clichéd woman on some solo self-discovery journey, mending a broken heart? Why did I even care what they thought of me?

I mouthed, "Hi" and forced a smile. I buckled my sternum strap and then closed my trunk. They nodded at me as I walked away from my car, wanting to avoid further contact with them. I didn't need them disrupting what was shaping up to be a lovely day.

I checked my downloaded map and set off in the direction of Sunrise Point to hike the loop counterclockwise, avoiding the climb up Queen's Garden. I walked a path through evergreen trees to a clearing. A short post-and-rail fence marked the boundary between safety and likely death. I stopped at the fence and peered out across a seemingly endless desert landscape and then peered down. It was as if I were gazing down upon a crystal cluster of every possible color of citrine. Crystal points of various shapes—tall and symmetrical to squatty, misshapen buttes—reached for the sky. All these points were hoodoos. Douglas fir sprouted here and there in between the hoodoos. This was the Bryce Canyon Amphitheater. A short, brown sign etched in white lettering read:

Sunrise Point

I snapped more photos before descending below the sign. A large, brown sign pointed farther downhill to Queen's Garden:

Queens Garden

← 0.8 mile
Descent 320 feet

Please
For your safety
Stay on trails
Have proper footwear
Avoid dangerous cliffs
Do not throw rocks

I digested the litany of warnings, aware that each had been created because some tragedy had occurred in the past that necessitated explicit caution. I descended. A loose layer of gravel and sand covered the compacted earth trail. I slid. I shifted my weight back and thrust my arms out to stop my slide from becoming a fall. I positioned my feet perpendicular to the trail and zigzagged the path, continuing my descent into the amphitheater's bowl. My head whipped around, soaking in the views as I sunk to hoodoo eye level. Up close, the hoodoos reminded me of stalagmites. Sweat-soaked, exasperated faces squinted up at me as they climbed the trail. I smiled and offered them words of encouragement:

"You are so close!"

"Almost there!"

"You're amazing. You've got this."

The temperature was perfect—like entering a sun-warmed car on a crisp, fall day. A dry breeze whipped my hair, drying my dewy face and christening me with sand.

As the trail descended to the bottom of the amphitheater, I gazed up at the hoodoos and firs. From this vantage, the hoodoos resembled pillar candles in various states of melted heights and thickness. Time shrank the hoodoos while it heightened the trees, but in the end, gravity claimed them both.

Everywhere I turned was photogenic. It was like Mother Nature's Venice, daring visitors to take a bad photo. My camera phone couldn't do it justice, so I unpacked my DSLR and hung it around my neck. While I stopped for photos at a vista, laughter roared behind me. I turned to identify the source of the noise. *Fuck.* The Jeep trio interrupted my solitude.

I continued down the trail and stopped at another view. The trio arrived not one minute later. They left the vista first, and I met up with them at another picturesque spot. The leapfrogging annoyed me. The more I tried to give them a wide berth, the more they encroached on my space. What about six feet didn't they understand? I hoped that they were only hiking down to the Garden and then U-turning their asses back up.

At the next vista, we snapped photos like Japanese tourists. The tallest, topless one shot with what looked like a prime lens. The other two openly drank from twenty-five-ounce Bud Light cans. I rolled my eyes. Had they no decency to disguise their drinking? With the sun blaring down at such a high altitude, they were going to be dehydrated, if they weren't already. I studied their small packs. I couldn't tell if any of them had water.

I picked up pieces of their conversation. They were decomposing the shot. *Travel photographers?*

I walked away while capping my lens. When the trail bottomed out, I stopped to take photos. After my third shot, the Jeep trio arrived at the same location. The tallest one reached into his shoulder bag and pulled out another lens. I couldn't fathom changing lens in the sandy, windy conditions.

I departed, contemplating not stopping at the next view with hopes of putting some distance between me and them. Five women traveling in the opposite direction stopped on the trail. They had coordinated their outfits: black leggings and bralettes. Three wore two French braids. Did hikers out West wear less? Wouldn't they want to protect their skin from the sun? Had their skin missed vitamin D during their more aggressive shelter-in-place orders? I couldn't fathom hiking in a bra no matter how warm it was. While I judged them in my mind, my Southern shone through when I smiled at them.

One woman in the group breathed out as if it used her last energy reserve. "Are we close?"

Hiker pleas; they needed some hope that their plight was almost done. "Well, you aren't far distance-wise, but it's all uphill. Just pace yourself and don't be afraid to stop and take breaks and hydrate."

They all groaned.

"I'm sorry," I said while frowning.

"No, you gave it to us straight. Thank you," another woman said. She wore a full face of makeup and reminded me of a telenovela star.

I veered right to complete the trail. It ended at Queen's Garden, which was named after a hoodoo that resembled Queen Victoria. I squinted my eyes, trying to picture the bustle dress shape. I didn't see the resemblance.

Not long after, I retraced my steps back to the Navajo Loop. My heart fell to my stomach when I spied the Jeep Trio stopped on the trail ahead of me. I slowed my pace, but there were no signs of them budging. I prepared to pass them again.

"Hey, you look like you know where you're going," the tallest of the trio said as I approached them. He reminded me of a tattooed version of my ex-husband: blonde, blue eyes, with a long nose that dominated his face. His accent-less voice even matched my ex's. His colorful tattoos covered his chest, back, neck, arms, and legs. Or was it one large tattoo with multiple warrior scenes spread across his body?

So, they didn't have shit to say to me when they were nipping at my heels, encroaching on my six feet, but now that I might be of some use, I was worth speaking to?

"I kind of know where I'm headed," I said.

"Well, we heard this was a loop, but it seems the trail splits."

"Yeah, you can piece together two separate trails to make a loop. The Queen's Garden Trail dead-ends where I just came from," I said, turning to look behind me. "You can turn around and retrace your steps hiking up the hill and be done."

"What are you doing?" the tall one asked.

My teeth clenched my cheek. I fake-smiled. "I'm continuing on to the Navajo Loop."

"We should probably follow you, since you really do seem like you know what you're doing," he said.

I wanted to hurl a glass punch bowl to the floor, clench my fists, and shout, "Damn, damn, damn," but I tempered my Florida Evans. There was no point in me being ungracious despite my disappointment. There had to be some way I could make the most of this. Show them some Southern hospitality. "Well, you're welcome to." I started hiking again. The three men followed behind me like ducklings.

The tallest one asked, "So, what brings you out to Bryce?"

I appreciated his willingness to engage in conversation instead of tailgating. "Just road-tripping to Zion."

"Wow, so how long have you been driving?" he asked.

I looked up to the cloudless sky, counting the days. It seemed like forever ago that I had left Chatt in the rain. "This is my third day on the road."

"Where did you start?" he asked. His companions remained silent.

"Chattanooga." Given most people had no clue where Chattanooga was, I added, "Chattanooga, Tennessee."

"I don't know if I know where that's at. I've been to Memphis and Nashville before. All the people were super cool."

I nodded. "Chattanooga is about two hours east of Nashville and about an hour and half north of Atlanta. How about you guys? Where are you traveling from?"

"San Diego," the tall one said and continued, "San Diego, California."

I chuckled. "I kind of figured you were referencing California." So, I was right. They didn't cloak themselves in Californian confidence and chill; they were the real deal. This was my first time allowing myself to see him beyond being the shirtless photographer of the group. I wanted to ask about his tattoos, but I didn't want to give him the impression I was being flirtatious.

"Are you only doing Bryce and Zion? Salt Lake is pretty cool if you can check that out," the photographer said.

"I was at Arches earlier today. I don't know if I'll have time to visit Salt Lake this trip since that's in the opposite direction, but I'll put it on my travel list. At some point, I need to drive home and get back to work."

"Oh, you're still working?" the photographer asked.

My cheeks burned. "Yeah, I'm fortunate."

"Yeah, it's strange coming across someone out here who's still working. Well, all three of us aren't working right now. I do set lighting for movie sets and whatnot. The movie industry is continuing, but things just don't feel safe, so I'm taking a break from that."

"I can respect that," I said. I looked at the other two, who still hadn't said a word to me.

The shirted one said, "I worked in marketing and sales. I'm furloughed." He wasn't as thin as the other two. Was he self-conscious about his size? He reminded me of how Ryan hid his weight under oversize hoodies.

The other shirtless one, about a five-foot-ten brunette, spoke. "I produce music, but I'm taking a break to recharge. You know, sometimes you've got to stop and check in with yourself. What do you do?" He sipped from his Bud Light can, licked the remnants from his dark mustache, and smiled at me. Two rows of perfectly aligned, Hollywood-white teeth, too perfect to be natural.

The breeze stilled. Leaves ceased to flutter. Birdsong paused. And while the world muted and faded to gray, my heartbeat pounded in my ears, and I struggled to speak. His smile seduced me with the allure of journeys unthought. He wasn't as thin as I had first thought. Rather, he was toned in the way you'd expect a surfer to be, with broad shoulders topping a triangular torso. I figured he surfed, based on the collection of stacked, rope bracelets on his right wrist. My eyes followed a happy trail down to an oversize rooster belt buckle that held up a pair of long, cerulean jean shorts. I wanted nothing more in that moment than for him to grab my face and pull me to him, my hips relenting, our breath syncing as our lips flirted with the idea of touching, my fingers freeing his glossy, black hair from his bun, his stubble brushing against my neck....

"You okay?" he asked, breaking my trance.

I tittered and tucked a curl behind my ear. Colors and sound resumed. "Yeah, I'm fine. I do software stuff for a supplemental insurance company. Supplemental like disability, critical illness, and life insurance. Business is slammed. I've been working from home since March."

"Cool," Rooster Belt Buckle said.

The trio stopped to take more photos while I continued on the trail. A large group congregated at the trail junction as I approached. I consulted my downloaded map and couldn't make heads or tails of where to go, so I conferred with the Bryce park pamphlet. It contained a few trail maps, and I verified that this was the Navajo Loop. I had just sussed out that I would take the outermost path, as I wanted to see Wall Street, Bryce's only slot canyon, when Rooster Belt Buckle caught up with me.

"Oh, you don't want to hike with your friends?" I asked with a slight taunt in my tone. It was as if I had been transported back to school because I wanted to push him away before he could hurt me.

"Argh, they're super into photography and light and getting the best shot. I mean, I'm not into that stuff. I'm Elias, by the way. What's your name?" he asked. His voice had a quiet strength. I had to stop and focus, as it was barely audible over the ambient sounds of nature.

"Allyn. It's spelled *A-l-l-y-n*. It's weird because I'm not named after any family members, but my dad was really into this local artist, and her name is Allyn. He actually commissioned her to do a painting when I was born." I nodded. "Yeah, I still have it. It's a pretty interesting surrealist piece. But, yeah, whatever. I'm sure you're used to unique names, being that you live in Southern California."

He nodded. We continued hiking together. Trees dominated that section of trail.

"So, did you all drive from San Diego?"

"No, we flew to Salt Lake," Elias said.

"Oh, how was that? Flying?" I looked at him. My cheeks flushed. I wanted to gaze upon his face for hours. I had lost all interest in hoodoos.

"It was really cool, actually. The flight was pretty empty."

"Yeah, I just didn't feel comfortable getting on a plane, so I hopped in my sixteen-year-old car and made the drive out, which was super interesting. I've traveled many places, largely all by plane, and the times I've road-tripped I was more exclusively focused on a specific area. Like the Pacific Coast Highway or New Zealand's South Island." I tutted at myself. *Stop stop stop with all the rambling!*

"That's your car at the trailhead? Sixteen years?"

"Yeah."

"That's cool. I drove across the country once."

"Yeah?" I glanced at him and wiped my sweaty palms on my pants.

"I found a truck I wanted to buy in Pittsburgh. I flew over and drove the truck back."

"What did you think of that experience?"

"Yeah, it was interesting. The landscapes, the people."

"Very different from California, huh?"

He smiled. "Yeah."

Gah, that smile. Desire swamped my panties the way it once had for Ryan. "I mean, I live in Tennessee, which most don't think of as a progressive state. I mean, it isn't, but where I live is. But even my visits to rural Tennessee never prepare me for the shock of, like, just how different America is."

"So, do you visit national parks often?" Elias asked.

"I hike in the Smokies a lot." Realizing he may not be familiar with those mountains, I added, "That's the national park closest to where I live, but other than that, I'd say no. You?"

"Not much at all. I spend a lot of time in the ocean and in studios, but I went to Yosemite a few months back. That was cool."

"I've been wanting to visit Yosemite for years. Maybe next year."

We arrived at a group of hoodoos that towered over both us and the trees. Our heads tilted back, admiring the orange sentinels. I stopped to take photos. Elias's friends caught up to us.

The photographer exclaimed, "Wow! These look like skyscrapers."

I didn't see skyscrapers, just like I didn't see Queen Victoria's bustle dress.

"Want a beer?" the photographer asked me, moving to open his pack.

"Oh, no, thank you. I have a drive ahead of me, and a big hike tomorrow, so I need to stay hydrated." I capped my lens and then waved goodbye to the trio.

As I put distance between me and the group, I hoped that they would catch up again. I needed more time with Elias. Who was this man who chose to not work so that he could reset? To afford to take time off work so he could travel? He had to be financially secure—or was he a trust fund baby? Was it COVID money? He exuded confidence, calm, and contentment. No conflict. No suffering. No fear. No end goal. He just was.

He captivated me. I wanted to slip Elias a note asking him to circle "Yes" or "No" if he liked me. I wanted to write

Allyn hearts Elias on my paper bag book cover. If I knew his last name, I'd practice signing my first name and his last name.

Trail traffic increased, and distant conversations that I once heard clearly were now garbled up in the white noise of people. I pulled out my phone and checked my location. I was close to the other Navajo Loop trailhead—the end of my three miles. I checked over my shoulder, hoping to glimpse the trio. Not seeing them, my stomach sank a little. I stopped to take photos of a hoodoo just off the trail. I'd prepared to move on and finish the loop when I spotted the photographer's head above the crowds of people. I lingered, pretending to fidget with my lens.

"Hey, we caught up again," the photographer said.

"Cool spot, huh?" I asked.

"Yeah," the photographer said, unable to take his eyes off the view. He peered into his bag, investigating his lenses, and then looked back up at the scene. He did this a few times before selecting a lens.

"Hey, are you shooting with prime lenses?" I asked.

"Yes!" The photographer's eyes lit up. "Do you also shoot with prime?"

"Oh, no, I'm definitely an amateur," I said.

"You have a nice camera. I mean, I do set lighting, so I have picked up a thing or two along the way about capturing scenes."

"Uh-huh." I nodded, pushing my thumbs underneath my backpack straps, not interested at all in the conversation.

He framed the shot and took a few photos. "You could look into Sigma art lenses."

My eyebrows knitted. "What Sigma?"

"Sigma art. Art as in *artisanal*," he said in an affected French accent.

We laughed.

"Cool. I'll check it out."

I glanced at Elias. He had checked out of the conversation and was using a tree limb that crossed the trail as a hang board.

"This is a great spot, but the lighting is bad," the photographer said to the shirted friend.

I eyed Elias, hoping he'd release his feet back to earth and hike on with me, but he seemed uninterested. I packed away my camera, said my goodbyes again, and pressed on to complete the hike.

I reached Wall Street. It was nature's version of walking a narrow, switchbacked street lined with skyscrapers. Vertical golden and orange sandstone reached to the sky. My neck strained gazing up. As I was switchbacking my way up the trail to Sunset Point, Elias caught up with me. I stopped to catch my breath.

He stopped next to me.

"This is just beautiful," I said. "I've hiked a few places in this world, and this place is pretty special." I inhaled, trying to ingest the bliss. I looked up, around, and then directly at Elias with a smile.

He smiled back. "Yeah, it is. By the way, your lipstick looks great. I've been meaning to tell you that."

I blushed and stared at my feet.

"Where's your favorite place that you've hiked?" he asked.

"Oh, well, it'd be hard to say. Well, actually, no. Definitely South America. There's just something magical about The Andes. I was planning to go back to Perú this year but then the pandemic." I rambled, "Honestly, my favorite place is Patagonia. I'm probably going to butcher the pronunciation, but I'd have to say El Chaltén in Argentina."

"Argentina," Elias echoed, but he pronounced it like a native Spanish speaker. Was he correcting my pronunciation or having a moment of fondness for the land? Maybe both? Whatever it was, his mind traveled for a second. His eyes flashed back to the present, back to me, back to Bryce. He was returning from someplace I didn't know yet knew. He smiled and then undid his hair knot. His hair fell a finger length below his shoulders. My own fingers twitched, wanting to smooth out the bump his hair tie had indented.

"Wow, *hablas español*?" I asked. My mind combed through the cobwebs of four years of high-school Spanish and random phrases I had picked up during my years working as a process engineer at a manufacturing plant. I uncovered almost nothing; it was nearly all forgotten. Was he a great speaker because of a large Spanish-speaking population in San Diego? Was he one of those Asian Peruvians? My perspiring palms grabbed my elbows. My stomach flipped and then knotted.

"*Sí*. I lived a year in South America right after college."

"Oh, like a gap year. My mother would've freaked out. Hell, I would've freaked out with the stress of needing to repay my student loans."

"Oh, my parents hated it, but given I wasn't going to be a doctor, lawyer, or engineer, I'd never make them happy. So I let go of their expectations and living my life for them a long time ago. It's not easy breaking free from the glidepath, but sometimes you've got to … to survive … to find your happiness."

I bit the inside of my cheek as he continued, "I'm sure your parents pushed education and a stable, economically insulated career."

I nodded.

He chuckled. "Almost all People of Color do. It's our safety net. That's the one thing they can't take from us. I did my four years, earned my degree, and then I went down to Argentina and bounced around the continent. I visited Ushuaia but didn't do any hiking in Patagonia. I'd like to go back. Maybe live there again or just a little place in México. I used to go to México a few times a month to surf but then the pandemic and all."

He possessed a duality that I found intoxicating. He was destination nowhere and everywhere. I didn't know him yet knew him. He calmed and excited me.

I yearned to know more. Who was this man who had lived in South America? Who had journeyed across America? Who had moved beyond his parents' expectations and seemed at peace, happy even?

"Oh, like a Che Guevara?"

He chuckled. "Not quite, but motorcycles were involved at times."

"You definitely should go back," I said. I glanced at his chest. I wanted to run my hands down it. I wanted to taste his sweat. My eyes continued down and fixated on his belt. "Cool belt." I needed to regain control of the emotions coursing through my entire body. My cheeks flushed. Could he see that?

"Hey, what are your plans?" he asked. "Did you want to have a few beers and hang out with us?"

I was flattered that he wanted to spend more time with me. I wanted to spend more time with him. There was this pull to know more of what he knew, to see what he had seen, to learn to be comfortable being me. I didn't want to leave him. I wanted his kisses. I wanted his embrace. I wanted his heart. I wanted his mind. I wanted his … detachment.

I sighed and frowned. "I really would, but I have this big hike early tomorrow involving a shuttle I prearranged, and I need to ensure I make it to Zion tonight. I also should stay hydrated."

As soon as the words escaped my mouth, I wanted to retract them. Should I abandon my plans? I had flagged three must-do hikes on this trip, and tomorrow was the biggest, most challenging one. I had made a commitment to myself to do those three hikes, but in front of me was what I had been chasing. The desire that Ben had awakened back at Virginia's Grayson Highlands was now raging like a wildfire for Elias. *Should I skip my hike? Should I hang out with him?*

He flashed his boyish smile. I stood there waiting for him to reach out and touch me. Or for me to muster the courage to grab his face and kiss him. I wanted to take in all of him. I wanted to know what his skin felt like. Were his hands rough? Were his lips soft? I wanted to know how he tasted. But we both stood there, frozen.

No. There was too much risk that spending more time with him would kill my fantasy of Elias. And what was I expecting to happen? Have a few beers, share stories about South America, maybe some vacation sex? Then, I'd wake up with a mild hangover, wishing I had gone on my hike instead. That was not how I wanted to usher in the return of my sexuality. Not with regrets. Not with the stains of disappointment. It was better for me to forever remember him like this, on the last day of August, on a picture-perfect day at Bryce Canyon National Park, in the middle of a pandemic.

I broke out of my trance and looked around. "I'm not quite sure how to get out of here." I nervously laughed.

He pointed to the exit, catty-cornered behind me. "I think it's there."

I hadn't spotted it, but he was in a great position to view hikers coming and going. "Wow. Glad you pointed that out." I bit my lips and then smiled before waving goodbye. He waved back. Was this like the other goodbyes? Would he pop up again?

I passed through a door-like opening in the sandstone and walked by Sunset Point. I snapped a few photos before I reached Sunrise Point, the start of my hike. I checked the time. My phone displayed 4:47 p.m. I wanted to be in Zion no later than 6 p.m. to give me time to settle and eat and get a nice rest before my demanding hike.

Bryce had taken double the time it should have, but it was worth it.

At my car, I set my pack on my passenger seat, removed my boots and socks, and slid my feet into my Chacos. I pulled my journal and pen from my pack.

Let me have this moment —
Let me have this memory.
Because I never want to forget
what you stirred in me.
Let me have this moment —
Let me have this memory.
Because on days when Hope hides
You'll find her for me.
God, let me have this moment —

Let me have this memory.
Because letting go of him
Is letting go of me.

My fingers traced the ink. I set my journal and pen next to my pack. I entered "Zion Lodge" into Google Maps and looked back for Elias. Would I see him again? Would he run over and tell me that he felt the same energy between us, that he could show me how to smite my doubts, that he wanted to join me in Zion? I put my car in drive. My eyes were glued to my rearview mirror, hoping for one final glance of him. As I turned the corner, I left Elias but held onto his memory.

The last rays of light illuminated the sky when I arrived at Zion's east gate, I handed the ranger my America the Beautiful pass and driver's license. In one day, I had visited three of Utah's Mighty 5.

In a high-pitched twang, the blonde ranger working the gate said, "Hixson, Tennessee?! I'm from Ooltewah." She returned my pass.

My eyes grew big with shock. "Shut the front door! Well, I actually live in Saint Elmo now, but wow, small world. How long have you been out here?" I placed my national park card back in the plastic hanger on my rearview mirror.

"Almost a year. I still have my Tennessee plates too." She beamed with pride.

"I love it! Tennessee girls!" I offered her my fist.

She fist-bumped me back, then handed me a map. "Enjoy your time here."

After five miles of zigzagging roads framed by mountains, I reached the Zion–Mount Carmel Tunnel. Six fortresslike windows ushered light into the mile-long tunnel, teasing me with glimpses of the canyon. After driving the thrilling peepshow mile, Zion Canyon unveiled herself. The road switchbacked, leading down from the red-rocked walls to the tree-covered valley floor. It was breathtaking, one of the most epic entrances into a national park I had ever experienced. A mountain goat relaxing beside the highway caused a traffic jam, and a huge crowd amassed at Canyon Junction for sunset. I turned right on Floor of the Valley Road. I entered the five-digit gate code and drove to the lodge.

It was just past 7 p.m. I pulled into a parking spot. I took a photo of my odometer. I had driven 1,959 miles from my home.

Me: *[odometer picture] Made it to Zion!! Going dark until I leave!*

An orange light flicked on my car's dashboard. The engine icon glared at me. That'd have to be a worry for another day. I turned my car off and then put my phone in airplane mode, severing the cord to the life I knew.

PART 3:

GENERATIONS, GENEROSITY, AND GENESIS

3.1 "GIVE ME YOUR TIRED, YOUR POOR, YOUR HUDDLED MASSES YEARNING TO BREATHE FREE."

When my dashboard clock displayed 6:45 a.m., I flung open my car door and pulled my pack from the passenger seat. It was heavier than normal, loaded to ensure overnight survival in the desert:

1. Hydration – a liter of plain spring water, another liter of water spiked with an electrolyte tablet, a liter and a half of sports drink, and my water filter just in case because I had read there was a spring on the trail.
2. Food – three peanut butter and jelly sandwiches, two apples, a few protein bars and energy chews in my snack stash.
3. Other essentials – first-aid kit, knife, poncho, space blanket, matches, headlamp, poles, plastic freezer bags, and DSLR.

The sun wrestled with the darkness, pinning down the moon to conquer the sky. I wriggled my shoulders, adjusting to the weight of my pack, and walked to the visitor center's flagpole, the designated meeting location for the shuttle to Lava Point. A young man waited alone in front of the flagpole. If I had to age him, I'd say he was in his early thirties. He stood around six feet. His hand rubbed his buzz cut. Stubble jutted from his square jaw as if it were a cacti meadow. His skin blended with the Southwestern landscape. He wore a gym tee, and his basketball shorts revealed that he didn't skip leg day. A running hydration pack rested on his back. His pack wasn't substantial enough to endure a sixteen-mile trek, so maybe he was there for a shuttle to Sinawava.

I slid my heavy pack on the ground, relieving my back. "Are you here for the Red Rock shuttle to Lava Point?" I asked.

"Yeah." His eyes sparkled like chocolate diamonds in the twilight. He smiled, revealing strong, straight-enough teeth. They weren't force-corrected like mine and Elias's. A small gap separated his upper front teeth, more like Arnold Schwarzenegger in *Conan* than Michael Strahan. His lips curled down to their resting position, forming a small frown. It made his smile that much more mesmerizing.

I licked my lips, unable to shift my gaze from his mouth. "Wow! Are you a trail runner? You make me feel like I overpacked."

"I am definitely *not* a trail runner. I plan to take my time and soak it all in. You hike much?"

"Yeah, you could say that. I've not really hiked in the Southwest, though. I figured with the world shut down, why not take a road trip out here?"

"Where are you driving from?"

"Tennessee. Chattanooga, Tennessee. How about you? What brings you to Zion?"

"Ah, so you pretty much drove cross-country. Impressive. I'm from all over since my dad's in oil, but I currently live in Austin. Similar to you, I'm taking some time to just travel. How long have you been in Zion?"

"Oh, today is my first day in Zion but fourth day of my trip. I arrived here last night."

"Oh, today's my first day too. Where are you staying?"

"At the lodge, in the park. With the crazy shuttle ticket system, I just felt it was less of a gamble if I couldn't get a ticket since the lodge has its own shuttle just for guests. How about yourself?"

In the busy summer months, Zion restricted vehicular traffic in the Zion Valley to shuttle buses and Zion Lodge guests, and only the buses ventured north of the lodge to the most popular trailheads. Since the pandemic, Zion had also implemented an online-reservation system for their shuttle buses. Their fee-based bus tickets were available for purchase only two weeks before the ticket's assigned date and time—the time indicating the earliest a guest could board the bus from the visitor center. Each time slot had limited quantities, so once those tickets were sold out, guests had to select a different time, a different day, or find some other means to get to the trailheads in the valley—walk or hire a private shuttle that had park permits.

"At this hotel in Springdale. I've been mostly camping on my trip, but I wanted a place with internet so that I could keep up to date with the fires in Yosemite. That's my next destination."

"Yosemite! I would love to go. What have you checked out prior to Zion?"

"I spent a bit of time in New Mexico. It was great."

"Oh, so you had no problem with the quarantine orders? I avoided driving I-40 out here because I was unsure if I had the stamina to drive through New Mexico without stopping overnight to abide by their fourteen-day quarantine orders."

His face contorted, and his mouth fell open in surprise. "Oh, I didn't know New Mexico had quarantine orders."

My eyebrows gathered. "Oh gosh, don't beat yourself up about it. What's done is done. Forgive yourself." I shrugged.

Concern remained on his face. He hung his head and rubbed the back of his neck, then scratched the space between his nose and lip.

"Seriously, don't worry about it, but just know for future reference," I said, shaking my head. "So I'm assuming you were able to drive through the reservations okay, right? I still haven't decided if I'm going back the way I came on I-70 or take the I-40 route." I sighed.

His shoulders relaxed. "Oh, I had no problems traveling through the reservations. They're open to drive through."

A passenger van pulled up, and an older man with a clipboard exited from the driver's side. He walked around the vehicle and opened its sliding door.

"Are you Red Rock Shuttle?" I called out.

Through his masked face, he said, "Yes."

The hiker from Austin, Texas, and I masked up and approached the van. I handed the driver two twenty-dollar bills. The reservation stated exact fare only. "Do you know how many passengers you're transporting today?"

"Four."

Austin pulled a hundred-dollar bill from his wallet. I contemplated offering to break his hundred since I had the cash, but when the driver refused the bill, he wrote him a check.

Who carries checks anymore? Is he older than I thought?

I counted four rows behind the driver's seat. Austin masked up and took the first bench. I slipped on my mask and then climbed in and settled on the second bench behind him. Austin and I peered out the windows trying to spy who the other passengers might be. A guy in knee-length jean shorts, a white tank, and round, metal glasses paid, masked up, and claimed the last row. He carried a cinch bag better suited for the gym than the trail. Had I overpacked?

Austin asked, "Where are you from?" to welcome him to our little crew.

"LA. Los Angeles." He pushed the bridge of his glasses up his nose and then pulled out his phone, folded his arms, and bowed his head to the screen gods.

Austin and I exchanged glances and shrugged. We resumed our positions, in silence, peering out the windows, waiting for the last passenger. Whoever it was, they were late. We fiddled with our packs and repeatedly checked the time on our phones. Would this last person be a no-show? How much longer was the driver going to wait?

Just then a tall young man, at least six-foot-four and in his mid-twenties, arrived at the van. He patted his pockets and chest and then surveyed the ground.

As he retraced his steps back to his vehicle, he stopped in the middle of the parking lot, bent over, and picked up his wallet. He was unfairly attractive, the kind of man whose face would launch a thousand ships, if women were the warring kind. The kind of man who attracted the attention of Greek gods like some blonde Antinous. He was beauty personified. He was the kind of guy who would never struggle to bed women, and I hated him for that as much as I wanted to bed him. He, too, had little to no pack. After paying, he pulled a mask from his shorts' pocket and covered his beauty. His blue husky-like eyes glanced at me before he crouched his swimmer's frame to glide onto the third row, behind me.

Austin asked, "Where are you from?"

"Seattle. How about you guys?"

"Austin."

"I live in Chattanooga, Tennessee."

"LA"

I then blurted, "What the hell, guys? You all have these tiny-ass packs. Two liter minimum when hiking in a desert, no? Are any of you even carrying two liters? You're making me feel like I overpacked."

Austin chuckled and readjusted his mask.

"Well, I packed a few snacks and everything I think I need," Seattle said, looking at his pack and shrugging.

"Gosh, well, I have a first-aid kit and other essentials, a six-inch knife, human pepper spray, and all sorts of trail goodies, so I guess if any of you run into trouble, you'll just have to wait for me to rescue you. You young men and your young men bodies. You think you're invincible."

"Hey, I'm not that young. I'm forty," LA said.

"Pardon me, you young men and the forty-year-old might need to get rescued by me."

They all laughed, including the driver who started the ignition and our journey to the trailhead.

"Hey," I said to the driver. "Do you do anything else besides drive the shuttle? I'm always curious how people make a living in park towns."

"Well, I was the Springdale sheriff for many years, but I'm retired now."

"Do you have any interesting stories?" Austin asked.

"Springdale is a quiet town. Nothing interesting. The most interesting thing really could be this pandemic. When the park implemented the timed, ticketed shuttle system, a lot of the private shuttle companies shifted to driving back and forth from The Narrows. Do you all have tickets to get back to the visitor center after your hike?"

The driver's eyes scanned us from the rearview mirror. Austin, LA, and I nodded.

"No. I need a ticket to get back? I thought I could just hop on a shuttle back to the visitor center," Seattle said.

"Yeah, you still need a ticket to get on the park shuttles even when exiting, but I can give you a card so that when you're done hiking, you can hop on a private shuttle back."

"That'd be great," Seattle said.

White + male + tall + attractive = birth lottery. Seattle had likely gone through life not having to prepare for or forge his own way because our society ensured his success. I wasn't faulting him for hitting the birth lottery, nor diminishing his intelligence or drive, but I was angry and jealous that I had to fight and claw my way to achieve what was bequeathed to him.

As the van passed a La Quinta, Seattle said, "I stayed here last night. I met this couple on the trail, and they offered me a spot to crash on their floor. The hot shower was nice after a week camping at Kolob."

I rolled my eyes, disgusted with his privilege.

"I'm at Kolob, too," LA said.

"Do you kids plan to hike The Narrows?" the driver asked.

"I hiked it yesterday afternoon," Seattle shared.

"If the weather allows, I'd like to try it tomorrow," I said. "I'm a bit worried about that toxic cyanobacteria blooming, though. The park doesn't want us in the river, but it's such an iconic hike." I didn't bother sharing my anxiety of a water hike.

"Bacteria?" Austin asked.

"Yeah, my friend's dog died after drinking from the Virgin River," the driver said. "If you go, be sure you cover up any cuts or scrapes on your legs."

"It's Zion. You've *got* to do it!" Seattle said and then re-adjusted his mask to cover his nose.

Austin cocked his head and looked at the van's ceiling. "I didn't even think about that. I was thinking of going to-morrow too." He surveyed his legs for open cuts.

The driver turned right, and we returned to the park through the Kolob Canyon entrance.

Austin rested his right arm on the back of his bench. I studied an indigo-inked tattoo on the back of his neck.

"Eye of Ra," I said aloud.

His left hand touched the back of his neck. "Yeah, most people think it's the Eye of Horus. I don't ever bother to correct them. You know a lot about Egyptian gods?"

"I wouldn't say a lot. I spent a few weeks there. I guess I remember more than I thought."

He nodded and then stared out the window while I ex-amined his arm the way I would a museum masterpiece. It was covered in many different colorful tattoos, unusual for melanated skin. Despite the various ages of his collection, they all popped with vibrancy and crispness. His arm tap-estry wasn't as cohesive as a sleeve, but there weren't many open slots for him to add to his collection. I passed the time, creating origin stories for each one.

Austin turned in his seat to better face us back passen-gers. "So, do you solo travel much?"

I tilted my head a few degrees, assessing if he was mak-ing the usual small trail talk or if he was interested in me.

"I guess recently. I was married for ten years, so I al-ways traveled with my then husband. Since then, I just don't have friends who have similar interests or the means to do the kind of travel I want. I've done a couple of friend trips, and they're fun, but there's just something freeing about solo travel. I mean, there's no compromise. If I don't want to eat breakfast, I don't have to. If I want to try a place on a whim, I can. Even if I find myself in a relationship again, solo travel is something I'll be unwilling to give up. There would have to be some sort of agreement like one couples' trip to—"

"Eight solo trips," he finished my sentence. Our eyes crinkled, and we filled the van with our muffled, masked laughter.

"There's pros and cons to traveling with your significant other and friends, but solo travel is amazing," Austin said. "The people you meet that you'd normally ignore back home in your routines, those unexpected experiences you are willing to take, and the vulnerability and openness. It all happens more when you are alone. You just really grow stronger, physically and mentally."

I nodded. "One thousand percent. You're, like, in my head."

Austin added, "About a year ago, I got into solo backpacking, and it's such an empowering feeling to have everything you need on your back."

Seattle said, "Yeah, backpacking is ultimate freedom."

I frowned in surprise. I wasn't aware that Seattle was listening to our conversation.

We fell silent, gazing upon the grandeur of Kolob Canyon.

"This topography is amazing," Austin whispered.

"Too easy," Seattle said.

Austin and I exchanged glances with furrowed brows. In a few seconds, our eyes communicated, "Yeah, you heard the same thing, right?" "What the fuck?" "Is this guy some super athlete?" Austin was 100 percent in my head!

Astonished, I asked, "Too easy? This topography is too easy? I guess you're the kind of guy who climbs Mount Rainier on just another weekend."

"Oh, I thought he said, 'Photography,'" Seattle said. "I meant photography out here is too easy because everything is beautiful."

"Phew. Okay, you had us going for a second there." Austin sighed.

We chuckled.

"*Buuut* my original plan was to climb Rainier this year, but then the pandemic," Seattle said.

"Wow, that's impressive. I visited that park a few years back, and since, I've thought of doing the Wonderland Trail but never dreamed of mountaineering," I said.

"Climbing Rainier requires mountaineering?" Austin asked. He and Seattle then had a deep conversation about the technical skill required to climb Rainier.

"What do you do for a living?" Austin asked Seattle. I was curious, too, as I was always intrigued by others who traveled and were outdoorsy, especially younger people. Were they earning a living from social media like the Smoky Mountains group, or were they working soul-sucking corporate jobs, living for the weekends like me? Did Seattle come from money, or was he a dirtbag?

Seattle shared, "I'm a nursing assistant but am taking time to explore nature, kind of a rite of passage."

Hmm, the American rite of passage to see our vast country and visit our protected lands. To disconnect in order to connect to that voice deep inside of you, uninfluenced by society. It all sounded romantic, and it was. I had gone to a few corners of the world to run away from American society so that I could find myself. I grew tremendously as a person by unplugging, but unfortunately, that level of disengagement was a privilege. While national lands were free(ish), public land was the greatest American luxury. And in these protected lands, we simply were not equal in our ability to embark on this proverbial rite of passage.

Because, oftentimes, "protection" was synonymous with "restricted access," some barrier with criteria that used to be based in color but was now some fee-based or first-come, first-served reservation system, which still disproportionately discriminated against People of Color who traditionally had more limited financial resources and time off to leave things to chance like the generosity of a stranger. How could this basic American *rite*, this free luxury, truly be available, welcoming, and safe for more than White men? It saddened me to think that not every American could have the freedom to explore, to learn who they were without societal trappings, to celebrate hard-earned accomplishments, to experience the purest bliss, and to grow.

"So where else have you been?" Austin asked Seattle.

"I started traveling down the coastal highway and detoured inland to spend a bit of time at Smith Rock in Oregon. You've got to go to Smith Rock if you're headed up," Seattle said.

"Yeah? After here, I was going to head to Yosemite, but the fires …" Austin's voice faded. He glanced at me.

"I was going to do Yosemite, too, but I avoided the area because of the air quality. Even if the park is open, the haze, your lungs. Man, it'd be brutal," Seattle said.

"Yeah, you bring up a good point. Maybe I'll skip Yosemite and meet up with friends in Yellowstone."

"I have a buddy quarantining in Squamish. I'd love to spend time there," Seattle said.

"Squamish? Where's that?" Austin asked.

"BC. British Columbia," I mumbled as if I were answering a game-show question I had overheard.

"You've been there?" Seattle asked me.

Snapping out of my trance, I said, "BC, yes. Squamish, no. I just know a bit about outdoor places around the world." I shrugged.

"So, what about you? What'd you all do pre-pandemic?" Seattle asked.

"I'm a laid-off fitness and Pilates instructor," LA answered.

"I worked live music and entertainment events, but all the events dried up," Austin said. "Instead of trying to jump into something else, I decided to take a year off from working and travel. Kind of a rite of passage, too, but I will be home for the election. I am not absentee voting."

"Yeah, with all the fuckery going on, I think that's smart. I work in software. Business is booming, as you can imagine," I said.

The van climbed steep, packed earth.

"I thought of driving to the trailhead yesterday, but now that I'm seeing this, I'm glad I didn't," Seattle said.

"Were you going to out and back it in one day?" Austin asked.

"That was the plan."

The van bounced, rolling over ruts and rocks. Seattle hummed the Indiana Jones theme music. We chuckled and then hummed along with him.

About ten minutes later, the van stopped. Our driver had transported us as far as he could. We climbed out of the van, ripped off our masks, and inhaled fresh air. A sign identified our location as the West Rim trailhead, not Lava Point:

West Rim Trail

Wildcat Canyon Trail .1 MI

Trail Register Box .1 MI

Potato Hollow 4 MI

Great West Overlooks 7 MI

Zion Canyon 13.5 MI

Our driver had reduced our hike by one and a half miles. He checked something on a clipboard while the guys stretched. I'd never stretched before a hike but succumbed to the unstated peer pressure.

"I'm going to hang at Zion Brewery after the hike. Feel free to come to celebrate completing an epic hike," Seattle said. He stretched his arms overhead.

We all nodded. LA abandoned us and started walking the trail.

"I shouldn't have drunk coffee this morning. I wonder if there's a toilet." Seattle searched for a place to relieve himself.

"It's interesting. I read that this place is 'leave no trace,' as in you're supposed to even pack out your poop," I said.

"Really? I did bring a shovel." Austin twisted his mouth. His eyes appeared more peridot-like in the brighter light.

What else had he packed in his small pack? "Yeah, just burying poop isn't enough here. It's a true 'leave no trace' where you need to pack it all out. I brought freezer bags just in case."

Worry lines returned to his face. "Why is it like that?"

"I think it's the landscape and volume of visitors they get here. This park isn't very large, so if everyone buried their poop, there's a high chance you'd dig a hole and uncover someone else's waste. But don't worry about it. At least you know now that some parks, including this one, expect you to pack your shit out. Literally."

We laughed, and then Austin and I started trekking together.

"You know we just talked to each other for an hour, and I don't know even know your name. I'm Zan," Austin said.

Should I share my real name? There was something nice about our anonymity and only knowing each other by the cities we left behind. If we wanted, we could leave it all in the dust and reinvent ourselves out here.

"I'm Allyn. *A-l-l-y-n.*"

He grinned. "I love your name. Allyn. Very cool. Unexpected."

We smiled at each other before he pulled ahead a few paces. I didn't expect any of us to hike together. Seattle ran past us. Zan stopped, turned around, and looked back at me. Our eyes grew tall, and in sync, our lips parted to bare our teeth as we doubled over in laughter, filling the desert air with joy. Of course Seattle would be the trail runner. Zan picked up his pace. His body grew smaller and smaller, and then it was gone. I was alone with all of my competing thoughts.

What is Elias doing? Why am I thinking of Elias and not Ryan? Why haven't I told Ryan about IVF? Am I afraid of losing him, or am I afraid of not having a backup plan? What would Ben think of me being out here? What if Owen has a girlfriend? My cheeks flushed.

I walked the tree-covered plateau, stealing glimpses of the sun rising over a canyon to my left and another canyon on my right. The trail narrowed to a path cutting through a field alight with gold rabbitbrush. The trail veered right:

Potato Hollow
← Lava Point 4 miles
Zion Canyon 9 miles →

A breeze shook the delicate leaves on the aspen-lined trail. As the trail veered right again, I climbed for the first time. The grade was so steep that it was more like staking my poles and pulling my body weight up. Climbs like this weren't necessarily hard, but my legs had spent the past few miles on flat terrain, so the increased exertion jolted my body into shock. Sweat, panting, thirst. When the trail leveled out, I stopped to eat an apple. I wasn't snacking or drinking as much as I should have been. I hadn't even drunk a liter of water.

I wrapped my apple core in a paper towel and stuffed it in the bag I had designated for trash. Leave no trace. The trail opened back up to an expansive view of Navajo sandstone peaks. I hadn't a clue what all the peak names were; hell, I hardly knew peak names back home, but it was beautiful. I couldn't peel my eyes away from the constant panoramic view to my right. I pulled out my DSLR camera and took photos.

Bush branches rustled. Birds flew. Something headed in my direction. Per my research, only one commercial shuttle traveled to the trailhead. No one should have been behind me unless they were using a private vehicle. Fight or flight? Branches snapped. I screamed.

"Sorry," a voice said.

I squinted, focusing on the movement in the bushes. LA emerged. My pulse slowed.

"I didn't mean to scare you," he said, approaching me.

"How did I catch up with you?"

He wiped sweat from his forehead. "I had to find a spot to do my business."

"Ah," I said, doubting he had packed up said business. "Isn't this beautiful? I'm not used to views like this back home."

"It is impressive."

I hiked away from him to give us a bit of solitude to take in the view. "Oh, the view from here is even better. Who knew it could be better?" He joined me and pulled out his phone to take a photo while I was snapping away on my DSLR.

"Man, my knee is killing me," he said.

"You know, I have a lot of drugs on me. I have ibuprofen if you aren't allergic and want some."

"Really? That'd be great."

Reaching in my pack to fish out the ibuprofen, I asked, "So, why did you decide to come to Zion? I don't think I heard your story."

"Oh, well, I just decided I need some space to think. I just got out of an eight-year relationship where I really thought she was 'the one.' We were living in New York City but moved to LA a few months before the pandemic. I thought things were going great and then the pandemic."

"Wow, well, I'm sorry. I've hit plenty of trails to process my thoughts. Just know that it's okay to have some days where you miss her and want her more than anything and other days where you hate her fucking guts. Give yourself permission to feel however without any judgment."

He nodded.

Healing heartbreak on some solo journey in nature wasn't only a woman's domain.

We hiked a bit together in silence. I refrained from unleashing my thoughts about "the one" on him. This man was in pain and adrift, searching for an anchor. Hell, a life raft. He had come out here for clarity. "The one," "forever," "my person," "my missing piece" were all trigger words for me now. Before my divorce, I had believed in them despite my parents' and friends' divorces, but now, I believed they stifled growth and happiness.

I scoffed at men's online dating profiles, advertising that they were looking for "wifey" or "my forever girl." This was unfair. I never made my friends vow to be with me forever, and some of my greatest love stories were with my friends, so why should I put those unrealistic demands on a partner? Why can't a partner also be a reason, a season, or a lifetime without any expectation that reasons and seasons *had* to be converted to lifetimes? If the lifetime happened, it should be natural. It wasn't that I was running from commitment, but I eschewed unrealistic expectations derived from societal pressures and feelings of ownership. I wanted everyone in my life to grow and find their happiness, and when it was time to move on, we could depart peacefully, thankful our lives had been enriched with each other's presence.

Lenny was right. I was a hypocrite. I was playing favorites on enriching other people's lives. Instead of being part of Owen's growth journey, I had cast him away, but I had further opened the possibility to grow with Ryan. Two very different men. Ryan saw my ugly. He wanted all the annual passes to whatever my life commanded and now that included a child. Owen had shown me his spirituality, his fervor, and his ugly, and I wasn't a friend back. Was it because Ryan was in my heart more than I cared to admit? Was it because I, a minority, also possessed White-male bias?

Was it because I had set another goal and, come hell or high water, I was going to insert a man in my life and Owen and Ryan were my safest, most stable options? Or was I waffling because, in reality, neither Owen nor Ryan were good partners for me? And what did it matter? It wasn't like Owen was an option anymore. He still hadn't responded to my text. Was I certain I wanted a relationship? *Did* I want a relationship or just good sex? Had Ben reawakened my sexuality, or had I misinterpreted what my interaction with him stirred?

LA outpaced me, leaving me alone in my swirling questions until I came upon a trail sign:

```
Canyon Rim Route →
← Telephone Canyon Route
```

I had studied trail recommendations to know that keeping right would provide sweeping views of the Canyon Rim. Not far from the trail split, my eyes feasted on nonstop views. I wasn't making great progress as I continued to stop to take photos, reminding myself to also experience the environment and not just catalog it.

At 1 p.m., I conceded that I wouldn't complete the hike by my target time of two. The hike wasn't difficult, so I chalked up my slow time to carrying more weight and being enamored with the scenery. As Zan had said, I was soaking it all in. I hit the part of the trail where the 3,200-foot descent began. I anticipated an angry knee.

After I passed Cabin Spring, I took a bathroom break. My orange urine reeked of ammonia. I hand-sanitized and then chugged water. As I pressed on, tree cover disappeared. I descended white, exposed rock—Little Siberia. I squinted and dug my hat from my pack to protect my eyes. I had forgotten my sunglasses in my car. Each step down, I winced. Forget my knees; my toes were killing me with pulsating pain.

The trail bottomed out at a small footbridge. I pushed my way through overgrown shrubbery, spooking a deer that dashed off the trail. The trail climbed, which was a welcome relief for my toes, but despite my hat, the sun zapped my energy. I stopped for a breather. I wiped the sweat puddling on my forehead with my swollen sausage fingers. I pinched my nostrils, craving moisture. I gulped my warm water, wishing it were cooler. The stifling air reminded me of opening an oven door, where the sudden release of heat singes your face and you instinctively hold your breath so that you don't inhale and scorch your insides. I smacked my tongue against the roof of my parched mouth and reminded myself to breathe. The heat was worse than I could've imagined, and today was the coolest day of the week, with the high only reaching ninety. I trudged on and lost the trail for about ten minutes. Back on the trail, I spied the first of many brown signs stamped with a white boot print; trail markers erected in the rock.

The wind carried laughter and conversation toward me. My heart raced. Angels Landing must be near. World-famous rock formations like Angels Landing and Delicate Arch elicited the same spark for me as did beholding masterpieces like Bernini's *David* or Rembrandt's *The Night Watch*, but they also carried the dread of viewing da Vinci's *Mona Lisa*.

People were exhausting. Society was exhausting. I groaned on my descent back to society, with its expectations and disappointments. On trails, that shit didn't matter. I wasn't Black. I wasn't female. I wasn't an engineer. I wasn't girly. I wasn't a Corporate America addict trying to kick the dependency of stable income and benefits. I wasn't a divorcée. I wasn't barren. I was just a person.

As human voices drowned out nature, I stopped and turned in the direction from which I had come. The trail less traveled. The trail unworthy of the social media shot. The trail I studied from a distance, poring over maps and trail reports. The trail that provided me no answers yet made me question.

I sighed, turned around, and continued in the direction of voices. They likely belonged to people who had just scrolled through pictures on the socials, drooled over a few, Googled "Top 10 Hikes of [insert national park here]," and then decided to go based on photos. I hoped those voices would abandon the mountains when the world reopened; the overcrowding and land abuse weren't sustainable.

I passed a couple resting in a hammock strung in a rare, shaded spot. Below their hammock, I spied Angels Landing, a wing rising over fourteen hundred feet above the canyon floor. They scrunched their faces upon seeing my exasperated state. Their puzzled faces looked beyond me. I imagined the questions plaguing their minds: Where had she come from? Will there be others? Should we check it out? What are the views like from there?

I choked down my bitterness. Who was I to have trekker superiority, making my claim to be there more valid? Sure, I likely respected and had a far greater appreciation for the land, but who was I to deny anyone else this experience? To hardcore outdoor enthusiasts, my connection to outdoor spaces might be undeserving. There was always a hierarchy, but I didn't want to be an exclusionist like so many others, denying a trail to hike, a wave to surf, a rock to scale, a slope to ride, a park to explore. Denying others the opportunity to form those connections wasn't the solution to protecting what I loved. If I had been denied thirteen years prior on my attempt to reach Charlie's Bunion, I wouldn't be here today. We all must start somewhere, and there shouldn't be hierarchies to navigate or barriers to entry.

It was a complicated problem: How to ensure our outdoor spaces don't get completely bastardized while still maintaining access? And who defines the bastardization? Is a paved trail too much alteration? A paved road? Blazes? Switzerland boasted a sophisticated trail system with many hostels and restaurants at its peaks. Was that bastardization? Did anyone think the Swiss Alps were bastardized because they were so accessible? Unfortunately, the pandemic had further morphed our national parks into amusement parks. Other protected lands, like national forests and wilderness areas, were wilder and less adulterated but also less accessible. Preserving our national parks was imperative for a safe, low-barrier introduction to the outdoors.

My feet needed a break. My toes cried in pain as they jammed against my boot's toe box:

> West Rim Trail
>
> Angels Landing 0.5 →
>
> ↑ West Rim Spring 3.0

I turned in the direction of Angels Landing. I dumped my pack on the ground next to a group of hikers gathered under the shade of a lonely tree. I studied the people illegally ascending Angels Landing. That section of the trail was closed to improve social distancing.

I was underwhelmed, like I had been many years prior when I arrived at Machu Picchu. Walking among the Incan ruins with perfumed, well-dressed travelers who rode a train or bus to the world wonder paled in comparison to my three-and-a-half-day trek that had preceded my arrival.

A male trekker, wearing a booney hat, reclining on a rock, said, "It's just not worth the five-thousand-dollar fine."

"Oh, wow, I didn't know the fine was that steep," I said. Even if I wanted to ascend Angels Landing and risk the fine, today would not be the day. My toes were done. Completely *done*. "Do you know how much farther it is to the trailhead?" I should have known. I could've consulted my digital map, but my brain wasn't functioning properly.

"I think it's about two miles back down," he answered.

I grimaced. "Thanks." I breathed in and winced every damn step down. Going downhill was supposed to be easy so long as your knees cooperated; my knees were great, but the most unfit people flew past me. My pride damaged, I zigzagged within the numerous switchbacks. I turned my body perpendicular to the trail and shuffled down. I used my poles to drag my legs. I did anything to avoid putting pressure on my toes. And the heat—oh my God, the dry heat. My hand was two shades darker and bore tiny, jagged lines as if my skin were a jigsaw puzzle. I groaned along with the unfortunate souls climbing up Walter's Wiggles. My heart leapt when I reached flat ground and crossed the Virgin River to the shuttle bus. Salvation!

I wanted to collapse, but I dug my mask out of my backpack and scrolled through screens on my phone to find my shuttle ticket. It was 4 p.m. when I sat on the un-air-conditioned shuttle. We stopped at Zion Lodge before skipping the Court of the Patriarchs, Canyon Junction, and the museum, with its limited pandemic service. We passed many unfortunate souls walking the valley floor, people who didn't have shuttle tickets but were determined to experience Zion. I disembarked at the next stop in service, the visitor center.

When I reached my car, I didn't have the strength to take off my boots as was my post-hike tradition. I opened the car door, expecting a backdraft. My plastic national park hang tag had melted and fallen on my dash. I started my car and cranked my air conditioning to its max. Once the plastic parts cooled, I slumped over in my car seat, resting my head on my steering wheel as my arms widely hugged it, blasting my armpits with AC. The orange check-engine light scowled. I reached over and shut the door, so that I could suffer in secret.

3.2 THE DAMMING OF AMERICA

The shuttles had been running since six, but I didn't make a practice of starting hikes in the dark, especially ones involving multiple water crossings. My heart thumped. *Fucking water crossings.* I slipped on my mask, walked up to a shuttle bus at the lodge's passenger loading zone, and flashed the driver the shuttle ticket on my phone. The shuttle was empty. I found a seat three rows behind the driver. He put the bus into gear and turned right onto the valley road.

"You traveling by yourself?" the driver asked.

"Yeah, it's been good so far."

"What have you gotten into?"

"Well, today's only my second full day in Zion. I hiked the West Rim Trail yesterday. I was really wanting to hike to Observation Point, but that trail's been closed for a couple of years."

"That's impressive. Most people don't even know about the West Rim Trail. You know that you can drive to Observation Point if your vehicle has enough clearance?"

"Yeah, but driving to a viewpoint feels like cheating to me."

"It seems you studied the park a good bit. Zion is great, but the best scenic spots in Southwest Utah aren't even in Zion. You should check out Escalante."

"Es-ca-lan-te?" I pronounced each letter as if I were in Spanish class.

"Yeah, it's east of here, but you need to go with someone. It's more wilderness. You'll enjoy The Narrows, though. It's magical."

I made a mental note of Escalante and then repeated my tally of places to see on my next trip out: Glenwood Canyon, Arches, Canyonlands, Moab, Salt Lake City, Escalante.

The shuttle drove past stops out of service due to the restricted COVID bus route. He pulled into the bus lane at the Temple of Sinawava stop. I thanked the driver and stepped off the bus. No one else was in sight. I had arrived early to beat the crowds, but now I had trepidation about trudging through water alone.

The Riverside Walk trail was flat and paved. As I hiked farther from the shuttle stop, I encountered a few people walking in the opposite direction. What time had they gotten on the trail? They looked dry. Did they go to The Narrows? The pavement ended where a packed earth and sand path began. Small hills rose from the flatness. The trail ended at a small beach, and I was left with two options: enter the water or turn around. I shivered. I hadn't packed a jacket. I dreaded my first steps in the water.

My tennis-shoe-covered toes relished the coolness, but then the water gripped my uncovered legs and injected iciness into my veins. I trembled and rubbed my hands up and down my sleeved arms. *Keep moving. When the sun rises and the heat comes, you'll be thankful for this.* I reached forward with my pole, testing the depth of the water before I moved my feet. I feared a misstep, sinking below the surface, exposing myself to the toxic bacteria, or, God forbid, drowning. At this pace, it'd take me over an hour to cover a mile. After five minutes of solitude walking upstream, voices echoed off the canyon walls. I stabbed the riverbed faster, eager to be around people.

Ahead, a petite, blonde woman of about my height disappeared into the water with each step. When the water hit her chest, she cried out—from fear or cold, I did not know. A man waded to her and helped her navigate out of that spot. He continued on with his group while the petite woman remained motionless. My heart raced. I wasn't expecting deep water so early on the trail, but from that moment on, I changed my strategy. Taller people afforded me the ability to observe how far the water rose on their bodies before I decided my route.

I caught up with the petite woman.

"Are you out here alone?" the blonde asked me. She wore all black, and her hair was gathered in a high ponytail, Ariana Grande–style.

"Yeah, I'm a bit nervous about the water situation, but I figure if I am always behind a taller person, I'll be okay," I said.

"Did you see where I almost was completely submerged back there?"

"Yes, it didn't ease my anxiety. I hate water crossings."

"Do you hike often?" she asked.

"Yeah, how about you?"

"No, never. This is my first time."

I stopped walking and snapped my head back. "Get out! Seriously? You *know* this will ruin all other hikes for you."

She laughed.

I continued walking next to her. "So, if you're not a hiker, why are you in Zion?"

"I recently got out of a really toxic relationship and was wasting time on Instagram. I saw photos of Zion and wanted to be here. I've never been by myself before, so this is all very new to me."

"Never been by yourself? What do you mean?"

"Well, I was a teen mom and bride. My girls are now eleven and thirteen. I went from living with my parents to living with my husband to being a single mom. So, after my last relationship ended, it hit me that I had never been alone. I thought, 'Amy, you've never done anything for yourself. You're finally in a financial position where you aren't dependent on a man, your girls are self-sufficient, your ex-husband is responsible and loves to spend time with your girls, so do something nice for yourself, by yourself.'"

"Wow, that's amazing. Good for you for doing something for yourself. Solo travel is so amazing."

"You travel by yourself much?"

"More so lately. It has pros and cons, but overall, I love it."

"Yeah, I can see that. I wish I could've tried this sooner," Amy said. "Do you have kids?"

"No. An ex-husband but no kids." My mouth hung open, hesitating to share more. I dreaded the typical follow-up questions to my declaration of not being a mom, given how our society normalized the most intrusive questions and judgments as it pertained to a woman's reproductivity. And truthfully, if she asked a question, I didn't know how I would respond. Would I say what I thought she wanted to hear, what I was doing with Ryan, what I had planned at the fertility clinic, or would I share my doubt? And what was my doubt? Confusion clouded my brain. Before Amy could react, I asked, "Hey, do you want to hike together? How far do you plan on going?"

"Yeah, that would make me feel much more comfortable. I really want to go to Wall Street. You?"

I wondered if all Utahan canyons with towering vertical walls were called "Wall Street." Both Zion and Bryce formed in the early twentieth century and could've pulled name inspiration from the skyscrapers of New York and Chicago. Maybe Latter Day Saints still had bad blood from the Illinois expulsion, or maybe outdoorsmen weren't very original or creative.

"I have no final destination. I'm just going to stay out here until I'm ready to head back." I had never done a hike without an end goal of some great vista. "Did you fly out here?"

"Yeah, I flew into Vegas and drove over. You?"

"No, I drove."

"From where?"

"Tennessee. Chattanooga, Tennessee."

"Oh, I know where that is. I'm from Charleston, South Carolina."

She had no accent, but neither did I. "Southern girls unite!"

We whooped and high-fived each other. The canyon walls echoed our jubilation.

Even though she was slower than me, my toes thanked me, and it was great having someone to strategize with and distract me from the water temperatures. We oohed and ahhed as the sun rose, revealing striations of golds, oranges, browns, and blacks in the canyon walls. We stopped and craned our necks, admiring the colors of the vertical walls set against a cloudless sky. Trudging through the water and sandbars, the destructive force of flash flooding was all around—watermarks etched on canyon walls and debris, including uprooted trees, deposited on the sandbars. As the sun peered into the canyon, we didn't warm up, and the water was never a welcome relief. In fact, we dreaded leaving the water to walk on a sandbank because re-entering the water shot fresh, icy prickles up our spines.

"How long are you out here?" I asked.

"Another week. I'm canyoneering tomorrow. I really wanted to do a helicopter tour, but the price is ridiculously expensive. Like five hundred dollars for fifteen minutes."

"What? I love helicopter tours, but they are super expensive." Because of the noise and air pollution, I no longer partook in helicopter tourism, but I couldn't deny how amazing the views were from the sky.

"Well, it's because I have to do a private tour since I'm traveling by myself. And after, I plan to visit the Grand Canyon. How about you?" Amy asked.

"You're doing all the things. Tomorrow's my last day in Zion, and then I'm driving home."

Trekkers wading in the opposite direction passed us as we took photos of each other. I was certain hers would be posted on social media before the sun set.

"Do you think we're close to Wall Street?" Amy asked.

"I don't really know. It's so hard to gauge how many miles we've walked because our pace walking upstream isn't like normal trekking." There weren't mile markers. How could there be? They'd get swept away in a flash flood.

A female solo trekker approached us.

"Hey, is Wall Street close?" I asked.

"Yeah, you're so close. When you see a big boulder in the middle of the river, you're right there."

I hadn't done any research on visual markers on this trail. To hike in water was all the information my brain could manage. After snaking farther up the river, Amy and

I encountered a large boulder in the middle of the Virgin River.

"Do you think this is it?" Amy asked.

"I'm not sure."

Upstream from the boulder, a cluster of people huddled as if they were watching a street performance. We picked up our pace, splashing over to them. They watched other trekkers traverse the narrowed passage where the canyon walls squeezed the river. Narrow paths reduced navigation options. Men approached the passage. The water swallowed their knees, their thighs, and lapped at their waists. The men removed their backpacks and hoisted them over their heads as the water claimed their stomachs and chests. Those men stood about five-foot-ten.

People who went in the middle of the passage stayed drier. Those who stayed closer to the canyon wall were sometimes baptized. A woman who stood about five-foot-five choose the middle path and submerged. Her partner pulled her to the other side of the passage.

"Amy," I said, transfixed at the scene before us, "I will watch your safe passage, but this is it for me."

She wrung her hands. "I don't know if I should do it." She chewed on her nail.

"Don't let my turning around dissuade you from continuing. You said you wanted to go to Wall Street."

She massaged her throat. "I did." She cocked her head. "You sure you want to turn around?"

I nodded. "Yes." I leaned over my poles. "I'm not a great swimmer, and I'm not trying to die by toxic bacteria. I'm sure you can team up with a tall person out here who would help you."

We stood in silence a few minutes longer. I wanted to support Amy. I would have waited for hours for her to conjure the courage to continue, but marching forward was not my path. We watched a few trekkers who had crossed the passage minutes earlier return.

"Back so soon?" I asked of a young man wearing a University of Minnesota T-shirt.

"Yeah, the waters got even deeper. It wasn't worth it for me," he said while adjusting his pack onto his back.

"How were the canyon walls? Were they narrower?" Amy asked.

"Honestly, they were about the same as here," he said before continuing downstream.

Amy turned to face downriver. "Let's head back."

"Are you sure? I want you to make that decision for you and you alone." I searched her face for understanding. "I don't want you to stay with me because we've bonded, and there's a sense of comfort. I don't want you to listen to some random-ass man and take his word as gospel, cheating yourself out of an experience. One of the first things you told me was you wanted to do this. You may never come back to Zion."

We both lifted our heads to the sliver of sun reaching down to us.

She turned to face upriver. "I'm scared."

"What would you tell your girls?"

She chuckled. "I'd tell them to be fearless but also bombard them with enough scary stories of death and dismemberment that they never think of trying."

Two tall women passed us, approaching the choked river.

"Hey," I called to them. They turned around. "Would you help her through?" I thumbed to Amy.

"Yeah. Sure. Of course," one of them responded.

I turned to Amy. "You've got to continue on, but it's time for me to turn around."

"You sure you don't want to come?" Amy asked.

"Today is not the day for me, and it may never be my day. I still stand by what I said ... you've ruined all other hikes after this." I laughed. "I hope you have fun canyoneering tomorrow, and I hope your girls are proud of you for choosing you."

She hugged me. I hugged her back. I watched the taller women pull her through to the other side, and then I turned downriver.

Walking downstream was easier. My pace quickened, but then I lost my footing. My ankle rolled. Water gripped my thighs and tugged. I clutched the top of my trekking pole, fighting gravity. *I cannot go under. I will not die today.* My feet struggled to find a stable part of the riverbed to stand. I pushed against my trekking pole, fighting the fall, and then my pole bent. If it snapped, the water would win. I'd go under. I unrolled my ankle and found stable ground. My heart rate returned to normal. I blotted the sweat that broke out on my forehead. Every hiker within fifty feet watched my struggle.

I nervously laughed and yelled, "I'm fine!"

I zigzagged back—river, sandbank, river, sandbank. The canyon was more beautiful as the late-morning sun lit its walls. Even though walking with the current was easier, there were hordes of people to navigate around. People who rented neoprene boots and wood staffs. Women in bikini tops with faux lashes. People carrying children. I remembered that Zan said he might hike The Narrows today. I tried to scan the crowd for him, but there were so many faces. Too many sheep to count. The Narrows was now littered with people. It was harder to find an appropriate path to walk while maintaining social distancing. I was no longer only fighting the current. I was fighting people for a place to step.

My eyes were peeled to the left bank, searching for the small beach where I could exit the river. What was a sandy expanse at sunrise was now teeming with people gearing up to walk the river. I pulled my mask from my pack and fastened it to my face as I departed the river. A continuous line of people pumped into the river: single file, three across, and multiple rows deep. I wanted away from there. Navigating the trail was like weaving through Bourbon Street during Mardi Gras, bumping shoulders with strangers and seeking the best walking path. My heart rate quickened. Between my neck gaiter on my forehead, my sunglasses, and mask, my entire face was covered.

Shuttle buses lined up, consuming and spitting out humans. I skipped the shoe wash, fumbled with my phone to pull up my shuttle ticket, and plopped into a seat. My toenails throbbed.

Driving away from the lodge, I spied two women walking the canyon floor in the distance ahead. Those poor, unfortunate souls didn't have shuttle tickets and were forced to walk. I glanced at my car's thermometer—ninety-five degrees. As I neared them, I slowed my car and rolled down my window. Heat engulfed me like a blast of hot air from a hair dryer.

"Do you want a ride to your car?" I yelled.

They lifted their weary heads, verifying the noises were directed to them. Once their brains registered that I was speaking to them, their mouths opened in shock.

"Are you sure?" the taller woman asked.

"Yeah, throw your things in my trunk. Do you have masks?"

"Yes!" the shorter woman said, checking traffic.

"Hop in!" I waved them over to my car.

I slipped on my mask and popped my trunk.

They loaded their gear into my trunk and sat in the backseat. I positioned my body to conceal my dashboard as much as possible. I didn't want them uneased by my attention starved check-engine light.

"Cool. Are you parked at the visitor center?" I asked.

"No, we're just outside the gate," the taller woman said.

A mile later, I exited the gate and pulled behind their camper van, which was parked across from the canyon floor gate like they said. "You lucked out on a great parking spot."

"Yeah, we were fortunate with parking but no luck on those tickets. Thank you so much for doing this," the taller woman said.

"You're very welcome."

I finished my drive to the visitor center and then walked to Zion Brewery. I wanted to treat myself to a belated beer.

I sat on the patio with a landscape view of the colorful canyon walls. Heat lamps stood dormant while fan misters waved down cool, moist air. I couldn't order a flight of beer because Utah had a two-drink max per person limit, so I ordered two sixteen-ounce sours to illustrate the short-sightedness of the law.

While devouring a hot pastrami Reuben, I rolled my eyes, unable to escape the conversation of the couple seated one table over.

"Google 'top places to see in the West,'" he said.

"Oh, that looks nice," she said, showing him her phone.

"Yeah, how far is it from here?"

"Three hours! Let me look back at the list." Her fingers danced across the screen. "Oh, where is this? Ah, California. We should check this out." She offered her screen to him again.

He squinted. "I think we've been there."

She cocked her head. "Really?"

"Yeah." He gulped his beer and wiped the head that collected on his upper lip.

She wrinkled her nose. "Humph." Her fingers massaged her phone. "Oh, look at this!" She shoved her phone back in his face. "It's called The Wave."

"Looks promising. Where is it?"

She retracted the phone and pushed her fingers up the screen. "Kay-nab, Utah," she said, overemphasizing the first syllable of the town's name.

"Is it close?"

She tapped her phone screen. "Looks like it's only thirty minutes away."

"Oh, we'll get nice photos. Let's do it tomorrow."

There was no discussion about trail conditions and considerations. I took a swig of my beer, washing down my disappointment. How would this couple react once they arrived at Kanab and learned there was a limited number of daily permits allotted for visitors or that they needed navigational skills to reach The Wave? They were the ignorant image chasers devoted to the screen gods. Was it too late to save the magic of our protected spaces? But what was I doing for my community other than bemoaning access and shunning those whose inspiration was sourced differently than mine?

I set my glass down. I yelled over to them. "The Wave requires a permit, so you might not get in."

"Really?" the woman asked.

I nodded. She tapped away at her phone, asking the screen gods to confirm what I had told her.

"You seem to know a lot about the area," she said. "Is there some place you'd recommend for us instead?"

I smiled. "I truly don't know this area, but I don't mind trying to help."

"Do you want to come over?" the guy asked, pulling an empty chair back from their table.

We spent the next hour trading stories of where we had been and how the pandemic had impacted us. We crafted a plan for them to visit Escalante. They invited me to join them, but I declined. The ache that had seized my toenails now spread to my heart. I feared a brooding in my forecast and didn't want to dampen their day. We exchanged contact information so that they could share their Escalante experience with me. Excited for their future plans, big smiles wrapped their sunburnt faces. I shivered in the desert heat—hesitant of mine.

3.3 LIFE, LIBERTY, AND THE PURSUIT OF HAPPINESS

My headlamp struggled to light the path. I thought I had put in fresh batteries, but maybe they were old. Fortunately, the full moon provided enough ambient light. My Chaco-strapped feet tossed up sand with each step. I wriggled my toes, exfoliating my skin and assessing the pain of my toenails. They could no longer tolerate being covered.

Light danced with darkness. I accelerated my pace. Fifteen minutes before sunrise, I arrived at Canyon Overlook. Chain-link fenced the cliff's edge, keeping visitors from falling over the side to a sudden death. A sign erected in the rock face named the peaks in view.

A breeze chilled the air. I turned off my headlamp and then pulled my neck gaiter over my ears. Desert extremes. Temperatures were predicated to soar to ninety-nine degrees today, which the news said was unseasonable for this time of year.

There were four groups of travelers at the overlook. One group was taking engagement or wedding photos. Another couple had bundled underneath a blanket. Two young women looked up to a phone and captured a selfie. Two middle-aged men snapped photos of the sign that named the peaks in view. I was alone, and for the first time in a long time, loneliness pierced my heart.

I closed my eyes and blinked out a few tears. I allowed them to fall, staining my cheeks. I climbed atop a boulder, reflecting on my solo-ness as I was surrounded by togetherness. I had been in all those groups: the wife, the lover, the best friend. Never the mom. And what was I going to tell Ryan? My first IVF consultation was in two weeks. I had cursory knowledge of the process, but shit was going to get real really soon. Hormones. Egg retrieval. The number of viable embryos to transfer. Unused embryos. Was I ready for that roller coaster? I pulled my legs into my chest and hugged my knees.

"Allyn?" a voice called from behind me.

I turned my head and squinted at the approaching shadow outline. "Zan?"

"Yeah, you remembered." He walked toward me, coming into focus. "Is it okay if I sit next to you?"

"Sure." I scooted over, affording him a spot. I wiped my face dry on my shirtsleeve. He scaled the boulder in one leap and sat next to me.

The full moon watched over the canyon, awaiting the changing of the guards. And then, the sun engulfed the West Temple in a fiery orange-red that ran down the canyon walls like a reverse ombre. The moon, in all her coolness, remained steady as the sun continued his peacockish arrival.

I shivered and then sniffled, wiping another escaped tear with my finger.

"You okay?" Zan asked.

I shrugged. He wrapped his left arm around me and pulled me into him. He radiated heat and smelled of mint and forest. Like raindrops becoming a drizzle and then a downpour, I cried. My shoulders shook. He pressed me into his body, absorbing my hurt.

Groups left. New groups came.

When the light was halfway down the canyon walls, I pulled away from Zan and wiped my face dry on my neck gaiter. "Sorry about that."

"No, it's okay. I mean, I wasn't expecting that, but that's okay."

"I'm such a fucking mess. This is my last day here, and then back to home. Back to that life I've carefully curated. The reality of what's waiting for me is just hitting me is all."

"Is it that bad?" Zan asked.

I laughed, then played with my Chaco straps. "I don't know how to answer that. I have a stable job that I devote too much of my time to. Awesome benefits. A home. Plenty of friends and family who love me, but there's just been this emptiness in my life. Like, what's my legacy? So, I started a fertility journey, and eh, well, that wasn't too successful. And, well, when I get home, I'm going to more aggressively pursue fertility."

"Like IVF treatments?" he asked.

I snapped my head back and pursed my lips. "Yeah, actually. I'm surprised you know what that is."

"I'm here because of IVF. My parents struggled with fertility, so I guess I get it."

"Wow." I exhaled like I was in yoga class, pushing my stomach empty. "I'm just super confused. For years, I've wanted a baby, but what if the hollowness is still there after a baby comes? And if there's no baby, how do I move on? Because I told myself I wouldn't do IVF, but here I am. And I don't know if I'm chasing my own dream to have a baby, or if I've become fixated on some societal expectation that I've been fighting to achieve?

"I don't even know why I'm pouring my heart out to you. This is insane. There's probably a million other things you'd rather be doing. Sorry."

"Sometimes it's easier talking to someone who doesn't know your history. My schedule's pretty flexible. Just have to be home for voting." His sad lips curled into a smile. "So, you want a child to fill some sort of emptiness?"

"I wouldn't say that." I continued to play with my Chaco straps, tucking and untucking them from the ankle hold. "I feel like my emptiness is because I don't have a child. I have a mostly 'successful' life per cultural standards." Reciting from memory, I said, "I have tremendous capacity to love, and I want to give that love to a child. I have financial resources to provide a child with a very comfortable life. I want to devote my life so fully and unconditionally to someone else's betterment. I want to create a healthy family unit, and I want to bring life into this world. Crazy as it is. And I know I don't need to have a child to achieve that, but I have this pull. And without bringing life into this world, I feel it'd be the one thing my mother would keep holding over my head as this almost-made-it-but-not-quite. So, in my mind, having and raising a happy, well-adapted child would be proof that I'm successful by every standard possible to everyone, including my mother. Like, in some way, it's my way of winning the game."

Zan frowned. "Parents influence their children's behaviors, but it's not the only factor. What if your child becomes a derelict? Would you consider yourself unsuccessful?"

"Probably. I know it's stupid. I've been working really hard to not focus on outcomes. It's hard to give them up."

"What do you mean 'not focus on outcomes'?" He bent his knees and circled his arms around his legs, mimicking my pose.

"Hmm. Well, it's like … take the American Dream. If I work hard enough, I, too, can attain it and be happy. My parents didn't really struggle, but I wanted to do better and be more secure than them. So I followed the formula. I went to college, I got married, we bought a home, we amassed things that we were told we should have, we saved as we were guided, but—" I shrugged.

"Happiness was fleeting, so we divorced. Looking back, I was always chasing something with an expectation that once I had it, I'd be happier. I was so laser-focused on some end goal. I'm trying to focus on the journey, enjoying the now, letting go of the expectation that if I do this, then I will get that. I should just focus on enjoying the doing."

"I think I get it," he said. "Are you happy now?"

I peered up at the sky and then looked ahead. The canyon was alight. A bead of sweat rolled down my back. I tapped my feet against the boulder and studied my big toenails. The red polish hid the damage I had endured. In a few days, the nails would probably fall off, exposing my trauma. "I'm happier now than I've been in my entire life, but I can't shake the feeling I could be happier. I don't know. Like, can you be happy if you can't share it?"

"And you only see yourself being happier if you can share that with your child?"

I laughed and punched his bicep. "Well, when you say it like that, it sounds fucking crazy. I mean, do you not want to be a dad one day?"

"No. No disrespect to you, but I think with everything going on in this country, with this planet, that having a child is the most selfish thing a person can do."

I frowned and bit my lip. "Do you ever think of why you are here? Your purpose or legacy?"

"Oh, absolutely, especially now that I'm not working. It's so easy to define yourself through your job or the role you are to someone else—son, brother, boyfriend—but those are just boxes. Mental shortcut associations that don't define who you are."

I nodded and looked at him. "Hmm. Do you feel you're on the path to fulfill your legacy?"

He nodded. "Me taking a step back from work has put me closer on that path. I loved my job, but it left me with so little time to think."

"You think you'll go back to it?"

He shrugged. "Probably. But I won't do those hours anymore. It's important for me to have time for myself, and I also want to devote time to music education. So many kids don't have access to learn to play an instrument, and that's what I see as my legacy.

"I was spiraling there for a few months," he continued. "I went from working a minimum eighty-hour week to nothing. A friend really helped ground me and got me to see the time as a blessing. He challenged me to think about what a perfect day would mean for me."

"Perfect day?" I asked.

"Yeah, from the moment I opened my eyes to the moment I slept. Every minute detail about what music I'm listening to, what I'm eating, what I'm wearing, the temperature."

My eyebrows inched up my forehead. "Wow, that's intense."

"Oh, it was. It took me two months to craft what a perfect day would be, and I still add small details and make tweaks."

"So, once you know what your perfect day is, what do you do?"

"You work to make it a reality. And, today, that's where I'm at. I want to reintroduce music education in schools, but I will have to work my job until I can execute my vision."

"That's so amazing, Zan. Like, I wish I had that clarity." I stretched my legs out and flexed my toes.

"You probably have it. It's just locked away in there" — he pointed to my head and then pointed to my heart—"or there. Start brainstorming what you're doing on your perfect day. You can sequence it together later."

I chuckled. "I'd definitely be hiking in South America, and at some point, eating a meal loaded in carbs."

"And where's your child? Is your child with you? Or at home? Do you miss him?"

I turned to Zan and narrowed my eyes.

He offered his palms to the canyon. "Or her."

Our shoulders shook with laughter.

"Hmm. There's not a child with me." This confused me. I had been on so many trails, fantasizing about sharing moments with my child, but now I visualized no child? "And this sounds horrible, but I'm not longing to get back to hear my child's voice or send a postcard. I just want to get back to a luxury hotel, order in room service, and look through my trip photos."

"That says a lot right there."

I pursed my lips. Hiking did impregnate me with a happiness that was so complete, so why did I invest so much in this other thing that I thought would bring me happiness? Maybe I couldn't imagine something I had never experienced firsthand. Or maybe this longing for a child was misplaced—symptomatic of something else I yearned for? "Damn, Zan. You've given me something to consider."

"You can thank the pandemic. I think we'll look back on this and see how much good came from it. It won't be all doom and gloom."

A family of five arrived at the Canyon Overlook. Two prepubescent boys and a tween girl ran up to the fence.

"Get away from that fence. Hold my hand," the woman said to the tween girl. I assumed the mother.

The tween tucked her hair behind her ears. Her head drooped. She shuffled toward her mother. The boys ran amuck, climbing and jumping from boulders. The dad was glued to his phone.

"Here, grab my hand if you want to walk by the ledge," the mother said.

She grabbed the tween's hand, and together they walked to the sign naming the peaks.

I groaned. "I hate that."

"What?" Zan asked looking at me.

I pointed my hand in the direction of the tween and the woman. "That. It goes on all the time." I lowered my hand to the boulder and studied the girl. "You probably don't even notice it because you're a man, but young girls are always being coached to not do things. To walk away from ledges, to get down, to 'play it safe,' to hold hands, to wear different gear—to constantly check-in, to not be alone, to not ruin your life and get pregnant too soon, to get pregnant at the right time with the right man. I'm damn near forty, and my family still deploys similar tactics. And look at the boys." My head whipped left and right, tracking their movements. "Just running wild. Freedom. It teaches women to be afraid to take risks. It teaches us we can't do what guys do. We hide. We play small. Fear chips away at our armor until we have nothing. Sure, I know that there are physical limitations to my body, but doing this to our girls, the words we say, it just kills their will to even try."

"I guess you have a point. My mom wouldn't let my older sister climb trees with me," Zan said, "but she'd sneak around and did it anyway. I always loved that about her." He stared into the distance, disappearing into some memory.

My stomach growled. "God, I'm starving. I didn't eat anything for breakfast."

"I have fruit in my pack if you want some." He pulled out oranges and apples. "I think I might have cheese and crackers too."

I was convinced he had a magician's bag with the amount of things he could stash in there. "Gosh, Zan, you don't have to fix *and* feed me. I should probably get going."

"What are you doing today? The Narrows?" he asked.

I stood up and stretched my back. "No, I did that yesterday. I have no plans today, really. I need to write a few postcards, but—" I looked down and wriggled my toes. There was no way I could do another hike. "I'm going to just lounge."

"I did the Narrows yesterday too. Funny we didn't run into each other." He bit into an apple, then licked the sweetness from his lips. *Those lips.*

I shifted my gaze back to the tween and her mother. Weren't my mother and I the older version of that duo— with my own mother guiding me to where she felt I should be—someplace ~~safer~~ more easily understood? And as much as she annoyed me, I allowed it on the basis of allegiance. Over the years, how had that shaken my confidence to explore, to try and fail and not shatter into a million pieces of doubt? I then smiled at Zan. "Hey, would you maybe want to just hang with me today?" I asked.

He looked up at me and smiled. A piece of apple lodged in the gap between his front teeth. "I'd love to."

We laid his picnic blanket underneath the eighty-foot-tall, lone cottonwood tree in the middle of Zion Lodge's lawn. We nibbled on fruit, cheese and crackers, and peanut butter and jelly sandwiches. He strummed his ukulele while I lay on my stomach, writing postcards, reading older journal entries that chronicled my loneliness, and reflecting on how it seemed another person had penned that anguish. I jotted a few lines that my future self would read, transporting her back to this lovely day:

I see lifetimes in your smile
The mountain whispers —
as you speak
The ocean lulling —
when you breathe
I know happiness through your eyes
All things change as Time is unkind,
Ravaging the body along with the mind.
But I'll take comfort when this life adjourns —
Because back to stardust we all return.

Deer, old and young, trod around us. The younger ones played, which elicited cries of excitement from some nearby human children.

Zan set his ukulele down and lay on his side. "What do you journal about?"

"Ehh, it's just whatever I'm experiencing. Sometimes, I just chronicle the day. Other times, I have so many emotions and thoughts, and that's what I write. It's cathartic to expel the dark thoughts, like all my gloom onto the page, or to capture the happy moments." I grinned and then bit my bottom lip.

"Zozobra," he said.

"Huh? What'd you say?" I scrunched my forehead and cocked my head.

"Zozobra. It's this festival in Santa Fe. It's actually happening pretty soon in a virtual format because of COVID. Essentially, a large man is constructed, kind of like Burning Man. They say Burning Man was inspired by Zozobra. Anyway, the man is called Zozobra, and all the people write their frustrations and worries from the past year on strips of paper. They place all this paper in a gloom box at Zozobra's feet and then set it all on fire, burning away all the gloom. It's kind of like you journaling out your gloom and moving on."

I righted my head and rubbed my chin. "Hmm, that's interesting. I like it, though."

"If it hasn't passed, maybe we should write down some of our troubles and cast them to the fire. I think we can submit it online, and they'll print it out to burn on our behalf."

"Sure. Why not?"

Our eyes locked. He pulled one of my curls, straightening and then releasing it. It sprang back to its original coil. I cut my eyes at him.

"Sorry, I like your hair. I know I shouldn't touch it," he said.

I laughed, turned on my side to face him, and rubbed my hand across his head. His soft, buzzed hair reminded me of a velour blanket. He closed his eyes, and I rubbed his head again. He rolled onto his back. I reached for his right hand and massaged it. A bandage covered his inner wrist.

My pointer finger traced the bandage's perimeter. "What happened here?"

"Huh?" He opened his eyes.

"Here. Your wrist." I hadn't noticed the bandage on the hike the other day. "What happened to your wrist?"

He smiled and pushed up to a seated position. His arms circled his bent legs. "So this." He pointed at his bandage. "I don't want to freak you out."

Was it a suicide attempt? I pushed to a seated position with my legs swept next to me as if I were riding sidesaddle. "Just tell me."

He peeled up a taped corner, unveiling the newest addition to his tattoo tapestry:

Allyn

My eyes mimicked a lemur's. Then I blinked and bit my lips. I read my name again and looked into his eyes. "Ehh, you don't even know me." I pushed away from him, allowing at least six feet of distance, and then I scowled. I searched his arms for other names. I only recalled images of various sizes like passport stamps. Was this the man on the trail that my friends and family had warned me about? The one who was trying to get me to lower my guard so he could torture and kill me in some van with no windows before dumping my body for some random hiker or hunter to find months later?

He frowned. "I get this seems weird. And no, I'm not some creepy trail guy—"

"Because that's exactly what the creepy trail guy would say," I said, folding my arms.

He shook his head. "Well, if anything happened to you, there's ink tying investigators to me." He reached into his pocket, retrieving his wallet. "Here, you can take photos of anything in here. My face. I'll record a video. If there was cell service, I'd have you call my mom. I'll even give you her number if you want to text her later. I can leave now if you want."

I snatched his wallet from his hand and combed through it. Debit cards. Credit cards. Insurance cards. I pulled out his driver's license and took a photo with my camera phone. His license was a Real ID, expiring in five years. He was an organ donor. His eye color was recorded as hazel. He had an Austin, Texas address. He was born the day my dad had died, making him younger than I thought, not even thirty, but old enough to buy me a drink. My fingers traced the laminated date.

I thumbed through his hundred-dollar bills and found a piece of stationery. I unfolded it. A mix of printed and cursive hand lettering filled the paper. The bottom was signed, "Love, Al with all my <3."

"Well, I don't think this Al person would approve of that tattoo," I said.

"She'd think it was hilarious."

"Really?" I said while narrowing my eyes.

"Al is my sister." He brushed his hand over his head, resting it on the back of his neck. "Was." He sighed. "It's taken a bit for me to get used to that. Al was my sister. She passed this year."

"Gosh! I'm so sorry to hear that."

"Thank you. Yeah. She's the one who got me into backpacking. She was a travel nurse and loved traveling and visiting all the parks. When she died, she wanted her ashes scattered at a few places. So, I have a route planned, mixing in her destination wishes along with a few of mine. Zion is my first stop for her."

"Wow, I'm—I'm ... I don't know what to say."

"And when you were schooling me yesterday about the New Mexican reservations and the pooping ..." He looked at me and laughed. "That's exactly the kind of shit Al would say. She was always educating me." He pulled out his phone and pushed his finger up, down, left, and right. He presented me with an email.

I read the email from the National Park Service, which granted him permission to scatter Alyssa Lynn's ashes.

As I read the email, he said, "Alyssa Lynn. She always hated it. She said it sounded like she was some super-Southern girl, so she adopted Al and commanded we all use it. And then meeting you here, and you're wearing this sparkly lipstick, which is awesome by the way. Very girly." He chuckled. "And you seem to be really confident in your name. Like ..." His nose reddened, and his fingers swept under his lower eyelid. "But she would've looked up to you. And, I wanted to capture that feeling, and umm, that's why I got the tattoo yesterday."

"I mean, I-I-I'm flattered." I tittered. "It's definitely a first." I stared at his feet.

"Allyn?"

I looked up and into his now honey-colored eyes, uncertain if I should walk away with the memory of Zan, like I had with Elias and Ben, or if I should plunge into deeper waters. I steadied my hands on the blanket, moving closer to him. I leaned forward, invading his space, and pressed my lips against his. His tattooed wrist reached behind my neck and pushed me into him as he pushed his tongue into my mouth. He tasted of peanut butter and mint. We lowered ourselves onto our sides, our hands rubbing each other's hair.

I pulled away, my eyes fixed on his lips, which I had made sparkly and dark pink. My chest heaved, trying to temper my desire. I inhaled the memories we had yet to create and parted my mouth to speak.

"Zan, would you like to go to my room?"

3.4 RELOCATION, REDLINES, AND REPARATIONS

The opening chords of "Lovely Day" played.

Zan stirred. "Can't you stay longer?"

I pressed my nakedness against his. "Couldn't I have met you sooner?"

He disappeared under the covers. Bill stopped singing, and then the opening notes of "Lovely Day" started anew. When Zan reemerged, I kissed my own sweetness from his lips.

I pulled away to breathe. "I've got to get on the road. I have, like, an eleven-hour drive ahead of me."

He traced my eyebrows. "You can just stay overnight in New Mexico. No one would know."

"*I* would know, and that's really all that matters." I flung the covers off me, offering my nakedness to the room. He kissed my breasts and then my stomach. "I've really got to go." Going home, to that familiar bungalow nestled at the bottom of the familiar mountain, to the laptop, to Ryan, to the impending IVF appointment.

And to something I couldn't quite yet name, but whatever it was, it was calling me back.

"Ten more minutes," he said as his smile moved below my waist.

I offered no further protests.

I drove by the Court of the Patriarchs, which were dappled in moonlight. The Watchman surveilled us as we exited the valley floor gate and turned left on UT-9. I lowered my windows and opened my sunroof when we approached the Zion–Mount Carmel Tunnel, where Zan and I screamed passing through its one mile. I pulled into the Canyon Overlook parking lot and pushed the gear shifter to park. Kurt Vile's "Pretty Pimpin" played.

Zan opened his door, collected his pack, ukulele, and picnic blanket, and stepped into the coolness. The door thudded closed. "You sure you don't mind sending my postcards?" I asked through the rolled-down window.

He crouched down to eye level. "They'll be mailed before our worries and Zozobra burn tonight."

I nodded. He flashed his smile. I smiled back, soaking him in along with the last twenty-four hours, allowing my adolescent dreams to wash over my adult reality, which lived a few states east. His smile. His confidence. His candor. His seduction.

"Can I have your number?" he asked.

I frowned. "Seriously? We can leave it all here. We don't have to pretend we'll stay in contact." In truth, the actions I had taken over the last day meant I couldn't leave it all behind. I couldn't keep this or IVF from Ryan. More importantly, Zion revealed the truth of my heart, and now I could no longer masquerade.

"I want to stay in contact if you do. I might be out of pocket until I'm back home, but I promise I will call you."

I stared at my check-engine light and twisted my mouth. I didn't want to sully the memory of our time together with whatever messiness the future held because, at some point, everything got complex and messy. *And, despite his wisdom, he is so young. I don't want to inflict my trauma on him.*

"Look, take my number, and if you want, call or message me," he said. "This way it takes all the risk out for you."

"Okay." I reached for my phone and entered his name into my phone as Zan Zion and transcribed his digits.

"I hope to hear from you, Allyn." He smiled.

I smiled back. He then loaded his gear into his vehicle.

I waited until he was seated. I waved. Then I turned off airplane mode on my phone. It stuttered with incoming messages and alerts. I scanned who had sent messages. My mother had sent over sixty. I sighed and didn't burden myself with reading or responding to anything. I was already behind schedule. I routed to Amarillo, Texas.

Within an hour, the sun rose, illuminating the landscape that was hidden in plain sight. It was vast and surprisingly green. I had always imagined American deserts would be more like North Africa, with sand waves mirroring the ocean, but this was different. Life existed in the barren expanse. Life flourished.

I freed my tangled and frizzy curls from their scrunchie. Out in a land where no one I knew knew where I was, I let go of all expectations for the first time in my life. I was free.

From US-89, my phone instructed me to turn left on US-160. I glanced down at my phone. My dot wasn't moving on the map. I tapped my screen. Nothing. I backed out of navigation and tapped "Start." The map didn't load. I had no signal. *Fuck. Why didn't I download this map?* My mind drifted to Zan's lips on my shoulder. *Because a sexy Texan was in my bed.*

I backed out of navigation again and zoomed out, scanning for I-40. Okay, I could take AZ-264 to AZ-87 to I-40.

At every road sign I approached, my heart lodged in my throat while my eyes strained, hoping to read AZ-264. Signs were few and far between. I glanced back at my phone. My blue dot moved, so I attempted to reroute to Amarillo.

There was still no option to download the map, and after I rerouted, my dot stopped moving again. My heart rate quickened. I turned my vents on high, blasting cold air under my arms. *Where the fuck am I? There are no vehicles around me. Should I turn around to find 264? Did I already pass it, or is it ahead?*

The time flipped back and then forward as the road weaved in and out of Arizona, a state that defied daylight saving time because it had no use for the construct. Had I left Arizona? Was I in New Mexico? Was I headed to Mexico? Argh, would I make it to Texas today?

"Stay straight for eleven miles," my phone said. My chest filled with hope. I grabbed my phone to view the turn-by-turn directions. I took a screenshot in case I lost signal again. Per Google, I'd take US-191 to Indian Route 12, to AZ-264, and finally hop on I-40. I was certain this was not the original route I had been prescribed. While it was a long, fortuitous route, all that mattered was getting to I-40.

When I turned on Indian Route 12, I entered Navajo Nation. I knew very little about the Diné. My formal education had significant shortcomings. My Louisianan-taught US history had heavily centered on the Louisiana Purchase and the Civil War. Beyond the Civil War, in the span of just three to four weeks, we learned about westward expansion, women's suffrage, the Great Depression, World Wars I and II, the Korean ~~War~~ Conflict, the Vietnam ~~War~~ Conflict, and civil rights.

In the grand scheme of my American education, I knew more about Europe than my own country.

When it came to the Diné, all I knew were Navajo Code Talkers, baskets, and turquoise jewelry. Given that I lived in Tennessee and crossed the Trail of Tears on most days that I left home, I was familiar with the troubles faced by the Cherokee and the Five *Civilized* Tribes. I was also versed in the more complicated side of their history, like slave ownership and how the Thirteenth Amendment didn't apply to reservations. They emulated White culture and were accepted as such until White society found more value in their land than in them as a people. And while recent history between some of the *Civilized* Tribes and Freedmen remained strained as they legislated whether tribal status was defined by blood or culture, I acknowledged that American Indians weren't any more monolithic than Blacks. The blemishes of one tribe didn't apply to all. Nothing is ever as clear as it seems.

Indian Route 12's asphalt surface gave way to packed dirt to cracked asphalt back to packed dirt to new asphalt to various states of disrepair. I dodged potholes as if I were driving on an oak-lined street back in New Orleans. Single-wide trailers wasted away on packed earth. Cars caked in dirt were peppered about the trailers. Some functioned while others sat defunct, as evidenced by missing tires and cinder blocks.

I passed a few one-story schools that rivaled school buildings in apartheid South Africa or a Cambodian village.

I was shell-shocked that I was driving through the United States of America. Sure, I had seen poverty. Sure, I had witnessed housing projects and run-down trailer homes, but this was different. Children living in a housing project or an Appalachian trailer park had greater access to interact with the larger world and had a chance, albeit small, to escape the cycle. Out here was almost total isolation.

Equal opportunity was the greatest myth of the American Dream.

I crossed faded, dotted yellow lines, passing trucks and cars that we'd call beaters back home. Even in poverty, there could still be a sense of pride in ownership: tidy homes, clean cars, fresh, bright faces. There was no pride of ownership here. Everything was downtrodden, wasted, and depressing. No fight. No dreams. An unseen smoke cloud hovered above, raining despair and smothering hope.

Did they own their land, or were they just renters on federal lands? I couldn't be sure, given the American government's history of establishing and enforcing racial hierarchy and claiming ownership to things that weren't for taking. I drove past Diné College as I approached Tsaile. So there was some hope. But similar to HBCUs, when are separate places a hindrance to progress? There was a time when there wasn't a choice necessitating separate spaces, but was some form of assimilation needed to achieve economic prosperity in America? When are segregated spaces supporting versus damaging?

Some said Black businesses prospered more during segregation and that Black children lost positive, Black role models after integration on account that consuming services from Blacks wasn't deemed as good when greater access opened up. Moreover, many Black professionals, like teachers, lost their jobs because many Whites balked at placing a Black person in a position of authority over White people. Recreationally, segregated resorts, like Lincoln Hills or American Beach or Idlewild, had encouraged Blacks to embrace outdoor pursuits free from harassment, a fostering that all but vanished with desegregation, and now Blacks participating in outdoor activities were often labeled as *acting White*. The Irish and Italians had successfully assimilated and still retained their cultural identities. Could they do that because they lacked melanin and looked more like their oppressors? Or was it a tale as old as time, where the oppressed maintains power by becoming the oppressor? Or was it because they came here of their own free will? My mind raced over these questions as my heart grew heavier.

And here the nation was, on another thirty-year cycle of White/Black racial tensions. Black Lives Matter was the latest rallying cry. We had seen it before with the LA riots, the civil rights movement, the resurgence of the KKK following *The Birth of a Nation*, Reformation. But how did other minority groups feel? Maybe there was a sense of shared pain and solidarity, but the transgressions of White America weren't only a Black experience. What about Native Americans? Middle Easterners? Mexicans and other Latin Americans? Asians?

This bias, this burden, these barriers extended to all People of Color. History has taught us that the majority of White compassion is often superficial and fleeting because when real change comes knocking on their doors, they turn off the lights; they close their window treatments; they do not answer our calls.

Tsaile, Arizona. Wheatfields, Arizona. I drove through nearly seventy miles of Navajo reservation, painted with the sins of the American government.

Fort Defiance, Arizona. Window Rock, Arizona. I turned left onto US-264, a four-lane highway. Golden arches. Billboards. The hallmarks of commercialism greeted me. Red lights. Small-town traffic. Google said, "Welcome to New Mexico." I didn't spot a welcome sign. Google Maps flashed an icon of an alien and a chile pepper floating above a park ranger's shoulders. My tired eyes perked up at the familiar red-and-blue shielded interstate sign. I-40! I turned right on US-491 and merged onto I-40. I accelerated, putting distance between me and the reservation's quicksand.

I-40 ran parallel to railroad tracks in miles of muted dullness. Music played, but I wasn't singing along. The drive through the reservation had drained me. I had envisioned New Mexico to be colorful and vibrant like the hot air balloons that soared its fall skies, but the sepia stretch of interstate was the land that time forgot. Or maybe the Navajo Nation had depleted my outlook for the next generation.

My phone buzzed. My mother had rung a few times. If I didn't want her to call the law, I needed to contact her soon, but I wasn't ready to talk to her or to anyone yet.

The interstate descended into Albuquerque, and three hours later I crossed into Texas:

Welcome to Texas
Drive Friendly – The Texas Way

Google Maps displayed a blonde cowgirl. Tejas. Texas pop culture flipped through my mind: Selena, *Walker, Texas*

Ranger, George Bush doesn't care about Black people, Big Oil, *King of the Hill*, cattle, barbecue, Tex-Mex, guns, football, cheerleading … Zan. Texas invoked images of cowboys and ranchers and untamed land, but there were also the major cities of Houston, which had become a haven for many New Orleanians post-Katrina; Austin, the gentrified, hipster poster child for feigned uniqueness; and the dichotomy of the glitzy glamour of Dallas and its casual neighbor, Fort Worth.

Texas, the state with a high likelihood of seceding from the Union. Truthfully, we were hardly united. I was shocked the nation hadn't splintered in two, three, or four by now. But was Texas's cultural identity as a Lone Star so different from Anywhere, USA? What did it mean to be Texan? Californian? Louisianan? Tennessean? American? Being American wasn't monolithic.

And even though the hate we had for one another was sickening, at the end of the day, weren't our core principles the same? To be honest, were our core principles that different than those of any other nation or peoples? In my travels, those in Africa, South America, Asia, and Oceania shared our same desires. Why couldn't we see that as a human species we had surprisingly more in common than we realized? We craved community and desired to set up the next generation for success. Mel and the 865 hiking community had gifted me that, and I hoped I could carry that torch forward.

But the United States that existed was not the America I wanted future generations to inherit. So, what was I going to do to change that? Was my legacy having a child, trying to change the world by investing in one person? Or was it larger, like Zan's dream of enriching children's lives with music? Both could be achieved, but did I want to bring life into a divided, dying land? With progress seemingly rolling back, would my child of color have my opportunities? Would she or he be as welcomed as I was in the mountains I loved?

My nose hairs singed, and my stomach lurched. I smashed the button in my car to recirculate air, but my retching didn't abate. I then drove by hundreds of barricaded cattle, likely being queued for slaughter. It was my first sighting of many cattle processing farms dotting the landscape. The sun sank lower on the horizon. It was twilight when I drove by Cadillac Ranch. I had made it to Amarillo.

I texted my friends and family, *In Amarillo, TX. What a heavy drive. Will text when I leave in the AM.*

My phone buzzed with responses. My mother called again. I ignored them all and crafted two messages:

Me: *Mel, so much to share with you. Attaching a few teaser photos. What's your work schedule look like this month? Let's make plans to connect soon.*

Me: *Hi Zan. It's Allyn. I'd love to hear about your journeys once you get a chance.*

3.5 HOMESTEADING

The air was crisp when I left the Amarillo hotel parking lot at six. Red lights pulsated against the pre-dawn sky. *Wind turbines. Alien invaders. Mind control. Shield your thoughts.* I skipped song after song on my playlist. Frustrated, I switched to local radio, scanning the stations until I landed on Tejano music. I smiled and bobbed my head to a language I didn't fully understand, but the accordion rhythm reminded me of zydeco. It wasn't long before the sun arrived, and I crossed another state line:

Welcome to Oklahoma

Google spoke to me a few seconds later. I glimpsed a man with a red bandana tied around his neck and a floating dreamcatcher before the Google Maps icon disappeared. I sang the title song from *Oklahoma!* It was my sister's favorite musical, and by virtue of the number of replays I was subjected to in childhood, I could sing the entire soundtrack. The storyline paralleled Oklahoma's journey to statehood with Laurey relinquishing her independence for matrimony. Our desire to be wanted and belong was strong.

I drove through one reservation after another. I passed several vehicles with American Indian license plates. This was the end of the Trail of Tears. While I had been to Oklahoma before, I hadn't reflected much of the state's history. The reality was that Oklahoma's land was stained with the blood that defined our country. The Indian Removal Act, the Slave Revolt of 1842, homesteaders versus ranchers, the Tulsa Massacre, the Great Depression, the Dust Bowl, the

Oklahoma City bombing, and unprosecuted violence against indigenous women.

When I reached Oklahoma City, I scanned interstate signs, searching for gas stations, few and far between. My radio succumbed to static. I drove in silence until I stopped for gas in Henryetta, OK, before pressing on. An hour and a half later, I read another state sign:

Welcome to Arkansas
The Natural State

Google interrupted the road noise with its welcome. A male guitarist dressed in black, with diamonds floating around his face, stared at me from my phone.

Me: *I did not have sexual relations with that woman. Crossed into Ar-kan-sas.*

I checked my odometer. Five hundred miles since Amarillo. My check-engine light glowered at me. At Little Rock, the speed limit dropped to 70 mph. Less than three hundred miles to Memphis. Hours later, I filled up in West Memphis, Arkansas. My skin goosebumped thinking of the tragedy that three boys, three teenagers, and their families endured in that town. I had driven over ten hours but wasn't groggy. Three and a half hours of daylight remained. Home was five hours away. *Stay the night or go for it?*

I crossed the Mississippi River:

Tennessee Welcomes You
The Volunteer State

I didn't need to glance at my phone to know that Elvis popped on the screen. Elvis was from Mississippi—what were his contributions to this state? Why not Dolly?

Why not a Tennessee-born icon who did so much for the community?

Me: *Feeling great to be back in 10-I-see listening to Three 6 Mafia to welcome me back. Going to push through to Chatta-nooga!*

My shoulders relaxed when I neared Nashville. I was in towing range. My car shook as I accelerated. I checked my rearview for parts my car might have littered on the interstate. *Come on*, I prayed, *three more hours, and then you can crap out.*

As I-840 connected to I-24, the sun accelerated its descent, but I was in the home stretch. This interstate corridor was my territory. I autopiloted as the interstate climbed and then descended Monteagle. I dipped down into Georgia for a few miles when my gas light came on. The interstate winded its way back into Tennessee. I exited at Lookout Valley/Lookout Mountain and stopped for gas.

When I inserted my key into the ignition, my Camry didn't turn over. I tried again with the same result. No other cars were at the pumps. I spotted one car parked away from the pumps. It was a beater. I figured that belonged to the gas station attendant. I was so close to home.

I called Ryan for help.

"Hey, my car isn't starting."

"Where are you?" he asked.

"Cummins Highway. At the gas station right off the exit," I said while trying to peer inside the gas station to see if the attendant was petite or burly.

"Can no one there give you a jump?"

"Well, it's not exactly safe to jump-start right at the pump. Ideally, I'd get help pushing my car away from the pump and then jump-start."

"So, what do you want me to do, Allyn?"

All I wanted was for him to rescue me. As a single, independent woman who paid all her bills, who filed her own taxes, who cooked, who cleaned, who grocery shopped, who took out the trash, who mowed the lawn and gardened, who washed the car and changed the oil, who troubleshot all plumbing and electrical issues in the home, who climbed ladders to free the gutters of leaves, who crawled through cobwebs in the crawlspace, who exterminated and evacuated all creepy crawlies, who had no backup, who made countless decisions every day, I wanted in that moment for someone else to step up and unburdened me. Strong women need help too.

"Don't worry about it," I said, frustration creeping into my voice. *Is it too much for him to see I am in need and want his help? Is it unreasonable to expect a significant other to be concerned for my situation and offer assistance? Why is everything always falling on my shoulders?*

"What? Just tell me what you want me to do, and I'll do it."

I sighed. The last time I asked him for help, he showed up late and didn't do what I requested, so what would make this time any different? Nothing had changed at all. "I'll call roadside assistance. I'll ping you when I get home."

An hour later, I drove over Lookout Mountain, peering down at the head- and taillights illuminating I-24 as it snaked around the Tennessee River. A few miles upriver was one of the trailheads for the Trail of Tears.

I backed into my parking pad around 10 p.m. Eight days. Thirteen states. Three thousand eight hundred fifty miles. I was emotionally and physically exhausted.

A pickup truck loaded with furniture parked in front of my neighbor's home, the ones who brought in my trash. Their yard remained uncut. The toothless neighbor approached my car. *God, I wish I had a garage!* I was not in the mood for conversation. I rolled down my driver's side window.

"You're moving?" I asked, hoping it would be a quick conversation.

"Yeah, rent's gone up, and Stevanie said she can't live like this anymore. She moved out."

"One second." I rolled up my window and opened my car door. I swung my tired legs outside my car and stretched over them. "What happened?"

"There was another roof leak, and another possum got inside from the crawlspace and died. That was Stevanie's limit."

"Did you talk to your landlord?" I asked.

Her tongue poked at her gums. "Yeah, he said he can't fix it for another two months. Our lease is up then, so we're moving to a trailer down in Georgia. He agreed to not charge us for breaking the lease if we don't report him."

I moved my seat forward and pulled my backpack from my car.

"And we're hoping Stevanie will move back with us since the trailer is much nicer."

"Where is she now?" I asked.

"At her boyfriend's, but they're fighting over money. The thing is, we can't afford to take care of Stevanie and the baby even with the assistance we get. So, if she moves back with us, she's going to have to quit school and work to support the baby, or give the baby up so she can finish school and go to college."

I hoisted my backpack onto my back, giving myself a whiff of my musty underarms that nearly gagged me. I reached down to pull the lever to pop my trunk. I just wanted to be in my home to shower and sleep. I hoped my neighbor wasn't expecting me to give her money. Maybe she just needed someone to listen. But I had no mental energy for other's people shit at the moment; I had enough to deal with on my own. "Well, I'm sorry to hear all of this. I'll miss having you as a neighbor," I said and then walked to my door.

My phone buzzed. I unlocked it. My stomach flipped at the message at the top of my inbox.

Owen: *Hey! Sorry it's taken so long for me to get back to you. Things have been hectic with all the protesting. My unit's been called to deploy overseas soon. I'd love to see you before I go.*

3.6 BACK IN SESSION

A baritone bark announced my presence before I could rap at the door. When Ryan cracked it open, his Lab mix squeezed through and launched his paws on my thighs. I crouched down to scratch him behind his ears.

"Nice whip," Ryan said, tilting his head toward my rental. My beloved Camry had almost gotten me home and was now waiting for me to decide if I was going to resurrect or scrap it.

I rolled my eyes. Ryan kissed me on my cheek, and then our lips met, and muscle memory prevailed. He tasted of marijuana and stout. He smothered me in his arms, cutting off my air supply.

"I can't breathe," I said, struggling to free myself.

Ryan stepped back. I rubbed my throat. His Lab sniffed the scented air and salivated, then galloped inside.

"We better get in before he clears the counter," Ryan said.

I pulled four bags of cannabis edibles from my purse. "Here, these are for you. I didn't want to forget them."

He studied the packaging. "You didn't even try them? Don't you want any?"

"Eh, just maybe a couple from each bag, but that's all."

We gathered on his back deck while he finished grilling. We then devoured the pulled barbecue chicken and grilled mac and cheese sandwiches without any conversation. He chewed an edible and cracked open a beer while I drank flavored carbonated water.

"You've been pretty tight-lipped about Zion. I was missing you, but I get it when we need that alone time," Ryan said.

I crisscrossed my legs. I picked at the bandage covering the tender skin that my toenail used to protect. His dog rested his head on my right calf, and I caressed his soft ears. "Ryan, I missed you too. And this dinner you made ... it's amazing."

"So, how was Zion?"

I raspberried. "I wouldn't even know how to describe it. Scenery unlike anything I've witnessed. The colors? Wow. I'd love to go back and experience a few more hikes and other places there, but I just didn't have the time to do. It was overcrowded but not like leaf-peeping season in the Smokies. Many novice hikers, but I met some cool people. And just with everything going on with me and America right now, I was really heavy in my thoughts."

"Heavy in thoughts?" Ryan asked, sinking deeper into his chair.

I uncrossed my legs and rubbed my hands up and down my thighs. My torso rocked to an unplayed rhythm. "I'm scared of what's to come. This country. The division. The hate. Is it going to improve? Get worse? Despite all my successes and resources to give, I don't know if I can guarantee a better life for my child, and if I can't, what's the point?"

"Allyn, you always come back from vacation all in your head. It'll settle. My philosophy is to be thankful for what I have and enjoy the everyday, small moments." He looked at me and reached for my hand. "Like sitting here with you on a warm summer evening."

I accepted his hand. "And that's one of the things I really love about you. You are content with where you are. You're happy, I don't know, working, drinking beer with friends, going to concerts, doing the occasional triathlon. You could fast-forward your life twenty years and be doing the same thing, and you'd be fine. You're, like ... predictable." I laughed. "A home base where everything is right where I've left it.

"But"—I licked my lips—"I don't want that. I want to be challenged. I want thought-provoking conversations. I want a home where comfort isn't predictability but rather the commitment to grow, to change things. Aliveness." I bit my lips and rubbed my thumb on his palm. I stared into his eyes, trying to gauge his reaction to what I'd said.

His face revealed nothing, and his silence unnerved me. Did he understand?

I continued, "Throughout our relationship, I was happy but struggled with the feeling that ... being with you was giving up a part of me. And ... and it's not that you ever asked me to be anything but myself, but I clipped my own wings to be with you. And I love you so much that I know the best thing I can do is to stop giving you false hope. I want you to find your person who will sit in this seat and enjoy all the sunsets and small moments."

He retrieved his hand from mine and snapped his fingers, calling for his dog. He roughed up his dog's scruff and face and then kissed his snout. He spoke into his dog's face, not looking up at me. "I definitely wasn't expecting this, but I just want you to find happiness, Allyn. I was hoping that would be with me, but it's clear that it's not."

"I'm really sorry it couldn't be, Ryan. Seriously." I stood up. "Well." I sighed and shrugged. "I guess I should give you some space."

He stood up and hugged me, pressing my face into his soft chest. He sniffled. I squeezed him tighter. The final rays of light disappeared behind Lookout Mountain.

On my drive home, I accepted that Ryan might need space from my friendship, and that space could become permanent. I wiped away my tears. I didn't want to lose him, but I couldn't keep trapping him in the hope of something that could never be. I wasn't capable of using him. It was dark when I pulled onto my parking pad.

The pickup truck sat empty and dormant at my neighbor's house. I studied my feet en route to my door and inserted my key into the lock. Before I could turn the knob, a low purr grabbed my attention.

I snapped my head in the direction of the sound. One-Eyed Willy sat in my patio chair, kneading kitty bread.

I walked over to her and scratched underneath her chin. She buried her head into my palm. Her name tag thumped against my fingernail. I edged my face closer to the metal tag, straining to read in the dim porch light. I squinted my eyes and read:

ZION

I gasped. My heart raced. My stomach leapt for my throat. Zion lifted her head from my hand and purred. I smiled and let my heart rate return to normal.

"So, how was Zion?" my therapist asked.

"Well, for starters," —I laughed—"I'm looking at a rather expensive vehicle repair bill or navigating a nearly impossible car market. I'll sort it out eventually." I started my ritual of walking the rooms of my home.

"Is that all you've taken away from your trip?"

"Definitely not." I exhaled. "Wow, it was unlike anything I have ever experienced. And typically, a few weeks after a trip, I'm settled back into my routine, remembering my time through pictures, but I can't shake Zion."

"What do you mean by that? Tell me about it."

"Sticking to my original plans would be like burying my head in the sand. Sure, I'm working, but I can't just go back to dating, hiking, and trying to get pregnant, so I've paused everything. I need to figure out where I fit in all of this." I stopped pacing. My mouth parted. My hand grabbed the crystal doorknob and twisted. Pushing the door in, I entered the second bedroom. I dragged my finger along the windowsill, clearing a path from the dust. My thumb rubbed my finger, rolling last year's grit into a ball.

"By pausing everything, you mean no IVF?"

"No IVF."

"What do you think caused this realization? What specifically occurred on this trip compared to all your others?"

"Hmm, I think being in a car, driving from state to state, feeling the divisiveness—the wealth of some cities, the interstate cutting through minority neighborhoods, the zeal for Trump, the overcrowded, outdoor spaces everywhere, the lack of diversity on the trails, the poverty of the reservations. This wasn't some faraway problem in another country. This was America. Those experiences took root. It wasn't like I could close a browser, turn off the television, or hop on a plane. Like, how can I keep turning a blind eye to all that? How can I inflict that on a child?

"And then I met some really cool people that prompted me to evaluate what really matters to me, and I wasn't wholly convinced in my pregnancy plans anymore."

"What about online dating?"

"I deleted my profile," I said.

"And Ryan?"

I exited my front door, stood on my front porch, flicked the dust ball into my flowerbed, and rubbed my hands clean on my shorts. My hipster neighbor's Black Lives Matter flag flapped. They still hadn't acknowledged my presence with a smile or a wave, much less a conversation. I rolled my eyes and then settled into a rocking chair. The ball of my right foot pressed onto the ground and lifted, creating a smooth, soothing rhythm.

"Allyn, are you still there?"

I cocked my head. "Ryan is my friend. Zion really made me realize that I didn't want what he offered. He's great. He's supportive. He's an excellent friend. But that's it." I paused. "When I got back from Zion, I visited Owen. I don't know if you remember him. Young military guy from Atlanta. He's back overseas now."

"I do recall Owen. How was seeing him again?"

My wind chimes sang on the breeze. I licked my lips. "It was strange seeing him again. I mean, we hadn't known each other long, but the connection was so strong. There was a lot of built-up tension; we had a lot to get off our chests. But we kind of picked right back up from where we left off."

"Does that mean you're dating Owen?"

"No, we aren't anything more than friends. We've acknowledged there's something deeper between us, but I'm not worried about what will or won't happen. I'm just enjoying our letters and calls. We have no expectations beyond friendship, but we agreed to see how we both feel when he gets back—" I stopped short of saying the word "home."

Owen's and my conversations had been heavier as of late. He discussed the growing, unsettling feeling that Georgia no longer felt like home. Hell, no longer felt like America. Lenny had shared similar thoughts with me, where foreign lands accepted her minority status better than America did. And I knew from my exposure to Vietnam vets that this unbelonging wasn't a new phenomenon. I'd find myself lying in bed at night, ruminating over how many minorities and financially disadvantaged people sought the military life to escape toxic cycles, sought a life that ripped them from their homes and often exposed them to unimaginable horrors. Wouldn't we all be better served if we refunded the Civilian Conservation Corp with an eye toward preserving the land for all Americans, including those who were forced from home, those who were stolen and had escaped from other lands, and even those who colonized and are still colonizing these lands? The Great Smoky Mountains, Big Bend, and countless state and local parks couldn't have existed without the CCC, and while many such programs were marred with controversy, we could do better this time around. Isn't it sometimes better to address the problem next door than half a world away?

"Wow, this is a lot of change from a couple of weeks ago," my therapist said.

"Yeah, it is, but it's necessary, good change."

My therapist chuckled.

"And I finally completed my homework assignment. I wrote a letter to my mom. And I realized that a lot of my expectations *were* wrapped up in what my parents introduced to me, which has been indoctrinated into them by our society. I've been so busy being busy, replacing one pursuit with the next, running away from a … a … an unfulfilled reality. And that works for some people, but it wasn't working for me. And so, I need this time to reset and forge my own way. I'm choosing to stop playing the game."

"So, are you giving yourself a time limit on your reset?"

"Actually, no. I spent so much of my life pursuing a false dream on a forced timeline that I want to give myself all the time and space I need to figure out my own direction. It's time to take my train completely off the track."

Zion trotted across the street, climbed my porch stairs, and sauntered over to my feet. I lifted her onto my lap and scratched beneath her chin. She kneaded into my thighs while her one eye studied me. Her purrs competed with my therapist's voice.

"I'm sorry, could you repeat that?" I asked.

"I'm excited for this new insight you've reached and this step you've taken."

"Right." I chuckled. "Because learning to rest and reset is an actionable step. You've been trying to tell me this for the longest time, but apparently, I needed Zion to finally get it."

We ended our session by scheduling my next appointment. Zion curled into a ball on my lap. I closed my eyes and inhaled fresh-cut clover and crabgrass on a young, autumn breeze.

3.7 SAUDADE

I draped onesies, knit pants, socks, and a quilt on the drying rack. I piled three sets of sheets into the wash and pressed start.

My phone buzzed on the kitchen counter.

I prayed it wasn't the meal delivery lady canceling again. I didn't have time to cook dinner, and I refused to have another pizza night. What else was there to do? Go to the post office, insurance quote for the new-to-me vehicle, and then story time.

My phone buzzed again. I walked to the kitchen, but I couldn't find it. I lifted Lenny's and Owen's care packages, searching for my phone. Where the fuck was it? It buzzed again. Finally I found it next to a pile of college applications. My heart fluttered upon reading the name on the screen. I bit my bottom lip and twirled a stray curl that framed my face as I picked up.

"Hey, I didn't expect to ever hear from you," I said.

"I made it home. I voted earlier today," Zan said.

"That's amazing. I plan to steal away and vote tomorrow." I leaned my back against the counter and fiddled with a few threads that had unraveled from the burp cloth draped over my shoulder. I had forgotten to throw it in the wash. "Wow, how was your time out West? Any updates on your job?"

"So many stories to tell you, but nothing as memorable as Zion."

I heard his silent laugh and imagined the small gap he showed to the world whenever he smiled. I blushed. "The lies you tell your conquests." I laughed.

"Not lying. Work's still dead. The West is overcrowded with people. It's just not fun with that many people."

"I get that."

"Well, I was thinking maybe it's time to head East. Maybe take in the last bit of fall color. The Smokies, the Blue Ridge Parkway, and Shenandoah look amazing. It seems pretty close to Chattanooga. I'd love to stop by and see you. And maybe you can show me your favorite places."

"Well, those places have always been popular with leaf peepers even before the pandemic. Who knows how insane it is now? So if you're looking to avoid people—"

"Come on, Allyn. Don't overthink it. Just say, 'Yes, I'd love to, Zan.'"

I scratched my forehead. "I don't know how to really say this."

"What?"

"I really would love to see you, but, well—" I breathed in. My heart raced. I breathed out and wiped my hands on my cheerleading shorts. "I'm kind of a guardian to my former neighbor's niece now. Stevanie. I think I told you about her."

"The pregnant teen?"

"Yeah. Right now, it's just an agreed-upon arrangement, but we're looking at the financials to see if it makes sense for us to legalize anything. There's so much to consider with health insurance, dependent care benefits, and Stevanie's financial aid for college." I sighed.

A sudden silence impregnated the call. I pulled the phone away from my face, checking that we were still connected.

"Wow, I'm so happy for you Allyn."

I chuckled, walked across the kitchen, and opened a cabinet, reaching for a wineglass. "Thanks." I smiled at the artifacts I had collected on the fridge: Stevanie's sketches, a weekly chore chart, a grocery list, emergency phone numbers, a college textbook fund goal thermometer, and a few photos.

I zeroed in on one photo taken two weeks ago. I had hosted a belated baby shower backyard barbecue for Stevanie. The photo captured Stevanie proudly holding her baby girl, surrounded by her current tribe: her aunt, her ex-boyfriend and his mom and dad, my mom, Mel, and me. It wasn't a gathering without risk and sacrifice. My mother called my relationship with Stevanie unnatural, but I still invited her to the shower. She said that she wouldn't attend and hinted at my lack of parenting experience. I reminded my mom that she had zero experience parenting during a pandemic and that Stevanie and I had had many discussions outlining the risks and determining if and how we could mitigate them. For me, it was important that Stevanie could solution through her fear instead of accepting avoidance as her sole option.

My therapist reminded me that my mother might never say the words I wanted to hear, but that people showed love and respect in their own ways. And maybe my mom deciding to quarantine and then driving eight hours to a baby shower for a young woman she'd never met was her way of acknowledging me as an independent, intelligent woman she respected and loved, even if she didn't always agree with my choices.

I smiled with the hope that my therapist was right and then opened my fridge door to retrieve a pitcher of filtered water. "I didn't expect for any of this to happen really. But driving across America, experiencing the landscapes and people in Utah, people like you, it just got me thinking about life differently. I'd spent my whole life painting by numbers and was pissed it never resulted in some master-piece. So I took a step back. I spent a lot of time thinking about my perfect day." I chuckled. "I'm still working on that, but a few things started taking shape. Like, I want to see more people who look like me in the mountains. I want more diversity in general to offer fresh perspectives, to have those uncomfortable conversations, to challenge all of us to keep growing. Because by questioning and gaining knowledge, we grow.

"And these are like Miss America 'I want world peace' goals, and there are plenty of organizations out there fighting to break cycles, to help tear down barriers. I've been researching and figuring out how I want to get in-volved. And then it hit me that I have a neighbor in finan-cial need, and I can help break their cycle. Stevanie thought she only had two choices: quit school to work to keep her baby, or give her baby up to stay in school. Those are choices no woman should ever face."

Zan responded, "It's wild that she didn't think she could have other options. I'm not saying she should've got-ten an abortion—I respect her decision—but I thought there were alternative schools, homeschooling, or even part-time student options."

"But that's just it, Zan. We're privileged, so it seems so obvious to explore alternate solutions. But we don't know what we don't know, and oftentimes, it takes someone else pulling us out of our ignorance and throwing us a lifeline. And so, when I approached my neighbor about providing some financial relief so that Stevanie could keep her baby and stay in school, Stevanie told me she didn't want my charity. So I asked her what she wanted."

"What did she say?"

"You know, I think it was the first time that anyone had asked her that. She asked me to teach her how to be financially independent so that when she looked into her next child's eyes, she wouldn't be filled with regrets. I told her that she should regret nothing and that I'd be more than willing to mentor her. And then, one day she said I was like the mom she never had, and it kind of grew from there." I filled my glass to the brim and sipped. "Gosh, Zan, she's a fantastic woman and an excellent mom. Oh, and her daughter makes my heart melt. I take care of Alyssa whenever Stevanie is studying or just needs a break from being a mom." I sighed. "It really does take a village."

"Alyssa?" he asked.

I couldn't read the tone of his voice. Was he confirming what I said because he didn't hear? Was he passing judgment? Did he now think I was the creepy trail woman? Was he lost in a memory of him climbing trees with his sister? "Yeah. Alyssa." I breathed out my nervousness. "I told Stevanie all about Zion, and she loved the name and what you were doing for your sister and how through your loss, you helped me through mine. I hope you're not upset that I shared that."

"Absolutely not. I love it. She'd love it. My God," he said.

"What?" I twisted one of my curls.

"All I did was wander around the West, wondering what you were getting up to," Zan said.

I giggled and then tucked a curl behind my ear. "Apparently, I've been getting up to a lot. I'm still learning, making plenty of mistakes, but you know, I'm happy with how full my heart is, and I know that in time, the next step will reveal itself to me."

That was true. For the first time that I could recall, I was marching to a destination that couldn't be pinned on a map or recorded on a list. There was a certain freedom in that.

"So, what's your address?" Zan said. "I just want to spend time with you in whatever capacity you allow, and well, if you'd be okay with it, I'd love to meet your family."

"Yes, of course. I'd love for you to meet my family."

I stood in the path of a sunbeam, streaming in through the kitchen window. I tilted my head up to the warmth. Dust particles danced around me. I closed my eyes, and a small, soft smile spread across my face.

NOELLE CUMBERLAND

was born and raised in pre-Katrina New Orleans and currently resides in South Lake Tahoe, CA. She earned an engineering degree from The Georgia Institute of Technology and a masters of business administration from The University of Tennessee at Chattanooga. She's never far from a mountain—hiking and running on local trails, paddling lakes and rivers, and gaining confidence with her new love of snowboarding. As an outdoor enthusiast, she's passionate about encouraging women and People of Color to embrace outdoor spaces. When not living her best mountain life, she works hard for the money in Corporate America, partakes in the lost art of porch sitting, and enjoys a good laugh with the real characters in her life.

Find out more about her projects at:
www.NoelleCumberland.com
and on IG: @noellecumberland

www.ingramcontent.com/pod-product-compliance
Lightning Source LLC
Chambersburg PA
CBHW051958240626
47153CB00005B/1810